Meera screamed as the mechanical bull bucked underneath them.

Jake felt her shift in the seat, and he tightened his hold on her hand, gripping her firmly at the waist to steady her. He had ridden this bull a thousand times, but riding it with Meera...*hmm*.

His body was now molded against hers, and they rolled and moved in unison as the bull bucked. She was laughing so hard, her head snapped sideways and she lost her balance. He reached for her and... They landed on wood chips, Meera first. He braced his arms so he wouldn't crush her.

The crowd went wild, cheering, whistling and screaming louder than ever. He looked into her glittering eyes. He didn't know if it was the adrenaline from the bull ride, or just...Meera...but his heart was galloping like a prize-winning race horse.

This girl is going to be the end of me.

Dear Reader,

Marriage makes us face the conflicting worlds of familial traditions, our own values and beliefs, and what we envision for the future. *First Comes Marriage* is the story of Meera, a woman firmly rooted in her family who grapples with her Indian cultural beliefs and the permanent ache in her heart that comes from wanting something she's never had...what we all want: unconditional love.

Meera is engaged to a family friend in London. It's a marriage arranged between families with ties so strong, breaking them will unravel Meera's whole world. So what's she supposed to do when she falls for an American cowboy?

While I was writing this story, I laughed, cried and snorted tea from my nose. I hope you'll enjoy the fusion of Western romance with epic, Bollywood-style drama.

To learn more about arranged marriages, past to present, East to West, or to find out where in the world Bollywood is, visit my website at sophiasasson.com. I also have a playlist by chapter of country tunes and Bollywood music to put you in the mood as you read. Plus free extras on the town, recipes for barbecue and vegetable curry, and more. I love hearing from readers, so please find me on Twitter (@SophiaSasson) or Facebook (SophiaSassonAuthor), or email me at Readers@SophiaSasson.com.

Enjoy!

Sophia

HEARTWARMING

First Comes Marriage

—

Sophia Sasson

HARLEQUIN® HEARTWARMING™

Recycling programs
for this product may
not exist in your area.

ISBN-13: 978-0-373-36778-8

First Comes Marriage

Copyright © 2016 by Sophia Sasson

Printed in U.S.A.

Sophia Sasson puts her childhood habit of daydreaming to good use by writing stories that go to the heart of human relationships. Sophia was born in Bombay, India, has lived in the Canary Islands, Spain, and Toronto, Canada, and currently calls the madness of Washington, DC, home. She loves to read, travel to exotic locations in the name of research, bake, explore water sports, watch foreign movies and hear from readers. Contact her through sophiasasson.com.

To my husband. You make me believe that love really does conquer all.

Acknowledgments

This book, and the ones to come, are thanks to my wonderful editor Claire Caldwell, who had faith in my writing from the start, and Victoria Curran, who finds me interesting enough to put up with. Their feedback is invaluable.

My writing has come a long way thanks to my fabulous critique partner, author Jayne Evans, who knows how to ground me without clipping my wings.

Also, thanks to the wonderfully supportive romance writers and authors I've met through Facebook and online communities. I'm grateful to be part of this group that shares successes, and to help each other achieve our happily-ever-afters.

CHAPTER ONE

"I DON'T MEAN to disturb you…"

"Then don't."

"Don't what?"

"Disturb me."

Meera sighed in frustration. *Americans! Does he have to be so rude?* She stood on her tiptoes, peeking over the stall door. She could only see his back. White T-shirt, snug jeans streaked with mud and a straw cowboy hat. He knelt in front of a black mare who whinnied as he lifted her leg.

Meera took a breath. The air was thick with the smell of animal manure. "Pardon me," she said more forcefully. "I understand you have a room to let."

He turned and her breath caught. *Too much dust in the air.* Green eyes sparkled mischievously, sandy-blond hair glistened angelically in the sunlight and a broad smile showed straight, white teeth. All perfectly packaged in a tall, athletic body. She blinked.

"'To let'? Is that French for 'toilet'?" he drawled.

Thank you for changing your image from American cowboy to Forrest Gump.

She put on her best finishing-school smile. When in Rome… She had to remember to speak redneck.

"Sorry, it's British for 'do you have a room for rent?'"

He stood, surveying her. She smoothed her black pantsuit, wishing for the millionth time she'd dressed more casually, especially in this oppressive heat. He patted his hands on his jeans, sending up clouds of dirt. She sneezed and instinctively brushed her arms. "Why would the Queen of England want a room at my dusty ranch?" The tone was sardonic, his eyes crinkling.

She pressed her lips together. She would rather leave than deal with such arrogance, but this was her last option for a place to stay tonight. This being her first time in America, she really didn't want to test her precarious, wrong-side-of-the-road driving skills to search for accommodations in the dark. "If you must know—"

"I must." He mimicked her tone and accent.

She took a short breath. *Keep your cool— remember you made the decision to be in this middle-of-nowhere town.* "I'm doing a medical rotation with Dr. Harper." Despite her frustration, she couldn't keep the excitement out of her voice.

Even if she couldn't be in New York, she would still get a month to herself and a much-needed break from wedding planning. She wouldn't let anything—or anyone—spoil it for her.

"Ah, lemme guess—Marty said you couldn't stay at his inn."

"And it seems you would be able to tell me why."

His eyes danced with amusement. "Because the town doesn't want you to stay."

She tapped a finger against her thigh. *I've only been here a day. What could I possibly have done to turn a whole town against me?*

He opened the stall door, and Meera took a step back. He leaned forward, and she took another step back. He towered over her. She was only five feet tall and he was north of six. He smelled of dirt, sweat and something…*manly.* She shifted. *Why must he stand so close?*

He wiped a hand on his jeans and held it out to her. "Jake Taylor."

He raised his eyebrows as she eyed his hand, still caked with dirt. She took it, meeting his gaze and feeling the gritty roughness of his skin.

"Meera Malhotra."

"Ah, what now?"

"Mee-ra Mal-hot-ra," she said more slowly.

"Well, that's quite a name. Welcome to Hell's Bells."

"Hell's Bells? I thought the town name was Bellhaven."

"The townspeople call it Hell's Bells. There's a story behind it."

He let go of her hand and picked up her suitcase. Apparently, she was not going to hear the story today. She followed him out of the barn, struggling to keep up with him in her heels as he strode across the field. The point of her heel kept getting stuck in the mud. He looked back, his lips curved in a smirk.

"Bollocks!" She reached down and took off her shoes, noticing the ruined heels. So much for the Manolo Blahniks. This was not the place for her London wardrobe.

"Are you coming, princess?"

"I thought I was the Queen of England!"

"You've been demoted."

She rolled her eyes; he would be a handful.

He extended his arm, offering his hand to her. She eyed it warily, not wanting to touch him again.

"Come on now, I don't have all day waitin' on your delicate feet to make the trek."

She sighed and took his hand. It was warm and large. Grass and clover tickled her feet as he firmly but gently tugged her across the field.

They arrived at a gravel road. She slipped her

shoes back on and eyed the big stately house at the end of it.

Wow! The place could have been Tara from *Gone with the Wind*, one of her favorite movies. Ivy grew up the white stone walls. There was a wraparound porch on the main level and a balcony on the second story. They climbed a set of brick steps that led to the front door. Jake opened it and set her suitcase down.

Her eyes widened as she took in the two-level foyer. A double staircase wound up to the second floor, and worn-out gilding begged to be shined on the banisters. Dark wood floorboards were covered in a light blanket of dust. A coffered ceiling replete with cobwebs finished the look. Meera's home was considered a small palace, especially by London standards, but this house was something else. Despite the grandeur, it lacked the stuffiness of aristocracy. Black-and-white family pictures, some yellowed with age, hung on the walls in different-sized frames. There was a spaciousness and welcoming charm that was missing in her family home.

"This is beautiful." Her heels tapped the floor as she walked over to a door and touched the handle. She immediately brushed the dust off her hands. "Why are these closed?"

"It's an old estate and very hard to keep up. We close the rooms we don't use."

Meera nodded as if it made complete sense. But why wouldn't you maintain your home?

"There's no kitchen in the guesthouse, so you can use the one in the back here." He pointed to the only open doorway. "I try to keep the fridge stocked for the ranch hands. Help yourself to anything you want." He grabbed a set of keys.

"Come on, your house is this way."

My house? He took her around the side of the building. Meera gaped at the small stone cottage. Pretty rose vines crawled up the side. The front yard was overgrown with weeds, but she could already see the possibility of a proper English garden. Jake opened the front door.

Inside, all the furniture was covered with white sheets.

"You'll have to dust things out…been a while since anyone was in here."

Was it her imagination, or did his face flicker with sadness?

He showed Meera two bedrooms, a living room and a bathroom.

"This is quite a guest cottage. Has it always been here?"

"It used to be the servants' quarters. I gutted it several years ago and made it into a house for…" His expression changed into something Meera couldn't read. "Into a guesthouse."

Meera looked around and felt excitement bubble through her. *This is just perfect—exactly what I need.* It would take some work to clean up, but it was quaint and peaceful and all hers. For a whole month she wouldn't have to answer to anyone, live up to expectations or deal with her usual obligations. Freedom! Spending a month in this small town was a small price to pay.

"This is wonderful, thank you. What will you charge?"

"How about an exchange of services?"

"I beg your pardon?" Meera's muscles tightened. Maybe she'd been too quick to judge Jake. She suddenly realized that she had walked into a place all alone, trusting a complete stranger.

"You're a doctor, right?"

She nodded, relieved.

"My ranch hands haven't seen a doctor in years. I have twelve people—three women and nine men. I'd like you to give them a physical here on the ranch, make sure they're good."

Meera frowned. "Why don't they have a primary care doctor?"

"They don't have health insurance. I've been looking into gettin' them some."

"Oh," she said simply. She knew America didn't have a National Health Service, but didn't people with jobs have benefits? What could she possibly do on the ranch without a proper clinic or medical supplies? Her father had given her his old-fashioned doctor's bag with a stethoscope and basic supplies when she completed medical school at King's College. She considered it a sentimental gift but was glad she'd brought it along. "I'd be happy to do what I can for them, but if they need blood work, X-rays or any tests, they'll have to come to the clinic or possibly the hospital. I really can't do much by myself here."

He nodded. "Most of 'em can't afford to see a doctor. Just having you do a checkup will be more than they've gotten in years."

Years without seeing a doctor? Her father's medical practice in London was full of affluent patients; that's why her supervisor had insisted she do this small-town rotation before he would sign off on the completion certificate for her research doctorate. She had tried to talk him into letting her go to New York—her father had even pulled some strings to line up a placement there—but her supervisor wouldn't budge. He'd said she needed to understand how "real" people received medicine.

Maybe this would work out better than she'd expected. "It's settled, then. And I insist on paying for my groceries."

He glanced at her appraisingly, and she warmed under his gaze. "I doubt you'll put a dent in our stock." Jake waved as he stepped over the threshold to leave.

She stared at him. Her best friend and cousin, Priya, would look at someone like Jake and get giggly. Meera could objectively acknowledge his handsomeness, but she saw the swagger that came with it. *Not at all like Raj.*

"Before you leave, could you tell me why the town doesn't want me to stay?"

He turned back and laughed. "Oh, you'll find out soon enough."

Her phone chirped, distracting her. She took it out of her purse and looked at the screen. Her mother probably had another wedding-planning crisis. She needed to take the call.

"HURRY IT UP, sun's almost up." Jake drained his coffee and stood. Most of his staff were gathered for breakfast. It wasn't quite six in the morning, but the room was brightening. He wondered whether Meera would be up early; she must be jet-lagged. He hadn't seen her since he'd shown her to the guest cottage last evening.

He would never forget the image of her standing in his barn. She wasn't what he'd expected. He'd heard about what happened in town yesterday. The way everyone was talking, he figured she would show up at his door eventually. He hadn't planned on letting her stay—he didn't need any more gossip about him going around—but something made him change his mind.

What was Meera's deal, anyway? Why would she want to come to his little town? From the clothes she was wearing, those ridiculous heels, not to mention the fancy luggage, she obviously didn't need the money.

He felt a punch on his shoulder. "Earth to Jake! What're the orders, boss?"

He shook his head to clear Meera from his brain, then quickly barked out the day's assignments.

"Billy John, it's your turn to make dinner. And please, none of that awful chili you made last time."

Billy John began to defend himself to a chorus of insults, and Jake slapped him good-naturedly. Suddenly, his eye caught a flash of yellow in the doorway.

"Ah, this is our new renter, or 'paying guest,' as she would call herself." He said the last part in a British accent.

She rolled her eyes. *What's wrong with me?*

She peered into the kitchen, her movements tentative. She looked different in a simple yellow sundress; the color complemented her milk-chocolate skin. Her big brown eyes were awestruck, her already petite frame even tinier in the soaring doorway. The room went unusually quiet.

He glanced around his kitchen and realized what an overwhelming sight they all made. Nine burly men and three loud women would intimidate anyone.

"Hello, everyone, I'm Meera Malhotra." Her voice was soft.

Silent stares greeted her. Jake started to say something when she gave them a disarming smile.

"If you couldn't tell, I'm not from around here. I'm from London. I'm a doctor, here to do a one-month medical rotation with Dr. Harper."

"Good luck with that."

Jake smacked Billy John on the back of his head. Meera's eyes widened.

Jake quickly interjected. "Now, listen up, I've asked Dr. Mal..." He frowned at Meera.

"Malhotra, but please call me Meera."

"I've asked Dr. M. to give you all physicals—" there was a chorus of groans and protests "—which will be mandatory if you want to work here. So shut it. Last one to get their checkup will have to clean the entire house top to bottom." More groans followed. "And I do mean the whole house."

"Please don't worry. I'll make it as quick and painless as possible," Meera said soothingly.

The protests and general grumbling continued as everyone rinsed their dishes and filed out. Meera stood in the corner watching the whole process, her brows creased, eyes dark.

"Don't worry—they'll come around."

"I'm not worried about them." She hesitated.

"No more so than the rest of the town, anyway. I still don't know what I did yesterday to make everyone so cross."

Jake smiled. *She's in for a surprise. I bet she'll be packing her bags this afternoon.*

"Why come here all the way from London?"

She shrugged. "I was required to do a one-month rotation and thought it might be fun to do it in a small town."

"But why here? Why not someplace closer to home?"

"I've never been anywhere outside the UK on my own. Or India—that's where my parents and I are from originally. I've always wanted to visit America, and this seemed like a good opportunity. Besides, it will be good for me to learn how medicine is practiced in rural areas like this one." She sounded rehearsed. There was definitely more to the story; it was written all over her face.

"That sounds like a mighty boring reason to be here all month."

She began twisting the watch on her wrist. Jake sensed she wanted to say more, but she didn't continue. *What aren't you telling me, Meera?*

"Well, you might get more than you bargained for, but I'm sure you'll make the best of it." She bit her lip, and Jake found himself staring at the way her mouth moved.

"Won't you give me a hint of what to expect when I go into town today?" she pleaded.

He laughed and shook his head. "There's no way to explain it. You'll have to experience it for yourself."

"Any words of advice?"

He grinned. "Yeah, give 'em hell!"

She laughed. It was a pleasant, tinkling sound, and for some reason he wanted to make her do it again.

"Well, thank you for giving me a room—the cottage is just what I need for the month." She got a faraway look in her eye. "Do you own this ranch?" she asked suddenly.

"My father does. It's been in my family for a long time, passed down four generations now."

"So you grew up here, then?"

He nodded. "I was born right upstairs and spent my whole life here."

"Must be nice to have roots." Her voice had a sad longing in it.

"It's what makes this my home." Jake was surprised to hear his own voice catch. *Home...this ranch is so much more than home.*

"Is your father still alive?"

Jake shifted on his feet; Meera was too nosy. He didn't like answering questions about his family. "Yes."

"Does he live here?"

"No, he's suffering from Alzheimer's. He's in a nursing home."

"What about your mother?"

He focused on the cattle grazing in the fields outside the window. His mother was a topic he didn't discuss, not even with himself.

"She doesn't live here," he said sharply, then turned away from her.

Meera stepped back. "I'm sorry—I was just trying to get to know you."

"You're renting a room at my ranch. We don't need to be friends."

She muttered something under her breath.

"What's that, now?"

"Nothing. Do you have any tea?"

He pointed to the pot. "Try coffee—packs more of a punch."

"It's okay, I'll pick some up in town today."

"Good luck with that." Mr. Cregg owned the only store in Hell's Bells, and he was about to lose a major bet thanks to Meera.

She leaned against the counter, pressing a hand to her head, as if massaging a headache.

He sighed. She was all alone in a new place. The least he could do was to be nice and stop giving her a hard time about everything.

"I left you a plate of bacon, sausage and eggs." He motioned toward the heaping plate on the counter.

She swallowed, and her nose twitched.

What now?

"Do you have any toast?"

He pointed to the bread box.

"I'll just have that."

He bristled. "I'm a pretty decent cook, you know, and the bacon and sausage are fresh from the ranch."

"When you say 'from the ranch'…what exactly do you mean?"

He looked at her quizzically. "I mean we raise the animals here."

"And then slaughter them?"

"That's what ranchers do."

Her lips curved downward. "Well, that's something to think about."

Now she was rubbing her temples with both hands. He studied her carefully. "Out with it."

"Out with what?"

"With whatever's making you look like someone's drilling your brain."

"Oh, it's just that…I'm a vegetarian."

"What?"

"A vegetarian. I don't eat meat or any product that requires killing a living—"

"I know what a vegetarian is. Look at you, all bones, it's no wonder."

"Please tell me you don't raise cows here, to be killed."

He looked at her in disbelief. "It's a cattle ranch!" He motioned at the grazing cattle outside.

She grabbed the back of a seat. Her caffe-latte skin paled. He pulled a seat out, encouraging her to sit down, and she slumped into the chair. The last thing he needed was for the doctor to require medical attention. She muttered to herself.

"What is it?"

She began to say something, then closed her mouth.

"Oh, come on."

"Well...just that... I was raised as a Hindu. We believe the cow is a sacred animal and hurting one, or being anywhere near where one is being tortured, may bring bad karma for an entire lifetime... and possibly the next several lives."

You've got to be kidding me.

"You're a doctor, right? You went to medical school? Where they teach you about the brain and science and how the universe works?"

She glared at him. "This isn't about science. Even if you don't believe in reincarnation, you're raising a living organism for the sole purpose of killing it."

"The animal provides us with food."

"There is plenty of plant-based food for us to eat. We don't need to live at the expense of another being."

"The animals only exist because I bring them into the world for food."

"And it's wrong to create something just to destroy it. In my culture, the cow is sacred because it gives us milk…it gives us life. We call it *gai mata*, mother cow. For generations she has fed us, and the karma of killing her—"

"Cows are considered sacred because your ancestors used them to plough the fields and didn't want people to kill them for meat in times of famine. It was a practical decision, not a spiritual one."

She raised a perfectly shaped eyebrow.

"I would ask that you not mock my beliefs. I'm not asking you to stop cattle ranching, just explaining my reservations. I'll see about finding some other accommodations in town today."

"Yeah, good luck with that."

She blew out a sigh of frustration and buried her head in her hands.

Jake suppressed a smile. *Why am I enjoying this?* He studied the small hands cradling her head. She looked so fragile.

Wait… He went to the pantry and rummaged around. He knew he'd seen this. He handed her a box, and she looked at him gratefully. She opened it and took out a tea bag, reading the label. "Fertility tea?" she asked with amusement.

He swore under his breath. *No good deed goes unpunished.*

He shrugged. "It probably belongs to one of the ranch hands. I don't ask questions," he said quickly. It was Jolene's tea. *Why was Jolene drinking fertility tea?*

"Well, I've got to get going," he said. "There's work to do."

She nodded and stood up. "May I rummage in your cupboards for a cup and kettle?"

"Yeah, good luck with that."

He didn't miss her pursing her lips as she turned around, moving about his kitchen, opening cabinets. He absently noted that she was wearing flat-footed sandals with a strap that went up her delicate ankle and ended in a bow in the middle of her calf. Did all women wear shoes like that?

He rubbed the back of his neck. *I should talk Marty into giving her a room at the inn. I don't need trouble.*

CHAPTER TWO

IT WAS A minor miracle she made it to town without crashing the car. She'd almost forgotten which side of the road to drive on. Meera pulled down the visor and studied her reflection, checking that her makeup was perfect. She adjusted the collar of her suit dress. She'd paired it with her favorite Jimmy Choo heels and a string of pearls. Her mother always said that dressing like a princess would make her feel like she could conquer the world. And Meera already had a plan to fix her situation. She would talk to Dr. Harper about how to handle the townspeople and convince Marty to give her a room. She couldn't stay at a cattle ranch. *And I don't need to tolerate that rude cowboy.*

She stepped out of the car and took in her surroundings. There was a barbershop with the quintessential blue-and-red-striped pole, a general grocer's displaying a table of fruits and vegetables, the silver-walled Betsy's Diner and a post office proudly displaying the American flag. The brick sidewalks were lined with pretty trees and flowering bushes. The air was slightly dewy and smelled of fresh-cut grass. A picture-perfect small town.

Meera lifted her face to let the sun shine on it. She liked warm weather; England was always too cold and India was too hot. If one dressed properly, this weather was just perfect. Perhaps it wouldn't be so bad to spend the month here. She would much prefer New York, but it wasn't that far away and she still had the month to herself. She would pack a lifetime of freedom into the next four weeks. Then she could go home fully content and lead the life that had been planned for her.

She walked up the steps to Dr. Harper's office but paused at the door, hand on the knob. *I can do this.* She turned the handle and stepped in. Chimes announced her presence.

"Ah, Rose, how nice to see you again." Meera smiled warmly at the receptionist. She had only met Rose for a moment the day before, but she seemed to be a kind older lady. Rose was wearing a flowered dress, her white hair neatly pinned in a bun. Meera could picture her serving tea and biscuits like a British grandmother.

"We don't need you here. Please go away." The harsh tone was so out of line with the smiling, friendly face that it took Meera a moment to process the words. Her stomach dropped.

"Rose, I'm sorry, have I offended you? I don't understand."

Rose wagged her finger. "We don't need your kind of doctoring here."

"But Dr. Harper…"

"Dr. Harper is an old coot who—"

"That's enough, Rose."

Meera turned to see Dr. Harper emerge from his office. She blew out a breath she hadn't known she was holding. He was a small man with bright blue eyes, a shock of white hair and a booming voice. She had seen him only briefly yesterday when he'd shown her around the clinic, then he'd left her to see patients on her own. She hadn't expected to start work her very first day in Bellhaven, but there had been an emergency with Mrs. Harper, who was suffering from lung cancer. Dr. Harper had asked Meera to tend to his patients. He'd been rushed and distracted, but affable enough, which made sense since he was a friend of her British supervisor.

"Dr. Harper…"

He held up his hand to silence Rose. "Now, I won't have you giving Meera a hard time. She did what was right."

Meera stepped forward. "Dr. Harper, I don't understand what the fuss is about."

Rose scoffed, glaring at her with open hostility. "Derek Jenkins!"

Meera blinked. "The boy who had a concussion?" She didn't understand. It was a simple case, and she had treated it with textbook perfection.

Dr. Harper sighed. "Meera, let's go to my office to talk."

Meera followed him and sat down in the chair opposite his desk. He took a seat beside her in the second guest chair. He was obviously trying to make her comfortable.

Did I miss something? She went over the details of the case in her head and ran through the treatment plan. She specialized in cardiology but had graduated at the top of her medical program and completed her consultancy training with commendations. She knew how to take care of a concussion.

"Was there a problem with Derek Jenkins?" She scanned his desk to see if he had pulled up the teen's chart.

Dr. Harper shook his head wearily. "Meera, you provided appropriate medical treatment."

Meera relaxed a fraction.

"But you didn't necessarily do the right thing."

Her heart stopped. "I beg your pardon?"

"Derek is the quarterback for the regional high school football team, and the first game of the season is this week. It's against our biggest rival in the next county."

Meera reminded herself that American football was not soccer. She had initially thought Derek's injury was related to heading a soccer ball, but then he told her he'd been tackled during practice and hit his head on the ground.

She stared at Dr. Harper.

He tapped a finger on the table. "This might be hard for you to understand, not being from around here, but football is like a religion in Hell's Bells, and Fallton is our arch rival. It's the most anticipated game of the season."

Meera furrowed her brows. "I know he was disappointed he couldn't play, but the treatment for concussion is pretty clear."

"You and I understand that, but the town doesn't. Derek wants to play."

"It's a school game! Compared to the lifetime risk of exacerbating the head injury—"

"To you it's just a school game, but as I said, to the town, it's…"

"Worth more than Derek's life?"

Dr. Harper took a breath. "They don't see it that way."

Her mouth fell open. He couldn't possibly be serious. If she allowed Derek to play, he could make his concussion worse, and there was even a risk of death.

"Dr. Harper, surely…"

"Meera, I'm not arguing with you on medical grounds—I am telling you why the town is angry with you."

Meera changed tactics. "What would you have done if you were here instead of me?"

"I would have done the exact thing you did. The risk to his life is greater than the importance of the game."

Meera spread her hands, her eyes wide.

"But I would have handled the communication differently."

He leaned forward and patted Meera's shoulder in a fatherly gesture. "You should have walked Derek home and then talked to his father. Marty was a football star—he's put a lot of pressure on Derek, but he's not heartless. If you'd gone over there to explain things, he'd understand why Derek has to sit out a game or two."

"Walk Derek home?" That was unheard of. If Meera did that with every patient, she would have no time left. She knew she was used to a different pace than Dr. Harper's practice. She'd seen only three patients yesterday, when back in her father's London practice, she would have evaluated five or six patients an hour.

"Meera, Dr. Thurm called me before you arrived."

At the mention of her supervisor, Meera stiffened. Dr. Thurm had added this month-long rotation as a condition of approving the final dissertation for her research degree. It was an unexpected blemish on her otherwise stellar academic performance. None of the other students in the class were required to do this rotation. He had personally set it up with Dr. Harper after he disapproved the one her father set up in New York.

"He told me you're the brightest student he has ever worked with. Your medical knowledge is outstanding."

Meera smiled and blushed. Dr. Thurm was very hard on her, as he was on all his students. Coming from him, the statement was high praise indeed.

"However…he said that while you know medical science, you need to learn the art and practice of medicine."

"I'm sorry… I don't understand what you mean."

Dr. Harper opened a drawer and pulled out a stapled document. He handed it to Meera.

She glanced at it, the title familiar. "This is the publication from my research study—I won an award for this work."

"But your brilliant research will never benefit patients."

She stared at him. "I don't understand."

"The chemical compound you found is incredible, but it counteracts with sodium. If, as you suggest in the article, you develop it into a medication to treat heart disease, how would you deal with the sodium issue?"

Meera didn't know where he was going with this. He had obviously read the article, and it was clearly explained in there.

"The patient would have to cut salt from their diet."

"And you do think someone could effectively do that?"

"If their health is important to them, they should. As I suggest, they can easily reduce salt intake by not adding any table salt to the foods they eat."

"I ask you again—who would eat saltless, tasteless food day in and day out?"

"It's for their health."

"If someone asked you to eat red meat every day for your health, would you do it?"

"I'm a vegetarian."

"Exactly. You couldn't make such a drastic lifestyle change, and yet you're suggesting that it's perfectly plausible that patients will."

"If there was a health reason to eat meat, then I would consider it." Dr. Thurm had brought up a similar point, so she had calculated the typical sodium intake of an adult and factored in things that couldn't always be controlled, like salt in natural and processed foods in a typical diet. She had figured out the probability of patients "cheating" on the diet. She had accounted for patient behaviors.

She sighed. "So you're saying Derek won't stick to the treatment."

"I'm saying his treatment is not just medical. He has to face an entire football team calling him a sissy boy for not playing. He has to face everyone in town who's placed significant bets on the game. Without Derek, Hell's Bells is certain to lose."

"I can understand that, but if you agree he can't play, what can I possibly do to make the situation better?"

"He needs you to be the bad guy. He needs you to go tell everyone in town that playing could kill him, that even though he's walking around like nothing's wrong, his injury is serious. You need to go talk to Marty, Derek's coach and his teammates."

Meera groaned. *I miss London.* Patients came into the clinic, received a diagnosis and left with a treatment plan. That explained why Marty had kicked her out of his inn, and why the town was so hard on her.

Dr. Harper stood. "I think you'll find that medicine is far more satisfying when you can actually treat the whole person rather than just the ailment that bothers them."

Meera left his office and went to the little corner desk in the waiting room that had been set up as her workstation. She put down her purse, fully aware of Rose glowering at her. She would not dignify the older woman's petulance with a response.

"When is my first patient?" she asked calmly.

Rose snorted. "You're not going to be getting any patients."

Meera stepped toward her. "Listen, Rose, I'm only here for a month. Surely, we can find a way to work together."

"*Only* a month! Ha! And how do I know you don't have your sights on Dr. Harper's practice? We all know the old coot'll be retiring soon."

"Stop talking about me like I'm not here, Rose," Dr. Harper mumbled as he went into an examination room.

The front door chimed and a woman walked in. She was wearing short shorts and a red halter top. Her auburn hair was perfectly styled in waves. An image of Jessica Rabbit popped into Meera's head.

"Gloria!" Rose walked around the reception desk to give the new arrival a hug.

Gloria eyed Meera. "Is she the one who…"

Rose nodded. "Can you believe it? Three days before the big game. I don't know why Dr. Harper hasn't told her to go home."

Meera seethed.

Stop talking about me like I'm not here! "Do you think it has anything to do with Jake?" Gloria asked.

Jake? What does Jake have to do with this?

"I wouldn't put it past her. Who wouldn't want the town's number-one bachelor."

I should set them straight. Meera would never date an American because she didn't plan to stay in America. Her parents, her research, her entire life was in England, and she couldn't leave them. Besides, she was most definitely not interested in Jake.

"If she goes after him…"

"I have a fiancé in London," Meera blurted. "My entire family is in London, and my father has a very successful medical center that I'll be taking over. I do not plan to live in a town like this. After my rotation, I'm going home." She looked pointedly at Gloria. "And I don't fancy Jake—he's not my type." She didn't need to know what her type was. With Raj in the picture since childhood, she'd always had everything she needed in a life partner.

Rose grunted. Gloria's pout disappeared, and she raised an eyebrow, appraising Meera anew.

"Like I said, I'm only here for a month. What do you say we find a way to work together?" Meera held out her hand to Rose.

Rose wrinkled her nose. "The people who live

in a 'town like this' don't want to see a doctor like you."

Dr. Harper came out of the examination room just as Rose huffed past her. Meera looked at him helplessly.

He shrugged. "You did say you enjoyed a challenging work environment."

CHAPTER THREE

MEERA GRIPPED THE steering wheel. After the day she'd just had, this was the last thing she needed. *I could step on the accelerator, just ram right through.* She had purchased the extra insurance on the rental car. She dropped her head onto the steering wheel. *Why can't anything go according to plan?*

"Don't even think about it."

She looked up as Jake stuck his head through her open window.

"Think about what?"

"About driving through that gate."

"I wasn't serious about it," Meera said guiltily.

He opened her door. "Come on, I'll show you how it opens. It's a guard gate to keep the cattle from getting out, so it's a little tricky."

After he was done showing her how the gate worked, he hopped in the passenger seat. "Drop me at the house, will you?"

He smelled like he had yesterday—sweat, dirt and something…Jake. Great. Now her car smelled like Jake.

She drove up the gravel road.

"How was your day?"

Was there amusement in his voice? "It was fine."

"Did you find another place to stay?"

"You know very well I didn't."

She couldn't see his face, but she knew he was grinning.

"The guest cottage is still available."

"And I'm thankful for that."

"What about bad karma?"

She took a breath. If her parents were here with her, or Raj for that matter, they would tell her it was wrong to stay. They would remind her that she couldn't in any way support the killing of animals. She looked ahead as the house approached.

If she didn't stay, Jake would continue his business. Her presence was of no consequence to him, but to her it was the difference between finishing her research degree and having this month of freedom or starting all over again with a new rotation.

She chewed her lip. "Do you kill them on the premises?"

He snickered. "You'll be happy to know we don't. We take them to a slaughterhouse."

She breathed out. At least that was something.

"Does that mean your karma is safe?"

She smiled. "I'm pretty sure this life is ruined, but you may have saved my next one."

Meera pulled into the carport next to the house and turned to look at him. "Why cattle ranching?"

"Excuse me?"

"This is such a beautiful property. You could do so much with it—why do you raise cows?"

He bristled. "You ask too many questions."

"I'm a naturally curious person, and surely it's not a personal question. Have you always raised cattle here? I thought I saw horse stables earlier."

He sighed. "Every generation has made its own mark on this land. My dad boarded and trained horses. Wasn't very profitable, so I went into cattle ranching. I like cows and steers— they're good animals, just need to be fed, and they do that mostly by themselves, grazing in the fields during warmer months. Horses need to be groomed and brushed and exercised and on and on every day. I do have a few horses left over from my father's days. Mostly, I lend them out to the town for events or when we need to get a tractor out of a ditch."

He stepped out of the car, then came around the other side and held the door open for her. The British were known for manners, but Raj had never held a car door open for her. She was surprised and pleased at the gentlemanly gesture.

"Do you want to come inside and have dinner? We made some delicious steak and cheese."

There you go again. She shot him a look of daggers. He was grinning.

"Oh, just go ahead and have a good laugh at my expense."

"What'd you expect?"

"How about some courtesy and kindness to a visitor? This is my first time in America, I'm all alone and I can barely remember which side of the road to drive on. Why must you be so unkind?"

"You do know we Americans threw the British out of the colonies."

Aaarrghh! This was useless. Her shoulders sagged; it had been a long day and she was tired. Why was she trying so hard? This was a bad plan. *Perhaps Raj was right and my expectations* are *too high.* Tears stung her eyes, and she turned to walk to the cottage. She didn't want to give Jake the satisfaction of seeing her cry.

She felt him grab her hand as she passed him. A jolt sizzled through her arm, and she froze, unable to explain the energy vibrating through her.

"Listen—come inside, have a cup of tea. I bought you a box of English breakfast when I went into town earlier." His voice was soft, somewhat apologetic.

A cup of tea did sound good. She could come up with a new plan, a way to salvage her ruined trip.

As she walked into the kitchen, Meera noticed the warmth, the smell of food mixed with dish soap. Pots and pans were laid out to dry on the butcher-block counter. Noisy clanks came from a dishwasher. She ran her hand over the large wooden dining table, where everyone had been eating breakfast earlier. It was scratched and dented in several places.

"I need to sand and restain this old thing." She looked up to see Jake's eyes following her.

"I like it—the table has character. Mum's kitchen is always polished, not a pot or pan in sight. Her appliances are those quiet ones that make this really eerie vibrating sound. We have a formal dining room where we eat, which feels a little sterile sometimes." She touched the dents in the table, enjoying the sensation of the little dips in the wood. "This feels like a home."

He smiled. "It is home, at least for the month you're here."

She felt as if someone had wrapped her in a warm blanket on a cold day. She liked the sound of a noisy, cozy home.

He walked into the pantry and came out holding a kettle and a box of tea bags. He handed them to her, and she noticed his lips curve shyly at her thanks. He could be a sweet man, when he wanted to be.

She went to the sink and poured water into the kettle. She would take a private moment to drink tea and think about what to do. To her surprise, Jake sat down at the table. She set the kettle to boil and pulled out two cups.

"I have a teapot somewhere, but I couldn't find it."

She gave him a small smile. "I can make do." She steeped the tea in the mugs then poured some milk and a little sugar into both, the way she liked it. She handed him a cup, and he took a tentative sip.

"This isn't half-bad. I think my mother took her tea this way."

His mother? She wanted to ask but decided not to.

"Listen, I know I've been giving you a hard time, but don't worry. The town will come around."

She shook her head.

"That's what I thought this morning, but I don't think they will. Dr. Harper had me go talk to Marty Jenkins about why Derek couldn't play. Marty just told me he hit his head all the time when he played and nothing happened to him. Then I went to see Derek's coach, who said Derek had to toughen up and that if I didn't clear him, he'd make sure I couldn't show my face anywhere in Bellhaven."

Jake's eyes crinkled, turning an interesting shade of green.

"The icing on the cake was when I walked into a locker room full of half-naked teenagers and had to cover my eyes while they snickered at my explanation." She took a breath. "I had no patients all day. All my appointments canceled, and everyone who walked in refused to even let me be in the room while Dr. Harper examined them. I sat around doing nothing."

He laughed. "Oh, give it a couple of days and something else will rile everyone up." He looked at her with warm, reassuring eyes, tempting her to believe everything would be okay.

"Hardly. When the town loses the football game, it'll start all over again." She ran her finger around the rim of the cup, feeling the cracked edge. "The grocer wouldn't let me buy tea. The diner was all out of veggie burgers and any other nonmeat items, and I got a ticket even though I was parked legally." She sighed wearily. "They hate me."

He pushed his chair back and stood up. She turned to see him put a pan on the stove and take food out of the refrigerator. "I'm still a vegetarian, you know."

He laughed. "I'm making you a grilled cheese sandwich, your highness."

Tears welled in her eyes. She wasn't used to someone taking care of her. Growing up, she'd had an army of servants at her beck and call, but she never asked them to serve her. She'd often gone without a snack when hungry, too ashamed to ask the cook to make her something. "Thank you. I appreciate it…you have no idea how much."

He cleared his throat. "Yeah, well, I don't want you fainting on me." She sipped her tea and watched him sizzle butter in the pan. She felt herself relax as the warm liquid went down her throat. "On top of it all, Rose seems to think I'm going to take over Dr. Harper's practice."

"Well, Dr. Harper has been talking about retiring. His wife is getting worse, but there's no other doctor in town."

"I told her I don't have my sights on his practice—I plan to go back to London to run my father's clinic."

"Yeah, they think you'll like it so much here, you'll stay. I mean, who would leave the good old US of A to go back to colonial times."

She pursed her lips to bite back a retort. He was trying hard to keep up the pretense of being a surly rancher; she wouldn't engage in his ribbing.

"Besides, if you haven't noticed, I'm the town's

most eligible bachelor and they figure you'll fall in love with me and never leave."

She couldn't help but scoff. He thought a lot of himself. "Well, she has nothing to worry about. I'm getting married a few weeks after I return." She winced. Her marriage wasn't a secret, but for some reason she didn't want to discuss it with Jake.

Crash! Startled, she turned and saw the pan on the floor. Jake recovered quickly.

"Sorry…handle slipped from my fingers. Don't worry, I saved your sandwich."

He set a plate down. She picked up the sandwich and took a bite. *This is the most delicious thing I've ever tasted.* She let the buttery bread and soft cheese melt in her mouth.

"Mmm. Thank you!" She saw him staring at her, his green eyes darkening to brown. She felt herself blush and looked down at her plate.

Jake sat down and splayed his fingers over his half-empty mug.

"I heard something about a fiancé, but this town has a way of embellishing." He gazed pointedly at her hand. "You don't wear a ring."

She chewed slowly. "In Indian culture, the engagement is part of the wedding festivities. My parents wanted it to be the first party of the two-week celebrations."

"Two weeks?"

"I'm their only child—they've always spoiled me." She kept her eyes on her plate. Her mother had been planning this event for over a year. She was quite upset at the timing of Meera's trip, but Meera hadn't wanted to put it off. She needed to do this before the wedding.

"So tell me about your fiancé." His tone was casual, but there was something new in his voice. She searched his face, but he was studying the table.

"Raj is a family friend. We've known each other since we were children. He's also a physician, and his family is also from India originally, but we both grew up in the UK. We have a lot in common."

"Is he also a vegetarian?"

She laughed. "Yes, he is. We are very well suited to each other."

A shadow flittered across his face. "Well suited. That's an interesting way to put it. Do you love him?"

She frowned. *What a strange question.* But suddenly her mouth was dry. She took a sip of her tea and rubbed her temples.

"As I said, I've known him for many years and we're quite fond of each other. We're research partners—we run a research project together, and after I finish my research doctorate, we'll open our own lab."

He raised his brows.

Suddenly, she didn't want to talk about Raj anymore. "Are you married?"

Was it her imagination, or did he flinch? He shook his head. "I was engaged once."

"What happened?"

"She left me." His voice was devoid of emotion, but she sensed bitterness and pain behind the words.

"Is the fertility tea hers?"

He laughed mirthlessly. "Yeah, that one took me by surprise, too." He was trying too hard to keep his voice carefree. The raw sorrow in his eyes gave him away. She wanted to reach out and touch him.

"How long ago?" she asked softly.

"Almost a year."

Meera placed her hand over his. "I'm so sorry." His hand felt warm and rough and somehow familiar. Meera pulled away.

He gave her a wistful smile. "It's probably for the best. I've let it go."

She finished her sandwich and stood up to wash the plate. She had a thousand questions for him, but it didn't feel right to pry. He seemed vulnerable…and heartbroken.

"Why're you marrying a man you don't love?"

Meera froze, the water pouring over her hands as she held the plate. Her head throbbed painfully. Was he asking because his fiancée had left him? "What makes you think I don't love him?" Did her voice sound shaky?

"You haven't once said that you do."

She turned off the water and sat down wearily. "There are all kinds of love, Jake. My parents didn't even know each other when my grandparents arranged their marriage. They discovered one another and fell in love after their wedding, and they've been together for forty years. Forty years!"

He didn't look convinced.

"Love is something you have to nurture…it grows over time."

"So what is this, an arranged marriage?" he asked contemptuously.

"You could call it that or a planned marriage. A carefully selected union between two people who know and admire each other. It's a sound basis for selecting a life partner."

He gaped at her, shaking his head in disbelief. "It's not a business merger, Meera, it's a life together. This is the twenty-first century. Your parents can't marry you off against your will."

She glared at him. "How American of you to think this is happening without my consent! Arranged marriages have been a part of my heritage for a very long time. The divorce rate in India is one percent. One percent! Compared to over fifty percent here. I'm not marrying Raj because my parents are making me—I'm marrying him because I want to. He's a good match for me, we've known each other for years…it only makes sense we would be good life partners." Was it just her, or was it getting stuffy in here? Her head was about to explode.

"What about love?"

What was with Jake and this love thing? "There are all kinds of love. At some level, Raj and I have loved each other for twenty years."

"That sounds like an academic argument to me."

"Well, I am a scientist."

"And yet you believe in karma."

She started to argue, then stopped. *He has me there.* "There are many things in this universe that science hasn't explained."

"Are your parents happily married?"

"Pardon me?"

"You said your parents have been married for forty years. Has it been a happy marriage?"

She had never thought about it before, but of course her parents were happy. Weren't they? She knew their inability to have children had created an underlying sadness for both of them, but beyond that? She suddenly realized she didn't know much about how her parents' marriage worked.

She stood up. "If you'll excuse me, I've had

a very difficult day and I'm exhausted. I need to go lie down and figure out whether I should return to London." She pushed her chair back, picked up her cup and took it to the sink. She was grateful for the food and tea; she felt fortified.

When she was done washing the dishes, she muttered a curt good-night as she stepped past him.

"Throw them a barbecue."

She turned in the doorway. "What?"

"The town. They can't resist a good barbecue—it's a good way to win them over. You can have it here, and I'll give you a grill and meat. Just…wear jeans and a T-shirt—you know, regular clothes."

She frowned at him. "What's wrong with my clothes? This dress is Gucci."

His eyes traveled up and down her body. Heat seared through her. "Most people here get their clothes at discount stores. Show them you aren't the Queen of England. Wear something regular folks wear, like that dress you had on this morning."

She began to argue with him, then stopped. He was showing her a way out. *A barbecue. I can use it as an opportunity to show them…and Jake…that I'm not so strange.* All was not lost. She could picture it already.

She clapped her hands and stepped toward him. "I'll have it the day after tomorrow. It's a

Sunday, so the office will be closed. I'll order everything I need online, overnight delivery. Yes, I'm sure I can make it work. I'll go make a list right now. Thank you so much, Jake."

Impulsively, she leaned over and gave him a peck on the cheek. Her lips tingled as they touched his prickly stubble, and she took in his scent. She stepped back, suddenly a little light-headed. Her headache was gone, replaced with comforting, elating warmth.

His eyes darkened. He shifted in his seat, clearing his throat. "Yeah, well, I'll tell Kelly to help you with all this. Let me know if you need anything."

Her cheeks burned as she backed out of the room. She mumbled another thank-you and fled to the cottage.

CHAPTER FOUR

JAKE SURVEYED THE SCENE. *Not bad.* Meera had gone to quite some expense, renting a tent, tables, chairs, even a dance floor. The tables were draped with red-and-white-checkered cloths and little vases of fresh-cut flowers. She'd turned his entire field into a photo-worthy barbecue.

He'd seen the light on in the cottage well into the night for the past two days, and she was up before sunrise today. She set up the tent right in front of the hay barn, the red structure providing a picturesque backdrop. She even managed a great day: partly cloudy sky, pleasant breeze and dry ground.

She had already loaded coal in the chimney starters of the grill he'd lent her, and he made a mental note to check that she'd opened the vent. Meera was standing near the grill with a clipboard in hand. He could see her checking things off. She was dressed in jeans and—*what do you know*—a T-shirt. She looked amazing, but then she always did—in whatever she had on, even the severe dresses she wore to work. Her dark hair was pulled into a ponytail. He liked it. It showed off her big, expressive brown eyes.

She's something, isn't she? He didn't know many people who would take on the town of Hell's Bells. Jolene certainly hadn't; she'd run away as soon as they turned on her, and she was born here. He admired Meera's gumption. Although she looked like a fragile little thing, he sensed an inner strength. She was a fighter.

He walked toward her.

"Need some help?"

She looked up and smiled. *Oh, wow.* His legs suddenly felt unsteady, and he slowed down. It was the first genuine smile he had seen since she arrived, and it was spectacular. He stopped when he reached her and stared at the ground, not wanting to meet her eyes. She was wearing flip-flops with sequins on the straps, calling attention to her bright red toes.

"I think I have the grill going."

He gave it a perfunctory look and nodded, unable to take his eyes off her. "You do—the coal looks nice and hot." She gave him another stunning smile, and he found himself grinning like a teenage boy. She had put it all together by herself. Given her obviously wealthy upbringing, he'd expected her to ask him or his staff for help on any number of little things, from moving tables and chairs to starting the grill, but she hadn't.

"People should be here any minute. I think I'll start the first round of hot dogs and burgers. I just need to check the package..."

"Package?"

"The instructions on how to cook them without burning."

Instructions? "What?"

She pointed to the cooler. He frowned. It wasn't one of his coolers; he'd assumed it held the beer. "Where did you get that meat?"

She smiled broadly. "It's meatless hot dogs and burgers."

Meatless meat? He gripped the cooler lid and lifted out a package. *Precooked?* This was going to be bad. Really bad.

"Tofu?"

She nodded excitedly. "They taste just like meat, but they're made of soy. Sustainable soy, I might add."

Why am I getting involved in this? She's her own worst enemy. He looked at her excited face. She had her convictions, and he respected her for that, but she was headed for disaster. "Listen, Meera, I appreciate what you're trying to do, but it won't work. Meat is meat, and nothing else tastes like it. You told the town you're throwing a barbecue; they'll be expecting meat, you can't just—"

"But that's the point—I'll show them they can

follow a healthy lifestyle and keep their traditions. They don't have to give up barbecues, just eat less red meat."

"This is a ranchin' town, Meera. You're not going to win them over in one night. I pulled out a bunch of meat from the freezer yesterday— Kelly was supposed to give it to you. It's all in the fridge. I'll go get it. You can offer up your tofu dogs and burgers as another option."

"No!" She gave him a sharp look. "That defeats the purpose. Part of my rotation here is to improve public health. I want to introduce the town to the notion that there are healthy, tasty alternatives to red meat. I have it all planned."

He shook his head. *Add stubborn to the reasons I shouldn't get involved.* "The whole point of this barbecue is to make up for not understanding what's important to the town. Meat is important."

"I'm trying to show them how to enjoy their traditions in a better way."

He threw up his hands.

He turned. "I'm not gonna waste my time arguing with you."

She looked defiantly at him. "It'll be fine, just wait and see."

"WHAT THE HELL is this?" Rose spit out the first bite of hot dog. Others followed suit, seeming equally appalled.

"It's a tofu dog," Meera explained.

"Toe what now?"

Meera looked at the disgusted faces. About fifty people were here—a good turnout, according to Jake. *What's wrong?* She'd tasted the first hot dog; it was delicious. Jake's advice on the mix of wood chips for the grill had given it quite a flavor. So why were they spitting it out?

She watched in dismay as people used her thoughtfully placed trash cans to toss perfectly grilled tofu dogs and burgers.

"Where's the meat? I didn't sign up for this veggie crap."

"Rose, remember how Dr. Harper has been talking about getting the town to eat healthier? Well, this is—"

Rose grabbed her arm and said in a low voice, "You don't mess with a barbecue. A barbecue is about meat—juicy, fat, red meat. It's not the time to introduce tofu. Dr. Harper meant to do some health seminars, hand out flyers, that kind of thing. You silly girl."

"I'm leaving! Should've known she was gonna screw this up," she overheard someone say.

"Why don't you go back to wherever they actually like this stuff," another local added.

"That's enough!" Jake's booming voice made Meera jump. "Meera's gone to a lot of trouble, so why don't we give her a chance?" There he was, tall and lean, cowboy hat and jeans and a T-shirt that showed off every flex of his sinewy muscles. He was towing a cooler behind him. "I've got some fresh meat here, and we'll grill it right up. And she's got some cold beer, so settle down."

There were cheers from the crowd. Meera's face burned. *How dare he?* "What do you think you're doing?" she whispered angrily when he got near.

"I'm saving you from yourself—you'll thank me later."

"Oh, you are such a pompous—" She took a deep breath and turned to the crowd. She was wasting her energy on Jake. "Listen, everybody, can I just take a second to tell you about some of the health benefits of eating soy rather than red meat? Studies have shown that eating soy can lower your risk of heart disease by as much as…" She stopped. Her guests were crowding around Jake, choosing meat, chatting away. Jake started poking coal in the grill, taking off the tofu burgers and dogs and throwing them in the trash bin.

She crossed her arms. She noticed something on the ground, near the grill. The clipboard. Someone stepped on it, and she heard it snap.

"Well, if you'll pardon me, I need to take care of something back at the cottage." No one listened. No one cared. She turned on her heels and ran.

She flung herself on the bed.

The nerve of him! She wanted the town to get to know her as a person, not "the Queen of England," as they'd all taken to calling her—a not-so-endearing name that Jake had no doubt perpetuated. Dr. Thurm and Dr. Harper had asked her to work on preventative medicine in Bellhaven as part of the community education component of her rotation. Teaching the townsfolk how to eat better was the perfect way to achieve that, and she'd been sure the party would convince them she wasn't just some clueless foreigner. She'd planned every detail of the barbecue so they could see how simple lifestyle changes could make a difference in their health. It was the basis for her research, a way to prove to Dr. Thurm that the development of her blood pressure compound could work. People would be willing to make a change for their health. Jake had ruined it all.

She let her tears fall. She could have turned it around, explained the benefits of soy…if Jake hadn't shown up with meat. How could she compete with that? Serving meat at her party! Her parents would be furious if they ever found out.

What am I doing here? she wondered. *This will never work. Maybe I should have waited until after the wedding, taken some time to talk Dr. Thurm into letting me do this in New York.*

Why am I trying to get this awful town to like me? I'm so in over my head.

But she couldn't go back to London, not after she'd fought so hard with her mum to come here now. This was her final shot at independence, to be free of the social obligations that came with being a socialite's only daughter, before taking on the duties of marriage. She'd seen the opportunity and jumped on it.

Meera would never have this kind of freedom again. Raj hated traveling.

Her phone rang, and she looked at the caller ID. *As usual, his timing is great. Maybe talking to him will help.*

"Hello, Raj." She tried to inject some enthusiasm into her voice; she didn't want to worry him.

"Hello, love, glad I caught you. I tried ringing earlier…" She felt a twinge of guilt. She'd been so busy planning the barbecue, she'd forgotten to return his call.

"Yes, I've been quite busy settling in. How are you getting along?"

He began talking about patients and giving her an update on the practice. Everything was falling into place. She and Raj would run her father's practice after they were married and eventually merge with the medical conglomerate Raj's parents owned. Her father was looking forward to retiring after Meera and Raj took over the medical center. Their research project was progressing well, and once they secured permissions and funding for their own laboratory, the sky was the limit.

She listened to his familiar voice, letting it soothe her as she lay back on her bed. The tension eased out of her muscles. This was why she was marrying Raj: he always calmed her. Given what had happened tonight, should she go back early? She could come back later and complete the rotation or maybe even transfer somewhere else. But then she wouldn't be able to apply for the funding she needed to start the lab. She squeezed her eyes shut.

Raj was talking about a new computer system her father wanted to invest in. Her thoughts went back to the barbecue. Jake had been right about it bringing the town together, and he'd been nice enough to let her host the party at his ranch. And even though she hadn't wanted him to, he'd been generous to offer up all that meat. She would pay him for it, of course. *Jake!* Why did he infuriate her so much? And yet, she couldn't hold on to her anger. No matter how wrong he was, Jake was well-intentioned. She thought back to a few nights ago when he'd made her a grilled cheese. Despite disagreeing with her about being a vegetarian, he respected her choice.

So why had he brought out the meat today? She thought about the way the town had reacted to her tofu dogs. Obviously, Jake knew the folks of Bellhaven better than she did. Maybe she had pushed too hard? She should go back; it was rude to leave her own party and perhaps a little grumpy. After all, the band would be there soon... Surely, there was a way to salvage the evening? The original purpose of the barbecue was to convince the townspeople she meant well; maybe she could still make that happen.

She interrupted Raj. "Listen, I'm rather in the middle of something right now—do you mind if I ring you later?"

He paused. "Well, I suppose that would be all right, although now is the best time for me."

"Sorry, but I really need to go."

"Meera..."

She stabbed the end button and immediately regretted it. Raj hadn't done anything wrong. Oh, well, she'd explain it to him later.

She walked back to the barbecue and saw the band setting up. People were sitting down and eating, and loud conversations drifted to her ears. There was general merriment in the air. It was exactly as she planned it, except it wasn't. Jake had done this.

She wrinkled her nose as she approached the grill. Jake was placing fat, bloody pieces of meat above the coals. Bile rose in her throat, and she clutched her stomach, resisting the urge to throw up.

He held out a plate to her and she stared at him in horror.

"Relax. I saved you a tofu burger before I put the meat on."

She smiled gratefully and took the plate. There was the sweetness again, the way he thought about her needs. Not many men would be that considerate.

"Who are they?" Jake pointed at the band.

"Don't worry, I thought the meatless meal would be enough of an experiment. The band is from Richmond—they do country music. The online reviews said they're quite good."

He smiled mischievously. "Well, then, you'll have to save a dance for me."

A shiver ran down her spine. She looked down shyly. "I don't dance very well."

He leaned forward and whispered, "Don't worry, I'll teach you." His breath warmed her ear.

"Jake, these burgers are yum-mum-mee." While Meera was staring at her feet, Gloria had sidled up to Jake and put her hand on his arm.

Meera smiled brightly at her. *Best fake smile, Meera—time to mend fences.* Gloria was wearing extremely small shorts again, showing off miles of legs that ended in wedged heels. *Ah, note to self: pointed heels get stuck in the mud, wedges are the way to go.* She would have to go shoe shopping soon; retail therapy might be a good antidote to the stress of Bellhaven. Gloria had paired her shorts with a red-and-white-checkered shirt tied in a knot above her belly button, and a pink cowboy hat completed the look. She and Jake would make a picture-perfect, all-American couple.

"Mmm… This is so good, Jake—what did you put it in?" Gloria purred. She leaned in, and Jake took a step closer to the grill, away from her.

"It's just beef, Gloria, nothing special."

Oh, I can't watch this. Meera excused herself, much to Gloria's delight and Jake's apparent dismay. She headed over to see the band.

"Dr. M., can I talk to you for a minute?"

Meera turned to find a young woman standing behind her. The girl was red in the face and heavyset. Meera frowned. The raised rash on her face could indicate a medical problem. "Of course. Come with me."

Meera led her to the cottage, and she looked around nervously as she hurried along. "Please don't tell anyone I'm talkin' to you."

Meera ushered her into the living room. "Don't worry. If I'm here as your doctor, I won't repeat anything you say unless you ask me to."

"Okay. My name's Lily…" She still seemed

anxious. "I have this problem, and I can't tell anyone else in town…"

Meera nodded and scanned the young woman's body, looking carefully at her face. "You're pregnant, aren't you?"

Lily's eyes widened. "You can't tell anyone!" Her voice was panicked.

Meera put her arm around Lily soothingly. "Like I said, this is confidential. Nothing you tell me will leave this room."

Lily relaxed visibly. "You promise? You can't tell a single soul in this town."

Meera nodded.

Lily collapsed on the couch. "How did you know?"

"The rash on your face looks like pruritic urticarial papules and plaques of pregnancy. And your weight."

"Everyone thinks I just got fat, but the rash is new and I… Is the baby okay?"

Meera went to her bedroom and brought out the medical bag her father had given her. She opened it and began taking Lily's blood pressure. She asked Lily some questions and did a brief exam, pressing on her belly. "The rash can happen with pregnancy, and I think you're fine, but I need to do an ultrasound to be sure. If you're right about your last period, you're about thirty-two weeks along."

Lily shook her head. "I can't come to the office for an ultrasound. Rose would blab about it to the whole town." She paused and touched her cheek. "I haven't told the baby's father—that's why I haven't seen Dr. Harper. I can't have this town knowing…" She stopped and looked down. "It's a little complicated."

Meera squeezed her hand. "If you haven't seen a doctor since you got pregnant, it's really important we do an ultrasound and run blood tests to make sure everything is all right. Come to the clinic tomorrow after twelve. Rose goes to lunch and Dr. Harper goes home to check on his wife around then. Wait in the car until you see them leave, then ring the bell and I'll come get you. They'll never know."

Lily nodded gratefully. "Thank you, Dr. M. I had no idea what to do or who to go to. Jake said you're a good person…" She sat up straighter. "I know the town doesn't want you here, but please don't let them run you off." She put her arms around Meera and held her tight, taking her by surprise. Meera had never been hugged by a patient before. *And I haven't even done anything for her.*

She let Lily leave the cottage and followed several minutes later, watching as the young woman rejoined the crowd.

She hasn't seen a doctor since she got preg-

nant! Maybe being an outcast isn't such a bad thing. Then people who need privacy, like Lily, can come to me, and I can focus on those who really need my help. She felt a spring in her step as she went back to the barbecue.

She had to remember to thank Jake for sending Lily. The fact that she'd gone to him when she hadn't told anyone else in town said a lot about the type of person Jake was.

The band was in full swing and from the look of it, everyone seemed to be having a good time. There were several people on the dance floor, yelling with delight and teasing each other. Perhaps all was not lost. She took in the gleeful faces and grudgingly wondered whether Jake was right. Maybe it was too much to expect the town to rethink their way of life with one barbecue. Where was Jake, anyway?

"Hey."

She placed a hand on her chest. "Could you not sneak up on me like that?"

"What was that about?" He nodded toward Lily.

Meera shrugged. "Nothing. She just had to use the bathroom and wanted to tell me how much she hates tofu burgers."

Jake smirked. "You're such a bad liar, it's written all over your face." Meera started to protest, but he waved her off. "It doesn't matter. It's time to do the two-step."

"I beg your pardon?"

His eyes gleamed. Grinning ear to ear, he put his arm around her waist and pulled her onto the dance floor. She squealed. He twirled her and began showing her the steps to the dance. She felt breathless as she followed his steps, feeling a little anxious at her clumsiness.

"I can't do this, Jake."

He shook his head. "Let go, Meera. It's about the music and having fun. You don't have to do it right—just try it, be free."

She grinned. *You don't have to do it right?* Then how was she supposed to have fun? She took a breath and started moving again, watching everyone else's feet so she could copy their steps perfectly. Several people on the dance floor were making eye contact with her, nodding encouragingly. Jake introduced her to old Mr. Leeland, who grabbed her hand and twirled her. She couldn't help dissolving into giggles as the elderly man tried to dip her. She caught Jake's eye, and he winked at her as she stepped on Mr. Leeland's foot. He laughed good-naturedly and led her across the floor. She couldn't keep up with the steps; everyone's feet were a jumble.

Someone twirled her and suddenly she was being passed from partner to partner, each one kind about her mistakes. She caught Rose staring at her, a smile on her face. Maybe Jake was right. She stopped worrying about the steps and started enjoying the music.

She felt completely carefree as Jake caught her hand and lifted her up when she began stepping on his toes.

She didn't know how long she spent dancing, enjoying herself with each breathless round on the floor. There were cheers and hoots from the crowd as she finally made a circuit without stepping on any toes. *I can't remember the last time I felt this free.* Jake had long since passed her off to another dance partner, but she searched for him in the throng.

Billy John had just grabbed her hand when a loud scream jolted her. Several others joined in, and chaos broke out as people began running in all directions. The band stopped playing. "Everyone clear out." It was Jake's voice, but she couldn't find him in the sea of arms and legs. *What's happening?* She looked around frantically and gasped. Flames! The grill was on fire along with the edge of a tablecloth.

"Move aside."

Meera saw Jake running toward the fire with an extinguisher. The tablecloth was now fully ablaze and lighting the roof of the tent. She took out her cell phone, but put it away when she heard the faraway sound of sirens. She ran out of the tent and stopped a safe distance away, noticing Jake had done the same. A few of the ranch workers were approaching with extinguishers, but Jake waved them back. The fire had spread too much. The slight breeze had carried the flames across the field, right up to the barn. The fire department would have to handle it.

The fire engines arrived in a blaze of lights, their sirens screaming. Several firefighters ran toward the fire, aiming their hoses.

Jake stood several yards away from her. As if he knew she was looking at him, he turned and caught her eye. *Oh, boy!* Even from a distance, she could feel his fury. He stalked over.

"Tell me you opened the vent on the back of the grill when you set it up."

Her mouth went dry. She put a hand to her forehead, trying desperately to remember. She could see his instructions in her mind's eye; she had written them down precisely on the clipboard. The paper said to open the vent after the coal heated up, but all she could remember was that she had been reading that very instruction when he walked up to her. And she had lost her train of thought. She didn't remember actually opening the vent.

"I…I'm not sure I did. Oh, God, Jake, I'm so sorry."

His eyes reflected the flames that were demolishing the barn behind her. "Do you have any idea how dangerous a fire is on a ranch? What it can do to the animals? Not to mention the fact that I may have lost a barn full of hay. Do you know how much bales cost these days?" He began pacing as the firefighters doused the fire. It seemed to be coming under control, but Meera could see a mess of soggy black ash on the ground and a black shell where the pretty red barn had stood. She thought that she'd ruined the barbecue earlier with the veggie dogs, but this? This was a complete disaster.

When Jake came close to her again, she touched his arm. "I'll pay for the damage."

He whirled to face her. "Are you kidding me? You can't wave your magic credit card and make this all okay, princess."

She inhaled sharply, trying to breathe against the tightness in her chest.

"Tomorrow morning, I'd like you to leave. I'll talk to Marty about giving you a room— although after tonight, I'm not sure you'll ever recover with this town."

CHAPTER FIVE

JAKE'S EYES KEPT wandering to the door. *It's still early—she may not be up yet.* He knew she hadn't left. Her rental was still in the carport.

"Earth to Jake! What do you want us working on today?"

Jake snapped to attention. "Go about your regular chores," he said dismissively. "I'll deal with the cleanup." He watched his staff file out silently; they had worked with him long enough to know he was in a mood.

"Kell, have you gotten your physical yet?"

Kelly shook her head and mumbled, "I'll get to it." She left quickly, and he fought the urge to throw something at her. He worried about her. She tried to hide it, but he knew there was something wrong. He couldn't let Meera go yet, not until she finished the physicals. *And there is absolutely no other reason I want her to stay.*

He hung around the kitchen, rearranging dishes in the dishwasher. After he was done, he went into the pantry. *I know Jolene had a teapot. A teapot she used to drink fertility tea while she was planning on leaving me.* He shook his head. *Every woman in my life is determined to torture me.* He couldn't figure Meera out. Why was she so desperate to have the town like her? It was as if some internal motor was driving her to make sure she was acceptable. She'd worked herself to the bone getting that barbecue organized. She hadn't snapped her fingers and hired an army to put it together. Though if she had, he wouldn't be calculating damages right now.

He gave up looking for the teapot and glanced at his watch. He couldn't waste away the day. He walked toward his ruined field and barn; he would hear her car leaving. His stomach turned as he saw the damage from afar. He'd had more than a hundred hay bales in the barn, and most of them were burned, charred or waterlogged and full of ash. With the drought this year, he didn't have enough grazing fields to get through the winter. He'd managed to get a good deal on hay to keep the animals fed.

He stopped and stared, painful knots twisting his stomach. He couldn't afford to replace that much hay, especially not at current prices. He wouldn't make a profit this year. Again. He did some quick calculations. With the loss of hay, and this field, he would have to sell at least fifty steers or send them to slaughter right now. He wouldn't get the same price he would get in a few months, but if he had to buy more hay and grain to feed them, he'd have to take out a loan and with interest—he did some quick math—he'd be screwed, anyway. Either way, the ranch was going to take a big hit.

He blew out a breath. *Meera's more trouble than she's worth.* Although truth be told, he should have checked the grill. That's what he'd been walking over to do when her smile distracted him. He was furious at himself. He didn't remember Jolene turning him upside down like that. But then, he'd never met a woman like Meera before. The way she'd come back from the humiliation of her tofu dogs…it took courage to face up to Hell's Bells like that. He had seen her retreat to the guest cottage. Most women would have stayed there licking their wounds, but not Meera. She'd marched right back as though she owned the evening.

As he approached the field, he squinted. *What the…* He ran the last few yards. Meera was standing at the edge of the field, tossing debris into a trash bag as big as she was tall. She was wearing a T-shirt and shorts, and her legs were covered in soot and dirt. He remembered the disdain in her eyes the first day they met when he patted his dirty hands on his jeans. *What is* she *doing getting her hands dirty?* He knew the answer even before he asked.

"What're you doing?"

"I've been taught to take responsibility for my actions, so I'm not leaving you with this mess."

Her determination made his heart speed up. Why didn't she just leave or hire staff to clean up after her? She was a princess; why break a sweat?

"You don't have to do this."

"Actually, Jake, I do. It's my fault, and I need to fix it."

He took in the firm set of her lips and locked on to her earnest, brown, almond-shaped eyes. She had guts coming out here to face him after the way he'd stormed at her last night.

Inexplicably, he wanted to take her in his arms and tell her it would all be okay, that he would take care of it. Manual labor was for hardy ranchers like him. She might have the heart for it, but she was too delicate to toil away in the heat.

He pointed to the big white tent that had fallen once the fire went out, then gestured to the area she was working on. "This is the easy part, you know. Wait till you see what's under the tent—it's ash and mud, and the barn has entire sections that'll need to be rebuilt. Any idea how many gallons of water they dumped?"

She looked down. "I can't undo what happened yesterday, but I'm going to make it right. I'll also pay for whatever damage I caused." He stepped closer, distracted by the ruined barn behind her. He pictured his last balance sheets. The numbers weren't looking good.

"Meera, this is not your problem. Let me handle it."

"I have to take responsibility."

"Look, I know your heart's in the right place, but you have no idea what you're doing here. This field, my barn, they're ruined. My father built that barn with his own two hands and no magic credit card can replace that."

She made a strangled sound, her lips trembling. "I should at least pay your building costs. And what about this field?"

"The fields are used to feed the animals—they graze on grass. Without grass to feed them, I have to either sell or slaughter about fifty head in the next week."

Her face crumpled. She took a shaky breath and sat down on the dirty tent, burying her face in her hands. "You're going to kill fifty animals because of me!" Something stabbed at his chest. She looked so heartbroken. What was he supposed to do? She didn't understand that this was how the cattle business worked. He let out a breath. *I'm so going to regret this.*

He sat down next to her. "It's not your fault entirely. I was going to check the vent on the grill and got distracted."

She gazed up at him with glistening eyes. "With what?"

"Huh?"

"What did you get distracted with?"

His mind brought up an image of her standing in nearly the same spot, smiling as if the world belonged to her. Inexplicably, he felt a kinship with Meera. They had nothing in common, at least not superficially, but beneath her uppity exterior, he sensed her kind soul. It made him want to know what else lay beneath the princess shell.

She was looking expectantly at him, waiting for an answer. "I got distracted with you." He reached out and took her hand, needing to feel contact with her.

Her eyes widened, then she squeezed back. He exhaled. It wasn't just him; she was feeling it, too.

"The point is, this isn't all on you. And I didn't mean what I said yesterday—I was angry at myself and taking it out on you. You're welcome to stay here. God knows you have your hands full with the town. You don't need to worry about this."

She sniffed. "I appreciate your generosity, really, but this happened because of me. I'll take you up on the offer to keep staying here, though. I still need to finish the physicals on your staff." She extracted her hand from his, then stood up and dusted her palms on her jeans. "If you'll be patient with me, I want to work on cleaning this up when I'm not twiddling my thumbs at Dr. Harper's practice."

Obviously, he wasn't going to be able to talk her out of it, but maybe it wasn't such a bad idea. It was one more hand to help clean the mess up, and he couldn't afford to increase the hours of the other staff. But did he really want her around, distracting him?

"Suit yourself." He tried to keep his voice nonchalant. "How much time do you have?"

She checked her watch. "I have another hour, maybe more before I have to get ready."

"I'll be back."

He went to the shed and returned with a forklift.

"You ever drive one of these things?"

Meera's eyes widened and she shook her head. "No! I have no idea how to operate that. I'll crash it."

He smiled and held out his hand. "Don't worry, I'm not trusting you with heavy machinery. I'll be driving."

She took his hand, and his heart thumped wildly as she squeezed into the cab next to him.

It was a tight fit and she was half sitting in his lap. He tried not to notice the way her leg touched his or how small she felt snuggled in beside him.

He put her hand on the clutch and showed her how to put it in gear, then he stepped on the accelerator. She yelped as they moved forward, and he couldn't take his eyes off the wild expression on her face.

Focus, Jake, focus. He showed her how to operate the lift and pick up the large tent in sections, moving it to the side.

Once they'd dealt with the tent, they parked the forklift and surveyed the damage underneath. There was ash mixed in with pieces of tables, chairs and the wooden dance floor. Flecks of the red-and-white-checkered tablecloth were strewn everywhere.

"The rental company is gonna charge you a pretty penny."

Meera shrugged.

"Did you call them and get an estimate?"

She shook her head. "No, it's fine, whatever it is."

Jake laughed mirthlessly. And there was another Meera contradiction. She was rich, so why insist on doing the dirty work herself? "Must be nice not to have to worry about money."

"I guess I'm lucky. My father has a very successful medical practice. He's never let me worry about money—it's one of the many things I owe my parents."

That's a strange sentiment. "Owe your parents? Why would you owe your parents?"

Meera smiled wistfully. "They're not my biological parents. They adopted me from an orphanage in India when I was ten." She looked out at the field, suddenly seeming a million miles away.

He stopped the forklift. He didn't know a lot about India, but no child belonged in an orphanage. He remembered what it had been like when his mother left, but he'd had his father and the townspeople to take care of him.

"Do you remember your biological parents?"

"I was three years old, or so the matron at the orphanage told me, when they left me at the doorstep. I don't remember them, the parents that gave birth to me." She paused, and when she spoke again, her voice was soft and so raw that pain seared through him. "I was living in squalor and poverty, conditions you can't even imagine until Mum and *Pitaji*—my father—adopted me." He could hear the voice of the little girl inside her, the one who was afraid and alone. He put his hand on hers, wishing he could take her pain away.

"They gave me a beautiful, perfect life. In the orphanage, all I could think about was getting my hands on a few rupees to bribe the cook to give me food. They did the bare minimum to keep us alive. Since my parents adopted me, they've given me everything any person could ever want."

That explained so much about her, especially the contradictions. Meera wincing at his dirty hands but then washing dishes in his kitchen and slinging mud to clean his field. He squeezed her hand, wanting her to know she wasn't alone.

"I can't begin to tell you how much I owe my parents."

Now he understood why she insisted on paying him back for everything. She had grown up feeling indebted.

"Have you spent your entire life trying to pay them back?"

Tears filled her eyes. "I don't think I could pay them back in this life, or my next several lives. I still remember the orphanage. The filth." He noticed goose bumps on her arms. "There was always dirt everywhere—in our beds, on the tables we ate at. And bugs. Sometimes when I close my eyes, I can still feel the mosquito bites, the cockroaches crawling over my feet as I tried to sleep. The grit between my teeth, like the food had fallen on the floor before they put it on my plate." She shuddered.

Jake put an arm around her and pulled her close. He wished he could ease her anguish, somehow erase the memories that still haunted her. She was a remarkable woman, more so because of what she had endured and overcome. He had nearly fallen to pieces when his mother left. Had it not been for his father, he wouldn't have finished high school. That Meera had spent so much time alone made his heart hurt.

She gently pushed away from him. "I had lost all hope. It was always the younger kids who got adopted. With their wealth and stature, my parents could've easily taken home a newborn baby. But they chose me, and in doing so, they saved my life. If I'd grown up in that orphanage, I would've ended up on the streets, or someone's mistress."

It sounded like a well-rehearsed statement, something rote. He wondered if it was how her parents relayed the story, and if that was what she had listened to growing up.

She fixed him with a look. "Instead, I have a life of luxury. My father gives me a generous monthly allowance that I barely spend in one year. I'm a respected doctor, and I have a wonderful future planned for me. I owe my parents everything. I owe them my soul."

Now he could see why it was so important to her to get Hell's Bells to like her. She'd spent her childhood wanting to be accepted.

"Your parents got something in return, you know," he said softly. "They got you."

She shook her head and inched away from him, as far as she could in the confined space. She was shutting herself off, retreating somewhere inside herself, and she wasn't going to let him in. She rubbed her temples.

"I got a lot more than they did, and I'm going to spend the rest of my life making sure they never once regret their decision."

He thought about this own father, and the hopes and dreams he had placed on Jake, the expectations that Jake had never quite lived up to. "A child is not an investment, Meera." His voice was soft but she tensed up.

"And my parents have never treated me as such," she said stiffly.

She stood and stepped down from the cab. She stalked to the garbage bag and resolutely went back to picking up debris, keeping her back to him.

CHAPTER SIX

MEERA TAPPED HER FOOT, listening for the sounds of Dr. Harper and Rose leaving for lunch. They were chatting and laughing while she stewed in the makeshift office Rose had created for her in a utility closet. She fanned herself. Apparently, the air-conditioning was broken. But just in her office-slash-closet. It seemed to be fine in the examination rooms, in Dr. Harper's office and everywhere else in the clinic.

She should leave, she thought, pack it up, find another rotation after the wedding. It would delay her lab application but so what? She was going to take over her father's practice; a small delay in starting her lab wouldn't change the course of her life. Still, her stomach churned at the thought. The one good thing about her timing in Bell-haven was being able to be by herself. A break before she added wife and daughter-in-law to her list of duties. In Indian culture, you didn't marry the man, you married the family, and Meera was already exhausted thinking about all the things

Raj's mother was adding to her social calendar after the wedding.

Besides, if she left, how would she help clean up the mess she'd made at Jake's ranch? Despite two hours of hard labor this morning, they had only cleared out the largest pieces of debris. Her arms and legs ached, but she knew she had to put in several hours tonight.

She had overheard Kelly talk about how short-handed they already were. Even if Jake was taking responsibility for not checking the grill, the barbecue had been her event. She couldn't inconvenience Jake more than she already had.

She wondered if she should go back to help out in the field rather than sit in the office doing nothing. She wondered whether Jake would be there. The work was grueling and boring, and it would be nice to have his company. As long as he didn't ask about her parents again.

What was it about his questions that had made her behave so defensively? She had panicked in a way she couldn't explain. She told the story of her adoption frequently—to relatives, colleagues and others who asked her private questions they couldn't get her parents to answer. Yet it felt different telling Jake. She sensed he disapproved of her parents. Why? All her life she'd been told how lucky she was, how incredibly grateful she should be. No one had ever reacted like Jake.

What was he trying to get at? And why did it bother her so much?

More than twenty years later, she still remembered the day at the orphanage that had changed her life.

It started out like any other day when visitors were expected.

Matron rang the bell while it was still dark out. That's how Meera knew it was visitors' day. She woke up in a twelve-by-twelve-foot room with cots lined wall-to-wall. At least twenty children slept in the room with her. She was always careful sitting up and stretching so she didn't hit the girl next to her.

Matron assigned chores to each girl, and they got to work cleaning floors, washing clothes and dishes, changing the bedsheets. By the time the sun came up, many of the children whined and complained. The ones who had been there awhile, like Meera, didn't mind because they knew what waited at the end of the grueling morning.

After hours of work, they were lined up in the back *maidan*, where the surly matron handed out soap, then hosed them down with cold water. The smaller children yelped and tried to run away. Meera stood still. The cold water would last only a few minutes, but the feeling of not having dirt and grime all over her skin would last the whole day.

They were given clean clothes to wear. She put hers on quickly and ran to the dining room. She eyed the plates and took the seat nearest to the biggest bowl of food. The bowl would be passed to each child, but the first person always got the largest scoop. It might be the only time all month she'd get a belly full of food.

The rest of the children filed in and took their seats. The visitors were shown in, and the matron went about serving the children. It was the only time she did that; on a normal day, the children were left to scratch their way to the last morsels of food.

The visitors watched and asked questions. They stopped to talk to the children about what it was like in the orphanage. They all knew their lines; they had been made to recite them over and over until they knew them by heart.

"The matron takes such good care of us."

"We eat like this every day."

"We're so lucky to have this place."

Meera knew her lines better than anybody else. She gave the tour of the sparkling orphanage and talked about the janitorial staff that cleaned the place every day. She happily showed them the toys that had been brought out that morning. She spied the stethoscope and used it to pretend she was a doctor. Once, she had hidden it under her bed after the visitors left, but the matron found it and gave her a beating. She proudly showed it to the visitors as her favorite toy, one that she played with all the time.

She hadn't noticed her father in the group of ten or so prospective parents that were there that day, but she had slyly admired the lady with the beautiful hair, dark red lips and pretty blue sari. She gaped at the diamond earrings glittering in her ears, wondering whether she would ever get to wear something so beautiful.

On the day visitors came, the children were allowed into the TV room. The matron often put on an English movie to show the visitors that her girls knew English. Most of the kids didn't understand the language, but they enjoyed the treat. Meera loved movies, even the ones she'd watched a dozen times.

Matron was clear on what life held for her charges. Meera could stay at the orphanage "for free" for another year, but then she had to get a job and pay rent. Meera's job prospects in a small town outside of Kolkata were nonexistent. She would have to go to the big city and become a beggar...or worse. If she were lucky, an old man in town might marry her. Meera spent every day trying to find a way out of her situation. The movies were her escape. They let her believe, for a short amount of time, that her life could be different.

She had been through enough visitors' days to know that the girls who were called to the matron's office during the movie were the ones the visitors had selected. The chosen ones. It was always the younger girls, the ones who were still in nappies. The ones who could barely say a word but cooed and giggled. If any of the older children were selected, it was the pretty girls, the fair-skinned ones. Meera knew she would never be her. She was too old, her skin was too dark and she definitely wasn't pretty enough. What she hoped for were the few rupees visitors sometimes gave the older children out of pity. On lucky days, she could hide the money before Matron confiscated it.

On this day, the matron twisted her finger and motioned for Meera to come to the office. Meera's heart raced. They must want more tea; why else would they call her? In the office, the lady with the blue sari sat with her back straight. There was a man with her, and he called out to Meera. She walked over to him, afraid she had done something wrong. What could they want from her? He got down on his knees so he was at eye level with her and asked if she would come live with them and be his daughter.

The man spoke English, a language she had taught herself but still didn't know fluently. Had she misunderstood?

He must have seen the disbelief on her face because he asked her again in Hindi. She couldn't believe her ears and stood there stunned until she heard Matron's harsh voice telling her to answer. She nodded excitedly. From there, things went quickly. She saw her new father hand Matron fat wads of cash.

Meera's life had never been the same since. Her mother had taught her how to dress and do her makeup so she always looked glamorous. Her father gave her everything she needed. No one would ever guess Meera had been a poor orphan girl. They had given her a fairy-tale life, but not once had she forgotten that orphanage or what her life could have been.

But was that because her parents never let her? She shook her head. She was letting Jake's reaction cloud her thinking. What was that *thing* she'd felt when they were sitting so close together in the forklift? And why had she let him hold her hand? More important, why did she feel so connected to him? She laughed at herself. *I have a silly schoolgirl crush on an American cowboy. I'll get over it.* The rest was her imagination running wild. She had watched three Western movies on the flight from London.

She heard the outside door close and stepped into the lobby. Dr. Harper and Rose were gone. She peeked out the front door, and they were nowhere in sight. Lily was parked down the street, and Meera waved her over. Lily looked furtively up and down the street before walking up the steps. She quickly entered the clinic, and Meera locked the door.

"I'm so glad you came," Meera said warmly, leading Lily to the exam room.

"Dr. M., you really have to promise Rose won't know about this. That woman is such a gossip—I couldn't bear it if people found out."

Meera handed Lily a paper gown and turned around while she got undressed. "Don't worry. I'll have to start a chart on you, but I'll keep it under lock and key in my desk. And before I leave town, I'll give it to you, and you only."

Lily sighed in relief. "Okay, I'm ready."

Meera turned and set up the ultrasound machine. She put some gel on Lily's stomach and began the examination. When she turned the screen, Lily gasped at the grainy black-and-white image of a head with a little nose and mouth. Meera pointed out fingers and toes. She took her time and printed several pictures for Lily, who sobbed loudly as she studied each one.

"Lily, everything looks normal, but I'd say you're closer to thirty-six weeks. Normal gestation is forty weeks, but you could deliver anywhere from two to four weeks from now. I know you don't want to tell anyone, but it's time you start preparing. You need to figure out how to get to the hospital, you'll need to buy things for the baby…"

Lily sniffed dramatically. "I can't. I just can't. You don't understand…"

Lily leaned her head on Meera's shoulder. Without thinking, Meera put her arm around the young woman. "Tell me. Perhaps I can help."

"About a year ago, my aunt Norma Jean's cousin by marriage came to visit—he's a soldier in the army. We started seeing each other and fell in love. Then Norma Jean tells me he's engaged to be married to his high school sweetheart back in Mississippi. So I tell him it's over between us. He goes away, then he comes back and proposes to me and we were both so excited that we drove all night to Atlantic City and got married. We were going to come back and make this big announcement to everyone, but he suddenly got orders and had to go overseas."

Meera bit her lip. "So this is his baby?"

Lily nodded. "It must have happened on our wedding night. He splurged on a hotel." She wiped tears from her eyes. "It was the best night of my life."

"How long did you know him before you were married?"

"About a month."

Meera's brow shot up. How did people make

such grand decisions so frivolously? When her parents suggested she and Raj get married, she took months to discuss it with him. She put together a list of pros and cons, and they had several thoughtful conversations, weighing each aspect before deciding. And she had known Raj all her life. She couldn't say any of that to her patient, of course.

Lily lifted her head as if sensing Meera's discomfort. "When you're in love, Doc, you just know."

"So why not tell people? You're a married woman, and being his wife, you should be getting medical care from the military."

Lily shook her head. "When he left, he made me promise I'd wait to tell everyone until he got back. He hadn't told his folks back home, and that girl he was supposed to marry—he wanted to break it to her himself. If I told people here, it would get to Norma Jean and she'd go and tell his momma and…you know."

"Have you spoken to him? When will he be home?"

"That's just it—I haven't heard from him in months. Since I figured out I was pregnant. We were emailing and writing and then it all stopped. I have no idea where he is or how to get ahold of him."

Meera's skin prickled.

"Have you contacted the army?"

Lily nodded. "They think I'm some crazy stalker. They asked me for proof that we got married, and I don't know where our marriage certificate is. Joe must've taken it."

Meera smiled tightly. She hoped for Lily's sake that Joe wasn't the scoundrel he sounded like. "The place you got married should have a record of your wedding. Call them and see if they can send you a copy."

Lily slapped her forehead. "I didn't think about asking them." She sat straighter and clapped her hands. "That would solve everything, and then the army can tell me where he is and I can talk to him."

"And you need to tell someone here. Do you have family in town?"

She shook her head. "It was just my momma taking care of me. The town didn't like her much 'cause she was a single mother. She died last year and I've been alone ever since. At least until Joe came along, and now all I have is my crazy aunt, Norma Jean, who doesn't even like me much."

Lily sniffed, then blew her nose. "The town doesn't like me much, either, but at least they're nice to me. If they think I'm having this baby out of wedlock, they're gonna write me off like they did my mom."

Meera patted her hand. "I know this might be

hard to hear, but you have to consider the possibility that Joe took advantage of you and the reason you can't get in touch is that he doesn't want to be found."

Lily shook her head vehemently. "I know what it looks like, Dr. M. I didn't just fall off the turnip truck. He loves me." She tapped her heart. "I know it in here. He's a good man, and he meant to make me his wife. I know he'll do right by me."

Meera took a breath. Lily was full of pregnancy hormones; there was no way to win her over with logic. Just like there was no convincing all the red-meat-eating, smoking, overweight people in Bellhaven that their hearts were ticking time bombs. She thought about how she handled her mother when she went overboard with the wedding planning. "Let's take it one day at a time. First, see if you can get the marriage certificate. Then we can try to get you medical benefits."

"Thanks so much, Dr. M. I feel better just talking to you. I've been holding this inside so long, I was gonna explode. And I know that isn't good for the baby...and I'm so glad the baby's all right."

Meera smiled kindly at her and began putting away the ultrasound equipment. She wanted to make sure Lily got out of the office before Rose returned from lunch.

"I'd never forgive myself if something happened. I don't know what I woulda done if Jake hadn't sent me to you."

"Do you want to know whether it's a boy or a girl?"

Lily shook her head, fresh tears streaming down her face. "I know it's dumb, but I'm still hoping Joe will make it back somehow. I want to find out with him."

Meera's heart went out to her. It was an impossible situation, one which she felt sure held heartbreak for Lily.

"I don't have a lot of money, Dr. M., but if we can come up with some monthly payment, I'll pay you for all this. I got a job as a waitress…"

Meera's chest ached at the desperation in Lily's voice. It had been a long time since she'd felt the pain of being poor. But she did know what it meant not to have money, and therefore her own freedom. What it meant to be at the mercy of someone else.

She shook her head. "No, Lily, I will absolutely not take money from you."

Lily shook her head in turn. "I'm not a charity case, Dr. M. I've got my pride. I have to pay you."

Meera considered her options. She didn't want Lily on her feet any more than she had to be. She chewed the inside of her cheek. Her eyes fell on Lily's clothes, and she snapped her fingers. She'd noticed that her clothes didn't have any tags on them. "Do you sew your own clothes?"

Lily nodded enthusiastically. "My momma taught me."

Meera thought back to Jake's comment about her clothes making her stand out in town. Well, then, I'll tell you what—if I get you some fabric, do you think you can make me a few things?"

Lily clapped her hands. "Oh, I've been wantin' to dress you since the moment I laid eyes on you. I can make you some real pretty dresses."

"Then it's decided. Sew me some clothes, and your account's settled."

She exchanged phone numbers with Lily and promised to come see her for measurements.

After Lily left, Meera snuck a look at the schedule for the rest of the day. Dr. Harper had six patients; she, of course, had none. *Forget it!* She wrote Rose a note to say she was leaving and to call her cell if she was needed. There was no point in wasting the day at the clinic when she could go back to the ranch and get real work done. *It has nothing to do with seeing Jake.*

CHAPTER SEVEN

MEERA PULLED INTO the carport at the ranch and noted that Jake's pickup truck was parked there, too. Her stomach fluttered with excitement. She smiled to herself and went to the cottage to change clothes.

As she made her way over to the ruined field, her pulse quickened when she saw Jake in a tractor. He was using a front loader to pick up debris and throw it in a dump truck. Meera studied Jake's confident movements as his eyes focused on the work ahead of him. He was quite the man.

She wondered about the woman in his life who had drunk the fertility tea and left him. She thought about Gloria and her claim to Jake. Gloria was a very attractive woman, but Jake hadn't seemed into her at the barbecue. He would want a simple girl, someone down-to-earth who would work the ranch with him. The image of Gloria driving the tractor in her red dress popped into Meera's head and she smiled. Not that a designer-clothes-wearing, dirt-averse vegetarian was any better.

He turned the tractor off and hopped down. She couldn't help but notice how sure-footed he was in his cowboy boots, and how his jeans fit him perfectly. *Boot cut indeed.*

"Couldn't stay away, huh?" His tone was light, but she noticed the worry in his expression as his gaze returned to the field.

"It was a difficult choice between staying in a tiny office with no air-conditioning and nothing to do…or coming here to do menial labor in the baking sun. My guilty conscience won out."

He gave her a small smile.

She shifted on her feet. "About earlier… I didn't mean to get so defensive."

He stayed silent but turned his attention to her, his expression thoughtful, inviting her to say more. What could she say to make him understand that her parents meant everything to her? They had literally saved her life. Would he get it? Her American cousin, Priya, often told her that cultural values were different here. Children grew up and left their families, eager to flee their childhood homes. This was the first time she had ever been away from her parents. She couldn't imagine a life without them.

"I love my parents very much. I can't stand anyone speaking against them."

His eyes locked on to hers. "Well, how about we leave it at that."

She raised an eyebrow.

"I love my father, Meera. God knows he's not perfect, but I don't let anyone talk smack about him. I get what it's like to be protective of your parents. I didn't mean to overstep."

Her heart responded to the sincerity in his voice. She wanted to open up more, to tell him all of it. Somehow she knew he would understand like no one else. She stepped toward him. "What can I do to help here?"

He looked as though he was about to say something, then shook his head slightly, as if he'd thought better of it. "Kelly said we need to get this field cleaned up today and lay down seed. There's rain in the forecast, and we might be able to grow something for the fall and be in good shape for spring."

"Does that mean you might be able to salvage this field?"

Jake shook his head. "Not for grazing. I'm still gonna have to send some steer to slaughter."

She took a step away from him. Years of her parents' lessons about the value of life hung over her head. "This is all because of me. Their deaths are on my soul."

He slapped his leg. "They're gonna go to slaughter anyway, now or three months from now. Get over it."

She took a breath. There was no point in getting angry at him. How could she expect him to understand? "I know it must be hard for you, but a lifetime of being a vegetarian won't undo the bad karma from this fire. That pain is real for me."

"I don't get how you're so logical in every other way but you can't get this through your head. They would have died, anyway!"

"But not because of me." *Why doesn't he see that I can't be responsible for their deaths?* It was a good reminder of how different they were, of the gap between their values and core beliefs. She'd been feeling too close to him lately. "Don't you want to save them?" she couldn't help asking.

His eyes hardened. "I do want to save them, but not because I want to spare my karma. It would be more profitable to slaughter them a few months from now."

She pressed a hand to her stomach, trying to calm it. Did she really expect him to change the way he lived his life? It wasn't as if he could change her mind about eating meat.

"Fine, then, save them for that reason. Isn't there anything else that can be done? Feed them grain or buy more hay? Could you use a neighbor's field?"

He made a frustrated sound. "Meera, let me worry about how I run my ranch. If there's something to be done, I'll figure it out. I'm gonna go ask Kelly to order the seed to replant this field. If you want to help, get to work."

She pressed her lips together. They were back on familiar ground, with him pretending to be the cocky cowboy. She wasn't going to give him the satisfaction of rattling her. "What would you like me to do?"

He extracted a shovel from the tractor. "Here. I need you to put all the garbage into piles. You'll dig up mud and grass, but don't worry about that. I just need to get all the pieces of burnt plastic and inorganic things off the soil. Understand?"

Meera nodded. She began to walk away but couldn't help turning back. "You want to prepare the land so you can use a seed drill to replant the grass."

The look on his face was so worth it. She enjoyed surprising him. She wanted him to see that she wasn't the princess he accused her of being. Maybe that was why she had shared so much with him about her adoption. Although it wasn't a secret, she didn't like talking about the orphanage. Raj knew all the stories, and he pitied her. Whenever her adoption came up, he treated her with kid gloves, as if she was still a victim, but that's not how she looked at her time there. She sensed Jake didn't feel sorry for her. She'd seen something else in his eyes, as if he understood that what she went through at the orphanage had shaped who she was today.

He walked back to the tractor and fired it up again, so Meera started shoveling with everything she had.

She didn't know how much time had passed; it could have been one hour or four. Her back and arms ached, and sweat dripped down her neck. Meera was no stranger to long hours and hard work, but this physical labor felt different.

Taking stock, she realized she'd cleared out a sizable portion of the field, much to her own surprise. And it felt good. Instant gratification—unlike her research, which took years to show even the hint of progress. Even in her medical practice, it often took weeks for treatments to work.

"WELL, BUTTER MY BUTT and call me a biscuit! Is that our hoity-toity doctor shoveling dirt?"

Jake turned around and grinned at Kelly. "Yeah, she's been at it all afternoon." He shook his head in disbelief. "She'd barely shake my dirty hand four days ago, and look at her now." He watched as Meera picked up the wheelbarrow and rolled it to the edge of the field to dump its contents in a pile. She was wearing a light cotton tank top and shorts that ended midthigh. Her clothes clung to her, and her legs were covered in ash and mud, as were her sneakers. She wiped sweat off her forehead. He hadn't expected her to literally get down and dirty, especially not twice in one day.

He wanted more of the woman who had dropped the princess persona and opened up to him. He wanted the real Meera.

He felt a kick on his shin. "What the…" He glared at Kelly.

She was shaking her head and wagging a finger at him. Kelly was almost as tall as he was and weighed just as much. She had grown up in Hell's Bells. More than twenty years older than him, she knew ranching better than anyone around here. She'd worked for his father ever since she was a teenager and had seen Jake grow up. She was a tough woman, stronger than most of the men on the ranch. And she was the only one who could boss Jake around…or kick him in the shin, for that matter.

"You best watch yourself. I see the googly eyes you're making at that girl and let me tell ya— you're headed straight to heartbreak again."

Jake opened his mouth to protest, but she stepped up closer until she was almost nose to nose with him. "You tell yourself what you want, but don't you even think about makin' up some bull for me. I know she's got a fella, and Rose says she's stuck up higher than a light pole. You send her packing if you know what's good for you."

Jake grinned mischievously. "When have you known me to do what's good for me?"

Kelly harrumphed. "Well, I'm not gonna waste my breath on you. I know that look in your eye. Just be careful—she's not our kind."

"Yeah, like loving one of our kind worked out for me."

Kelly went quiet. Jolene had grown up in Hell's Bells; she'd been the safe choice, and Jake had thought she'd stick by him no matter what.

They stood side by side, watching Meera. "She gave me her credit card to pay for the hay and seed."

"She what now?"

Kelly shrugged. "She said it's her fault and she wants to pay for it—told me to make sure it's charged to her."

He wasn't surprised, but he wasn't going to let her take sole responsibility. Jake shook his head. "Give me the card and forget about it. Tell Tom to put it on the ranch's tab."

Kelly put her hands on her hips. "Now, you listen here—don't think I don't know the books. I do all the ordering and selling… I know the numbers and you aren't making them. This is her fault—let her fix it. Don't you go gettin' all stupid about it."

Jake shook his head. "It's not right, Kell. I was supposed to check that grill. It's not all on her."

"If it weren't for her, you wouldn't have had the barbecue. Jake, you got enough of your own problems. You don't need to put yourself out for a foreigner who's gonna leave in a coupla weeks." She looked at him appraisingly, but his gaze was drawn back to Meera. "With your heart, I might add."

Jake began to argue, but she put up her hand. "You don't have a choice. Tom says you're over-extended from the antibiotics we had to order for those sick cattle. He can't give you more credit. We're in the middle of a drought—we can't afford to replace all that hay."

Kelly nodded toward Meera. "She's got the money and she's not payin' rent. Let it go."

Kelly was right, but Jake wasn't going to take advantage of Meera. "I can't. I'll fix it with Tom."

She shook her head, "Boy, you're too poor to paint and too proud to whitewash."

"She asked if we could have a neighbor look after the cattle."

"She's tellin' you how to run the ranch?"

Jake turned to face Kelly. "The last thing I'd do is take ranching advice from her, but it got me thinking—Mrs. Hayes might have a field she's not using. What if we asked her to let us use it? We can give her some meat later for the winter."

Kelly tapped her chin. "I heard something 'bout Mrs. Hayes selling a whole herd of sheep last week. She might have grazing room." She looked at Jake. "You gonna let her save your soul, then?"

"What's that now?"

"She gave Rose a whole lecture on bein' a vegetarian."

"I'm not doing it for her, Kell. You know it's better if we fatten the steers before selling them." Because of the drought, the price of beef was through the roof, and they sold animals by the pound.

Kelly nodded. "As long as that's what it is. Don't let her make you feel bad for being a rancher. I'm not saying her beliefs are wrong, but they're not yours."

"Kelly!"

"Okay, okay. I'll go talk to Mrs. Hayes now."

He nodded. "Thanks. And hey, I want you to let her give you a physical. I don't like the way you've been huffing and puffing when you're carrying feed."

She scowled. "You pay heed to my words, boy—that kinda girl doesn't go for a boy like you." She stalked off.

He opened his mouth to protest, then turned back to Meera. He noted the lithe and graceful way she worked. She must be tired and hungry, but she kept at it. He wondered when she would stop surprising him.

He couldn't deny he was attracted to her, though he couldn't explain why or how it had crept up on him. But if he'd learned anything from the experience with Jolene, it was that he had nothing to offer a woman, especially not a worldly woman like Meera. Lucky for him, there was no risk of him losing his heart. She would go back home. She had a fiancé, a family, a career. She was most certainly not the kind of woman who would be interested in a man like him. Was she?

CHAPTER EIGHT

"WHEW! HAVE YOU been rolling in manure?" Rose scrunched her nose as Meera walked into the clinic. Meera hadn't wanted to waste time showering after Rose's frantic call to come to the clinic. She'd cleaned up with a wet towel, but she knew she looked awful. *And yet, I don't care.* It felt liberating not to have to worry about her appearance or how she carried herself.

Rose was waving a hand in front of her nose. Irritation twitched through her. There was nothing she could do to make Rose like her, so why bother trying? The same went for the townspeople. She was only here for a month, and it wouldn't be the end of the world if, for once in her life, she wasn't Miss Perfectly Pressed Meera.

"If you must know, I've been helping Jake clean up the mess from the fire. I could've spent an hour getting cleaned up, but I figure taking care of the patient is much more important." She put her hands on her hips. "If you're done turning your nose up at me, perhaps you can help me do just that."

Rose stared at her.

"Where's the patient?"

Rose jerked her head toward an examination room.

Meera paused at the doorway. "And please fix the air-conditioning in my office." It was freeing to accept the fact that Rose would never like her.

Derek Jenkins was on the exam table, his father holding a cold pack to the boy's head.

Meera braced herself for Marty's anger. The last time she'd seen him, he'd told her she was a quack.

"Dr. M., will he be okay?" Marty's face was creased with worry.

She began examining Derek. "What happened?"

"He went to practice and fell."

"He did what? I didn't clear him for the game. How was he allowed to play?"

"It's not Dad's fault. I talked Coach into it."

Apparently, medical forms were a mere formality in this town. "Tell me how you fell."

"I had the ball and I was running for the fifty-yard line, then all of a sudden I couldn't see in front of me and I fell. The guys tackled me."

Meera flinched. She finished examining Derek, then turned to Marty.

"He seems fine now, but I'd feel much more comfortable if you went to the regional hospital and got a CT scan of his head to make sure he doesn't have a bleed. The blurred vision is a sign of concussion, but the fall and tackle could have made it worse."

"Will he be able to play in the game tomorrow night?"

Meera stared at Marty. "Definitely not." She lowered her voice and pulled him away from Derek. "I can't stress how serious this is, Mr. Jenkins. If he already has a bleed, it could be life-threatening and made worse if he plays. You need to get him checked out."

"He can't get a CT scan."

Meera took a breath. *What's wrong with these people?* Normally, her patients begged her to do more tests than necessary, convinced they had ailments she couldn't diagnose.

"Mr. Jenkins, you must understand—"

"I can't afford a CT scan, doctor. We have no health insurance, I can barely pay for his travel games…where am I gonna get the money to pay for an expensive test?"

Meera closed her mouth.

"Can't you help him?" Marty pleaded.

The boy needed a CT scan. She couldn't diagnose anything else without the test. Head injuries were serious in children, and a misdiagnosis could cost Derek his life.

"Is there a program for medical assistance here?" she asked.

Marty shook his head. "We're not poor enough for medical assistance, but health insurance costs more than I can afford. Please, Dr. M., Derek's all I got."

She could hear the desperation in his voice. But what could she do? She thought about Dr. Harper and Dr. Thurm's admonitions that she had to learn the *art* of medicine.

"Stay here."

She walked to her closet office and called Raj.

"It's late, love."

Meera explained the situation. Raj was a pediatrician; maybe he had ideas.

"There's a lot of new literature that says a CT scan is not absolutely necessary for head injuries in children. The risk of radiation could outweigh the diagnostic benefit."

"But what about the blurred vision?"

"It is a concerning sign but may be the result of a hematoma that will resolve itself. If a CT was available, I would recommend it, but since it's not, I suggest you do a complete neurological exam on him. If he's fine, I think it's also okay to watch him closely for a few days."

"Thanks Raj." She stared at the phone as she hung up. Raj was always there for her. It was past his bedtime in London. She knew he had to be up early to do rounds at the hospital, but he hadn't complained. He was, and always would be, the person she could count on most. Her parents were right; it was important to have someone who could support her career.

She went back into the examination room and repeated the neurological tests on Derek, just to make sure.

"He looks good for now, but I can't stress enough that he must not play again. He does have a concussion, and he can get very badly hurt." She gave him instructions on what to watch for and wrote down her cell number in case Derek's symptoms worsened.

She ushered them out of the room, hoping Derek wouldn't try anything stupid.

Marty gave Meera a hug. "Thank you, Dr. M."

Meera stiffened as he enveloped her. "Just make sure he doesn't play," she mumbled.

"So, Doc, two, three more days until I can play?"

"Derek…"

"How about you come back in three days," Rose chimed in. "Dr. Harper…or Dr. M. will give you a physical and then we can decide." Meera frowned at Rose. She'd been about to remind Derek that he might not play for weeks but that she should see him in a few days just to make sure he was okay.

"That sounds good."

Derek and Marty left.

Meera spun on Rose, but before she could say anything, the older woman held up a hand to cut her off.

"When he comes back in three days, you tell him it'll be another three days," Rose said sagely. "It's the only way you're gonna keep him off the field. Oh, and the air-conditioning in your office is fixed."

Meera smiled, relieved. "Thank you."

Maybe there were a few things she could learn from her medical rotation in Bellhaven.

After confirming there were no more patients to see, Meera walked out with a spring in her step. If she hurried back, Jake would still be out on the field. Maybe they could have dinner together. She stopped. Why was she thinking about Jake? She was perfectly happy with Raj. His assistance today showed how well-suited they were.

And yet, she couldn't stop thinking about how she felt working alongside Jake. It unleashed something inside her she couldn't explain. She was buzzing with a strange energy. And it felt good. *Really good!*

Maybe it was just endorphins from working in the fields. Her legs, arms and shoulders felt as though someone had run a truck over them, and she was dirty, sticky and in bad need of a good bath—a physical state she'd avoided ever since she left the orphanage. But it felt real, not orchestrated.

She lifted her head to the sky and let the hot sun and warm breeze kiss her face. *This is how I want to feel every day. Totally free!*

Brriiinnnngggg...

It was probably Jake. She looked at her screen and an internal balloon deflated.

Mother!

CHAPTER NINE

"COULD YOU REPEAT THAT, please?"

"It's a Bull Blazin' Festival."

"That's what I thought you said." Meera tilted Billy John's head so she could look into his ear.

"It's my favorite town event. We've got bull riding, a grillin' competition, a pie-eating contest, moonshine…you have to come, Dr. M."

Did he say moonshine? "I would love to, but I'm going to New York City this weekend. I have an appointment I can't miss. If I go to the festival, I'll miss the last bus to the city."

"You can drive."

She shook her head. "It's fine to drive around town, but I'm still not used to driving on the wrong side of the road. I hear drivers in New York City are quite aggressive."

She put a cuff on his arm to take his blood pressure.

"But you can't miss it! Everyone's gonna be there. We get people from all across the county showing up for it."

Meera smiled indulgently and put a stethoscope on his chest.

"Maybe Jake can drive ya."

"Pardon me?" Meera had been focused on listening to his heart.

"I could drive you where?" She turned to see Jake walk into the room. Her heart immediately responded, thumping faster.

"Meera needs to go to New York," Billy John answered for her.

"I've been meaning to go up to Jersey, right outside the city, to see someone," Jake said.

"About what, boss?"

Jake narrowed his eyes at Billy John. "About some used equipment." His eyes shifted. What wasn't he saying? He turned to Meera. "I can get Kelly to cover the ranch. Might be fun."

Meera tried not to show her panic. Drive to New York City with Jake? It would take seven hours. She took a deep breath, forcing air into her lungs. *I'll be all alone with him for a weekend. Two whole days.* She had already arranged with Dr. Harper to take Monday off so she could sightsee. Her heart fluttered like the wings of a bee, buzzing with excitement.

"Yeah, that way you can come to the festival." Billy John looked at her earnestly.

Meera felt Jake's eyes on her. He was leaning casually against the kitchen counter, long legs in tight-fitting jeans. His T-shirt couldn't hide the muscles underneath, and a cowboy hat completed the fantasy-worthy look. Her cheeks reddened as his sparkling green eyes locked on to hers. "Why not, Meera? It'll be much faster than taking the bus. It's the practical solution, isn't it?" He raised an eyebrow in challenge.

Meera swallowed. *Why not indeed? Only a million reasons.* Including the fact that Raj was already upset at her. She'd barely had time to return his calls in the past seven days, and she hadn't told him about Jake. Not that there was anything to tell.

Her eyes reconnected with Jake's. Her breath stuck in her chest, her entire body warming deliciously. What was this *thing* between them? Was it just physical attraction?

Her mother once told her that souls were matched in heaven. Meera had asked how she would know if she met her soul mate. Her mother responded that her *janam kundli*, her astronomical birth chart, would match her soul mate's chart. When her parents suggested she marry Raj, they pointed to the fact that their *janam kundli*s matched perfectly. Not that she completely bought into the birth-chart thing, but given how compatible she and Raj were, it wasn't surprising that they were somehow meant to be together. *Then why does Jake make me feel this way?*

"So…?" Billy John's voice broke the spell.

I can't spend an entire weekend with him. I don't need him planting silly doubts in my head. My plans are firm.

Billy John was looking at her expectantly. She didn't dare make eye contact with Jake again. She smiled graciously. "Let me think about it."

Billy John punched the air. "Wait till you ride the bull, Doc—it's gonna rock your world!"

Meera laughed and shook her head. "Let me tell you now, that *if* I come to the festival, I won't be riding any bulls. I've seen enough Western movies to know it always ends badly for women like me."

Both Billy John and Jake grinned. "We'll see about that," they said in unison.

Meera gave Billy John a clean bill of health, and he headed back out to finish his chores.

"By the way," Jake said, "you'll be happy to know that our neighboring ranch let us borrow a grazing field, so you don't have to worry about those cattle haunting your karma."

Meera clapped her hands. "Oh, that is such good news! Thank you, Jake." She was strangely elated at the thought that he had done it for her.

"I didn't do it for you," he said, as if he'd read her mind. "It's better for me if I sell them a few months from now when they're fatter."

Her smile disappeared. *There's snotty Jake*

again. He didn't understand the lifetime karma of killing cows. "Must you raise cattle? There are so many possibilities. Why can't you do other things here, like go back to raising horses or—"

Jake stepped closer, his nostrils flaring. "Meera, I'm a rancher. That's how I've chosen to live my life. You asked me not to mock your beliefs—please respect mine."

She moved back and swallowed. He was right. He might have teased her, but he'd never asked her to stop being who she was. So why had she challenged him? His life was obviously in Bellhaven, and she was going back to London. What did it matter how he ran the ranch? She was here for a few more weeks. That was all.

He mumbled something about work and walked out. She started after him but held back. She had to get to Lily's house. She'd called her earlier that morning, sounding worked up, and Meera had promised to stop by on her way to the clinic.

When she arrived, Lily was waiting at the doorstep, her eyes rimmed with red. She fell into Meera's arms. Given how large she was, Meera almost fell over.

"Let's go inside and sit down. You can tell me all about it." Meera had a gnawing feeling this was about Joe.

"Well, I called the chapel where we got married, and they sent me a copy of our marriage certificate but the Army won't accept it—says it isn't legal." Lily sobbed uncontrollably and handed Meera a crumpled piece of paper. Meera hugged Lily close until she could speak again.

"We had to apply for a license first. Turns out Atlantic City isn't like Vegas. They'll marry you for fun, but you need a license along with the marriage certificate for it to be legal. Says it right there on the certificate, in nice fine print."

Meera gently smoothed out the paper and read the little italic note at the bottom. It clearly stated that the certificate was not legal without a license from the state.

Meera held Lily while she cried, wondering how she could find Joe and throttle him.

Lily needed an outlet for her grief, but Meera also thought it was time for her to face the cold, hard facts.

"Lily, you didn't know the marriage wasn't legal. It doesn't help you with the army and getting medical benefits, but you must be able to tell *someone* now. They would understand your intentions were pure. If anyone's to blame here, it's Joe. And if you tell Norma Jean, maybe she can help you find him and make him take responsibility. You shouldn't have to keep this secret anymore."

Lily shook her head. "Joe wouldn't do this on

purpose. I know him and I'm telling you, Dr. M., something happened or he's off someplace where he can't write to me. He wouldn't willingly do this to me."

Meera looked at her in wonder. "How can you still believe in him, Lily?"

"I believe in our love. It's real." She clutched her chest. "I know it, Dr. M. I just know it. It might sound stupid, but I know it in my heart and nothing will convince me otherwise."

Meera sighed and decided to change tactics. "Regardless, you will deliver soon. You need to make preparations, tell people in town so they can help you."

Lily nodded. "I know I have to tell folks…for my baby. I don't want anything to happen to him or her, and I'll need help. I have to take time off work, and I'll have to get a car seat and stuff. I've been reading all about preparations online."

Meera nodded encouragingly. "It can seem overwhelming, but I'll be here to help you, too."

"Will you be here for me? Will you deliver my baby?"

Meera began nodding then stopped. *I can't promise that, can I? I have a plane ticket for three weeks from now.* She looked at Lily. The younger woman couldn't afford a hospital, so if Meera didn't deliver Lily's baby, who knew what she would do. And with no prenatal care,

Lily could be at high risk. *Surely I can stay a few extra days if need be. Mum and Raj will understand if I need to postpone the celebrations, won't they?* Even as she rationalized it, she knew there would be hell to pay if she didn't get back on time.

"I'll be right here for you, Lily." Her voice held more confidence than she felt.

"I'll announce it at the Bull Blazin' Festival."

Meera raised her eyebrows. "Are you sure you want to tell the town in such a public venue?"

"Yes! If I tell them one at a time, they're each gonna want to hear the story from me directly. If I make a big announcement when they're all there, at least it'll save me from all the nosy ladies showing up at my door expecting their own private version."

"Perhaps you should tell Norma Jean first— she wouldn't want to hear it at the festival with everyone else."

Lily bit her lip. "I guess you're right. She'll be mighty mad at me, but it's gotta be done." She met Meera's eyes. "You'll be at the festival, won't you, Dr. M.?"

"Actually, I won't… I was going to…"

"Oh, please, Dr. M., I can't do this without you. I need at least one friendly face and someone to pull me out if they all turn on me. You know what this town is like. Please—I need you there."

Meera stared at her tear-streaked face. She could skip the trip to New York City, cancel her appointment…but her mother would go ballistic. It was one of the reasons her mother had finally relented and allowed Meera to come to the States before the wedding. So, she could cancel and face her mother's wrath…

…Or she could go to New York with Jake as he'd suggested. Her heart hummed at the thought. She had three more weeks of freedom; she should take full advantage of it, explore the feelings she was having for Jake and figure out what it was about him that made her throw away reason and logic. If she didn't, would she wonder about him when she was married to Raj? Maybe she owed it to all of them to get Jake out of her system.

"Please, Dr. M."

She turned her attention back to Lily. No one had ever counted on her like this. Wasn't this why she had become a doctor in the first place? To help those who were alone, who needed a helping hand? She finally had a chance to make a real difference. How could she abandon Lily now?

Meera nodded and squeezed her hand. "I'll be there." *I better make sure I can keep my word.*

She spent the next several minutes asking Lily about her health and doing a quick exam to make sure she and the baby were doing well. After extracting a promise that Lily would come to the clinic to get another ultrasound, Meera left.

She couldn't get Lily off her mind as she drove to the clinic. How could she believe so vehemently in Joe? All signs indicated that the boy had taken advantage of her. And yet Lily truly believed they were in love. How could she know that? How could she be connected to someone at such an emotional level? Meera shook her head. It didn't make sense.

She thought about the reasons she wanted to marry Raj. He was her best friend, her stabilizer, the calm waters that kept her boat steady. He shared her values and understood how important her parents were to her. She always felt normal with Raj, completely calm and in control. *And utterly bored.* The realization surprised her. Jake was anything but ordinary; she enjoyed talking to him, even disagreeing with him. He fired her up. Maybe that's what her time in Hell's Bells was about—to get the restlessness out of her system so she could go back to London content and live the life she wanted...the life she'd planned.

What was that American saying? *I need to blow off some steam.*

CHAPTER TEN

"OH, NO NO NO, you're not talking me into that." Meera stepped backward, straight into Jake. He automatically reached out and grabbed her shoulders. She was standing so close that her hair touched his chest, and if he wanted, he could rest his chin on her head. He caught a whiff of her hair; she'd left it loose around her shoulders. It smelled of lavender and vanilla and something intoxicating, just like her.

The sunny day had the town square bustling with excitement over the Bull Blazin' Festival. The smell of fresh-popped corn and sugary cotton candy sweetened the air.

Meera tensed as she came into contact with him. He kept his hands loosely around her arms, putting just enough pressure to let her know he wanted her there. She shifted on her feet. He longed to reach up and run his fingers through her hair, to pull her against him and fold her into his arms. *Better take it easy, Jake. She's not ready.*

Jake bent his head to talk in her ear so she

could hear him over the noise. "Come on, now, I know you can do it. We can go together." He kept his tone light and airy, willing her to let her guard down. He felt her relax just a fraction and his heart pulsed with excitement. Then he felt goose bumps on her arms and grinned. *You feel it, too.*

"I just can't!" Suddenly, she turned to face him, her big brown eyes sparkling. He looked at the mechanical bull behind her.

"Okay, why don't we work on gettin' you some liquid courage." He took her hand and led her through the rapidly growing crowd. She resisted, but he held on firmly. Her hand felt small and delicate in his, like it always did. He twined her fingers with his and it felt familiar, as if they'd been doing it forever.

Jake couldn't stop thinking about Meera lately. When he closed his eyes, he saw her standing in the sunshine and smiling at him, shoveling dirt, sitting in his kitchen drinking tea, rolling her eyes at a comment he'd made. And he was always on the lookout for her, even when she wasn't at the ranch.

This was not how it had been with Jolene. There was something going on here that he couldn't explain. And, whatever it was, he had to figure it out and get it out of his system. Meera's questions about why he raised cattle were thinly veiled. She would never accept him the way he was. Maybe she had more in common with Jolene than he realized. The sooner he got over whatever was between them, the better it would be for him. He couldn't go around...what had Kelly said? Googly-eyed. And there was no better way to do that than convince her to go to New York with him. Two days alone, without the distraction of prying eyes, was just what they needed to get whatever...*this*...was out of their systems.

He rolled his shoulders, easing the tension out of them. It had been a hard week on the ranch, cleaning the field in addition to the regular chores. Meera had done more than her fair share, spending every minute of her spare time helping out. He marveled at her stamina, fueled by sheer determination. Even Kelly grudgingly admired Meera's efforts. Everything was taken care of, and he had put Kelly in charge of doing the weekend chores so he could go to New York. The letter from his mother was in his pocket. He'd put it off long enough.

He just had to convince Meera to come with him; she was insisting on driving herself.

They reached the drinks tent, and Mrs. Hayes greeted Jake. "Oh, now, it's been a while since I've seen a smile that big on your face."

Jake grinned even wider. He had known Mrs. Hayes all his life; she ranched the land next to him and was as close to a mother to him as anyone could be. He hadn't seen her much since Jolene left.

She looked at Meera. "And you must be the new doctor that's got this town all in a tizzy."

He turned to see Meera give her a wary smile, and he squeezed her hand.

"You can thank Mrs. Hayes for taking in my cattle." He reassured her with his eyes, and she smiled at the older woman with more genuine warmth.

"Don't worry, dear, I know the town's been hard on you. But if you're what put that smile back on this boy's face, well…" She handed them each a red plastic cup. "The drinks are on me." Meera thanked her and began to move away.

Mrs. Hayes grabbed Jake's arm. "Son, that look you got in your eye right now… I haven't seen that since you were a little boy of twelve and ate the entire pie I had cooling on the window. Since before your momma left." Jake choked on his drink. Mrs. Hayes hadn't mentioned his mother in years. He saw Meera watching them from a little ways off, but it was noisy and he was pretty sure she couldn't hear what Mrs. Hayes was saying. "I mean it. Jolene's my baby girl, but I know she never put that gleam in your eye."

Jake picked up a water cup and took a long swig. She was still clutching his arm and now fixed him with a motherly look. He gulped. "Mrs. Hayes, I loved Jolene—you know that."

She shook her head at him. "You and Jolene… I told that girl it was all wrong. I told you the same thing, but you're both too stubborn. Take it from me, son, when it's the real thing, you know it." Mrs. Hayes let him go. "I'll pray you come to your senses," she said loudly. She smiled warmly at Meera. "And you, too, darlin' girl. Now both of you go have a good time."

Jake waved at Mrs. Hayes and bumped his red cup against Meera's.

"Bottoms up, Meera."

She looked at him. "What is this, anyway?"

"Moonshine—it's homemade liquor and no one does it better than Mrs. Hayes." Meera smiled and took a small sip.

"Sounds like you've known her a long time." She tilted her head toward Mrs. Hayes.

Jake nodded. "She lives on the ranch next door. We're like family. She looked after me when my—" He stopped. Meera's eyes bored into his, their brown warmth reaching into him. She held his hand and stepped closer to him. The smell of the raspberry drink mingled with the heady scent of her lavender and vanilla. She smiled encouragingly. "—when my mother left us." *There!* He had said it out loud and the world hadn't come to an end.

"What happened?"

He took a sip, swallowing slowly. He wanted to tell her, to have Meera understand this part of him. "She just packed up and left one day, didn't tell anyone. Left a note saying she couldn't take it anymore. Things were never the same after that—I don't think my dad ever recovered from that betrayal. He just kept going downhill."

Meera inched over to him and rested her head on his chest. She broke her hand free of his and placed it next to her cheek.

He put his arm around her shoulder, holding her tight, and she burrowed into his chest. His breaths slowed as his heart lightened. The entire town knew what happened with his mother—he never had to discuss it—and his own words surprised him. He had never connected his mother's departure all those years ago to what ultimately happened to his father. At least not out loud.

"Well, isn't this cozy."

Jake felt Meera stiffen, and she pulled back immediately. He winced at Gloria's high-pitched voice.

"It is cozy, Gloria. Meera and I are good friends." He narrowed his eyes at her. He found Meera's hand and tugged her toward him.

"Hmm, her fiancé must be missing her, don't you think?"

Jake glared at Gloria. Meera extracted her hand from his.

"That is none of my business, just like what I do is none of *your* business." He found Meera's hand again. He needed to get away, go someplace where he could have her to himself. Gloria was saying something, but he didn't care; all he could think about was that he needed to be close to Meera, to be alone with her, before she retreated again.

He pulled Meera away from Gloria and led her back to the mechanical bull.

"Let's do this!"

She shook her head. "No, there's no way. I can't…"

He fixed her with a look. "You can't, but *we* can."

"You'll ride with me?"

He nodded. A few people cheered as they stepped into the ring. An attendant helped her mount, then Jake swung his leg and settled in behind her. Townspeople were gravitating toward the ring, eager to see them on the bull. The midday sun was shining down on them, and his head felt hot underneath the cowboy hat. There were catcalls and shouts of encouragement. It should've made him run. Normally, he would be desperate to find a place to hide, somewhere far from prying eyes. Ever since Jolene left, he'd avoided the sympathetic expressions of the busybodies in town. The same pitying looks they'd given him when his mother left. But now, he didn't care—he wanted them to see him. To see that he was okay. That he was happy.

He snaked an arm around Meera and she grabbed the bull's grip. He placed his hand on top of hers. Suddenly, nothing mattered—all that existed was Meera and the beautiful, sunshiny day.

Her soft hair tickled his nose as he bent to whisper in her ear. "Ready?"

He felt her shiver. "Ready as I'll ever be."

A cheer went up from the crowd as the bull started. Meera screamed as it bucked underneath them. Jake felt her shift on the seat, and he tightened his hold on her hand, gripping her firmly at the waist to steady her.

She shrieked in delight as they both jerked with the bull. The crowd roared. Suddenly, he felt the seat drop below them as the bull lurched forward, suspending them in midair. Meera screamed as they both slammed back onto their seats, slightly unbalanced. He was sure they were about to fall over, but he somehow managed to pull her back into the right position. He had ridden this bull a thousand times, but riding it with Meera was something else.

His body was now molded against hers, and they rolled and moved in unison as the bull bucked. She was laughing so hard her head flopped sideways and she lost her balance. He reached out, desperate to save her, and found himself falling to the ground. They landed on soft rubber, Meera first, and he braced his arms so he wouldn't crush her. The crowd went wild, cheering, whistling and screaming louder than ever. He was right on top of her, so he used his arm to prop himself up. He looked into her glittering eyes. He didn't know if it was the moonshine, the adrenaline from the bull ride or just... Meera, but his heart was galloping like a prizewinning race horse. *This girl is going to be the end of me.*

"Kiss! Kiss!" the crowd chanted giddily. Meera's lips were slightly parted. *Tempting.* But this was not how he wanted to do it.

He stood and held out his hand. Disappointment crossed her face, but she let him help her up. He picked up his hat and put it back on his head.

They stepped out of the ring and someone handed her a straw cowboy hat. Jake placed it on her head.

"It's official now—once you've fallen off the bull, you've earned entry into this town." The crowd was closing in on them, people wanting to chat with him, to meet the doctor everyone was talking about. He needed to get them out of here.

"Jake, wait…where are we going?"

Jake didn't answer. He kept walking, pulling her with him. They crossed the town square, and he took her down a path that cut through the park. She protested, but he kept going. He was ablaze with an intensity he couldn't explain. The only thing he could think about, the only thing he craved, was to hold her, and to do it away from the nosy townsfolk. He needed to be with Meera—just her. He wanted to tell her what he was feeling; he had to hear her say she felt the same way. Whatever had been set aflame inside him was her doing.

He took her down the stone path to the stream and stopped when they got to the bubbling water's edge.

Her eyes were wide, her breath coming quickly. Her hair was wild and loose; wisps stuck to her cheeks. A rosy tint crept up her neck to her cheeks and ears. Their eyes connected. There were a million things Jake wanted to say, to blurt out, to ask her, to tell her. Her eyes were wide with wonder and anticipation. His heart drummed in his ears. She took a small step toward him.

Here goes nothing. He closed the distance between them and put a hand on the back of her head, pulling her close. He had imagined what it would be like to kiss her, to feel her, to be connected to her. He planned to do it sweetly, lightly; he didn't want to scare her away.

As his lips touched hers, an unknown force took hold. She responded with an urgency that took his breath away. She tasted of raspberry moonshine and a buttery sweetness that could only be…Meera. He was coupled to her soul, and he felt her reach in and touch his heart.

THE NEED FOR air brought Meera back to her senses. She broke the kiss and stepped back, gasping. What had she done? How could she let Jake kiss her? And why had she kissed him back? She knew this was wrong. *Then why does it feel so right?* That kiss was like nothing she had ever known.

She'd never kissed anyone other than Raj, and when they did, it was always pleasant. This was something else. She stared at Jake. For a moment, it felt as if their souls were entwined.

She stepped back and turned around, desperate to break eye contact with him. This couldn't be happening; not to her. It must be the moonshine or something else. There was no rational explanation for the way she felt right now, no words to describe it. Nothing in her plans accounted for this strange sensation overtaking her. She was leaving in a few weeks. Surely, this was nothing more than a summer flirtation?

And what would she tell Raj? Or her parents? How could she do this to him? She clutched her stomach. She had betrayed Raj in a horrible, selfish way, and she had no excuse for why she'd done it. Or why it felt so good. Jake was totally wrong for her.

He put his hands on her shoulders and gently turned her around. His eyes were a sparkling green, mirroring the confusion, exhilaration and pure joy she felt.

"I don't know what this is, either, Meera. It's not just you."

She took a sharp breath. "Jake, I can't believe I just did that."

She collapsed against him, and he held her tight. She felt warmth and comfort flow into her, and it quieted the tempest in her heart.

She looked up at Jake, his green eyes wild and wide. Her parents would never approve of Jake, even if Raj wasn't in the picture. He was not the type of man they had set her up to marry. But part of doing this trip before the wedding was about feeding the wild side of her soul so she could return home grounded. Even Raj had encouraged her to explore, to be free from her usual rigidness. *If I stomp on my feelings right now, how is that fair to Raj, or to me? I'll go back discontent and wondering what might have been.*

Maybe it's time I let loose a little and think with my heart. I won't let myself get carried away.

She smiled at him. "I need some more liquid courage."

He laughed. "Yes, I don't think we should be alone right now, either." He led her back to the town square. This time when he took her hand, she didn't resist.

The festival was in full swing when they got back. People from several towns over had come to celebrate, and Jake seemed to know all of them. There was good-natured ribbing about his holding her hand, but he navigated through the crowd completely unconcerned.

She should care; the Meera she knew would worry about how she looked right now, fret over what her parents would say if they found out. But for once in her life, she couldn't bring herself to give in to her usual anxieties. Her heart had never felt lighter, and until this moment, she hadn't realized what a heavy load she always carried.

She touched her lips, still tingling, and flushed as she remembered the feeling of Jake's mouth on hers. He squeezed her hand, and she glanced up at him. *He feels it, too.*

The rest of the festival was a blur. She looked for Lily but didn't see her. Meera texted her and got a cryptic reply saying she wasn't coming.

Meera made a note to check on her later. They went back to Mrs. Hayes for more moonshine, and Jake fed her something called funnel cake. They shared a bag of kettle corn and cotton candy. By the time dusk came and the festival was wrapping up, Meera realized that this had been the happiest day of her life. She felt liberated, free from her parents' smothering plans, unbound from the burdens of their expectations, released from her never-ending to-do lists.

The next few weeks are mine alone. Why shouldn't I do what I want and enjoy it while I can?

She turned to Jake. "Do you still want to go to New York with me?"

"Two days with you and no one around to gossip about us? Heck yeah!"

She beamed. She wanted to spend time with him. To get to know him better, to find out what it was about Jake Taylor that made her heart beat faster. Impulsively, she put her arms around him, and he picked her up and twirled her around. She squealed in delight and several onlookers hooted encouragingly.

Then she remembered why she was going to New York in the first place. She tapped him on the shoulder and asked him to set her down.

CHAPTER ELEVEN

"YOU KNOW HOW many pictures I've seen of this skyline? To actually be here…" Meera bounced in her seat, not caring how juvenile she must seem. They were crossing over the George Washington Bridge into New York City. Jake was driving, a big smile plastered on his face. There were so many lights, even at this late hour, and his face glowed.

"I've never seen it, either."

"How could you not?"

He shrugged. "I don't know… I've never felt the need to leave Hell's Bells." He looked pointedly at her. "Until now."

She was glad he had come with her. She had originally asked Raj to come to New York for their honeymoon, but he had refused, saying he didn't like to travel so far. Her parents were the same way, only visiting India to see family, which was why, despite their wealth, she had hardly seen the world. She intended to travel the globe, but for the first time, she wondered how that would be possible. Raj certainly shared her career goals, but could he share her life's passions?

She reached out and squeezed Jake's arm, glad she had had the courage to come with him. "Stick with me, kid, I'll show you the world." He laughed at her bad Brooklyn accent.

"Promise?"

She winced at the seriousness in his voice. They'd spent the past seven hours in the car talking nonstop. Somehow they managed not to talk about the kiss or her appointment in New York. And yet, that simple word brought reality crashing down on her.

"I can't make you any promises, Jake. You know that."

He nodded. "You're right. That was unfair of me." They were stopped in bumper-to-bumper traffic; the bridge was a sea of red lights. He put the car in Park and reached over to place a hand on her cheek, turning her face so she had to look directly into his eyes.

"Meera, I know it's complicated between us. Honestly, I have no idea what it is I want from you or what I can give you, but I'll tell you this—there's something between us and I'm not willing to give it up right yet."

She nodded, unable to speak. He had voiced exactly what she was thinking—the uncertainty of what the future held, despite the strength of her feelings for him. It wasn't as if she could give up her entire life's plans on the fleeting skip of a heartbeat.

"So how about we just see what happens, do what comes naturally."

"How do you do that? I've planned every single moment of my life. I know what I'll be doing ten years from now, and you're asking me to just…"

"I'm asking you to throw your clipboard and checklists away for the next three weeks. Blow off some steam!"

She took a sharp breath. *Blow off some steam.*

"Trust me."

She took in his sincere smile, felt the warmth of this hand on her cheek and let some tension seep out of her muscles. Her entire body felt light and free, as if it belonged to someone else. *Is there something wrong with allowing myself to feel this way for a little while longer? This is my chance to discover life, to live the way I want and not the way I'm expected to.*

She nodded. "Why the heck not."

He laughed at her terrible accent—Southern this time.

"Where else do you want to go?"

She smiled. "You won't believe it, but I've always wanted to see the Taj Mahal."

"Wait, didn't you say you've been to India as an adult?"

She nodded. "We go every year, but it's always to see family. We never seem to have time to go sightseeing. It's supposed to be a beautiful monument."

"Wasn't it built by some love-crazed king?"

She swatted him playfully. "It was built by Shah Jahan as a monument to his wife, who died in childbirth. It's the ultimate symbol of love."

"I thought you didn't believe in love."

"That's exactly why I want to see it. It represents the type of love…" She paused. The Taj Mahal symbolized the kind of grand love that didn't exist anymore. Perhaps in Shah Jahan's time, such love was possible. "It's the type of love I've never known and therefore can't imagine."

He smiled. "When will you stop surprising me, Meera Malhotra?" It was the first time he had pronounced her name perfectly.

She giggled. "When you stop pretending to be the stupid redneck you most definitely are not."

"Yes, ma'am!" Jake laughed. "What if you could have that Shah Jahan type of love, Meera? Would you let yourself enjoy it?"

The seriousness in his voice stabbed her heart. As her mother had pointed out, Shah Jahan lived in simpler times. Her mother was full of "young love" stories that ended in divorce because couples couldn't agree on the basics. Her mother made a good argument for what it took to make a marriage work in the modern world—an understanding of each other's career goals, shared interests and similar lifestyles. Everything she had with Raj. She knew that even if their *janam kundlis* hadn't matched, her mother would have still used this rationalization to lobby for their union.

"It doesn't exist, Jake, at least not in our complex world."

It was almost two in the morning when they pulled into the hotel she had booked. Jake gave the car keys to a valet and took both their bags out of the trunk. Meera walked up to the check-in counter and gave her name.

The clerk looked at her apologetically. "Ah, Dr. Malhotra, I'm very sorry, but you're so late coming in that I had to give one of your rooms away. I only have one room left."

"What? Where are we going to go this late at night?" Meera stared at the clerk incredulously. She had reserved the rooms just before they left Bellhaven. Most of the city was booked up; she knew there weren't likely to be other hotels in the area with two rooms available. How could the hotel give away a room that had been reserved a mere seven hours ago?

"Perhaps you and Mr—" she looked at Jake "—and your friend could share a room?" The clerk raised an eyebrow at Meera as if to say, *I'd share a room with this man any day.*

Her parents would never approve. They would throw a fit if they ever found out. Raj would go ballistic. What would she tell him? How would she explain this…in addition to the kiss? *Especially* because of the kiss. And Jake! Share a room with him?

"I'll be a perfect gentleman." Jake's breath tickled her ear, and her nerves trembled. It wasn't *his* resolve she questioned.

"Oh, in for a penny, in for a pound."

The clerk looked at her in confusion.

"She means we'll take it."

Meera opened her purse, but Jake handed over his credit card. She shook her head, but he ignored her protests. "I don't let a woman pay."

Meera tensed. She plucked Jake's credit card off the counter and firmly handed the clerk her own. "This is my trip, Jake, and I'm not your woman." She cringed at the harshness in her voice.

Jake's jaw twitched. Meera lifted her chin. The clerk was eyeing them with open curiosity, Meera's credit card poised in her hand. Jake closed his mouth, his expression pinched.

Meera nodded to the clerk, and she ran the card through the machine.

They took the elevators to their room in silence. Meera tried to make eye contact, but Jake stared stonily at the doors as the elevators rose.

When Meera opened the door, Jake groaned. "Is this a room or a closet?"

Meera took in the small room, which contained a single queen bed, a desk and a TV. There was a small bathroom. The window looked out on the brick wall of the building next door, so close you could reach out and touch it. A sharp pain pierced her chest. There wasn't enough air in here. She took a deep breath to try and calm herself, but it didn't go in.

It's fine. It will be fine. Her breaths were coming faster. Her chest hurt. She dropped her purse. She needed more air. Now!

Jake's arms came around her, and he squeezed her against him. The air left her lungs completely, but then she took a breath and it went in, just a little, and her heart slowed. Jake held her as she took several new breaths. She didn't know how many minutes passed, but when her breathing returned to normal, Jake released her.

"Where did you go just now?"

She closed her eyes, "I don't do well in tiny rooms." They reminded her too much of the orphanage. She didn't like the feeling of being trapped, of not having enough room to move about.

"I'm here, Meera." His voice was soft. "You have me."

She felt tears welling up, and impulsively she turned and put her arms around his neck. He hugged her back, and she let his warmth soothe her. She didn't care what it meant or didn't mean. In this moment, she just needed someone to take care of her.

Eventually, she extracted herself, and they took turns showering. When she came out, she noticed Jake had set up a makeshift bed on the floor. She gave him a grateful smile. "Should I even bother asking if we might take turns?"

He gave her a look that brooked no argument.

They settled in for the night; both of them had been up for almost twenty hours. Yet Meera couldn't sleep. Her mind buzzed with a thousand questions. Despite spending all that time in the car, she still wanted to talk to Jake.

"Why do I feel like I've been sleeping all my life and I'm just now waking up?"

Meera sat upright in bed. "I know! I can't explain this energy I have. I should be exhausted."

Jake was sitting on the floor grinning. He sat with his back against the window, so she propped herself against the headboard to face him. They chatted about the sightseeing they would do after their respective morning meetings.

"So what kind of equipment are you buying tomorrow?"

He shifted. "Actually…I'm seeing my mother."

She sat up straighter. Jake was usually so closed off about his mother. "I thought you were out of touch with her."

"I was. She sent a letter out of the blue a couple months ago and asked if I'd come see her. She lives right outside the city, and I've been thinking about it. Guess I just needed an excuse to drive all the way out here."

"Why does she want to see you now?"

He shrugged. "She didn't say." He was making an effort to sound casual, but Meera could hear the angst in his voice. He'd been putting this trip off, unsure of what to do or how to face his mother.

"How old were you when she left?"

He took a sharp breath. "About twelve."

Her eyes found his, silently letting him know she was there for him. A comfortable silence blanketed the room.

"I remember her clearly. Beautiful long blond hair, sparkling blue eyes… She had a really nice smile and she made the best apple pies. I remember her sitting on the front porch, reading books all day. I heard her begging my father to take her to see a movie in town or to save up to go to Europe." He smiled wistfully. "She was always bugging him to take her shopping in New York."

Meera felt her arms and legs go numb. His tone was light but the pain behind his words tore through her. What was so wrong with wanting to see the world?

She longed to reach out and touch him, but she didn't want to break the moment. She needed to see the ghosts he held in his heart.

"One day, she just up and left. She said she'd fallen in love with someone else and she wanted a divorce. She left a note, but I don't even remember her saying goodbye to me. It's like we didn't exist anymore and she couldn't wait to start her new life by leaving us behind. I heard my dad tell Mrs. Hayes that she sent divorce papers and asked for nothing, not even visitation rights. We hadn't heard from her at all until she sent me this letter." He pulled out a well-creased paper from his pocket.

"So you haven't talked to her since you were a child?"

He shook his head, and Meera shuddered. She couldn't imagine not being able to talk to her parents; they were her whole life. Even now, she texted or talked to her parents every day. Meera remembered what it was like before she had a mom and dad, when she spent every day wondering why her biological parents would discard her like trash, why she was so unlovable. Staying connected to her parents staved off the self-doubt that plagued her. She could see the same insecurities had haunted him all his adult life, too.

She wished she could reach out and hug the little boy whose mother had abandoned him.

"I don't remember my biological parents," she said. "My earliest memories are of the matron at the orphanage. She told me I wasn't worth anything and that's why my parents left me. But they must have loved me at one time. *Pitaji*—my father—always says that whatever made them drop me off on a stranger's doorstep and never look back…it was something beyond me, an obstacle that my presence couldn't conquer."

Jake nodded, but his gaze was a thousand miles away. She recognized the look; he was processing things he'd never allowed himself to think about. "She and Dad were high school sweethearts. They married when they were just eighteen. Dad's always been content with just the ranch. I've always been happy there, too. He doesn't talk much about it, but I think my mom wanted more out of life, and he didn't want to leave."

"Why not?"

"What?"

"If your father loved her so much, why wouldn't he give up the ranch for her?"

His eyes cut to her. "The ranch isn't just some place, Meera. It's a part of who we are, both my father and I. We work the land to provide for our families…"

Her mother's words came back to her. *Unlike the movies, love doesn't conquer all. You must be practical and be with someone who understands the life you want.*

"But if it's ripping your family apart, why hold on to it?"

He frowned. "You don't get it. Can someone convince you to eat a bloody red steak tomorrow? No, because that's who you are. Being a rancher is who I am—it's who my dad was. If he'd given up ranching, he wouldn't be the man my mother married. He'd be some puppet she created."

She didn't know why it mattered. Why was she so interested in finding out whether there was a solution, some compromise his parents hadn't thought about. Something that would prove her own mother wrong.

"There wasn't a middle ground?"

He shook his head. "She wanted to see the world. When you're a rancher, you can't just take off for weeks or months. Animals need to be fed and cared for every day, and my dad had horses.

They require a lot of work. I think she felt suffocated with us, like we'd taken her choices away."

Meera went cold. This time the silence stretched between them.

"I wouldn't want you to make the same mistake."

And there it was. The elephant in the room that was sitting on top of her. The one that choked the breath out of her.

"It's not the same situation, Jake."

"Isn't it? Do you feel like you're in control of your life? Like you're making your own decisions? Why don't you want a love like Shah Jahan had for his wife? Why are you willing to settle for something less?"

She picked up the bottle that was sitting on the nightstand and took a long swallow of water.

"If your father had taken your mother to travel the world, would she have stayed?"

He shrugged. "That wasn't the point. She needed to accept who he was."

"And he needed to respect what she wanted out of life. These are exactly the modern-day dilemmas that couples face. My marriage to Raj is strategic—we've already worked out the issues that make most couples incompatible."

"Are you physically compatible? Do you kiss him like you kissed me?"

Something painful stabbed at her chest. She burrowed under the blankets.

"It's been a long night, Jake. I'm going to sleep."

She was just drifting off when her phone buzzed. She sighed and reached across the nightstand to check her texts. Her mother hadn't yet figured out the time difference.

Let me know how the appointment goes.

The appointment! That's what she was here for, and it would serve her well to remember it.

CHAPTER TWELVE

MEERA HEARD JAKE tossing and turning most of the night. A little past dawn, she gave up on sleep and went to the bathroom. She showered, dressed and put on the dress she had picked for the appointment, a turquoise sheath with long, butterfly-style sleeves and a boat neck.

Jake was sitting on the bed when she emerged from the bathroom. His eyes traveled the length of her body, his brows creasing.

"What?" She was still annoyed at him for spoiling a good conversation last night.

"Nothing." He went into the bathroom and slammed the door. He opened it again a second later and stuck his head out. "I was going to say you're really dressed up to go sightseeing."

Bollocks!

She should have found a way to tell him earlier. He closed the door, and she heard the shower running.

She slipped on gold leather lace sandals. She had to look the part; she couldn't very well show up wearing a T-shirt and jeans. She called room service and ordered coffee, a pot of tea, cereal for herself, and eggs and bacon for Jake.

Room service knocked on the door just as Jake came out of the shower. He smelled like clean soap and aftershave, a heady scent. She took a deep whiff when he wasn't looking.

"Hey, thanks for ordering breakfast." The waiter laid the tray on the bed. Jake poured coffee for himself and tea for Meera. He put milk and sugar in the tea and handed her the cup.

"So where is this fancy appointment of yours?"

Meera took a sip and picked up her toast. "I need to go see Sienna Simone."

"Is she someone I should know?"

Meera brushed nonexistent crumbs off her dress. "She's a famous designer. My mother had her design a special wedding dress for me, an East-meets-West design, and I have to go try it on. She's only here today."

"So you came to New York to get fitted for a wedding dress."

"I did." She swallowed, the tea burning her throat.

"Well, good luck with that."

They ate breakfast in uncomfortable silence.

Finally, Jake put down his fork with a clank. "What I meant to say last night was that I have some experience with women who settle down. Jolene thought she wanted me 'cause it made sense—we were high school sweethearts, too. But when it came down to it, she didn't want a life on the ranch. If you want to marry that Raj fella, I'll come dance at your wedding—" she gave him an incredulous look "—okay, maybe not, but I'll be happy for you. You say you're here to do a medical rotation, but I think you're really here to figure out what you really want."

"I know what I want," she said with feigned confidence.

He swallowed and went back to eating.

What if Jake was right? What if she was here to figure out what she really wanted? And if the answer was that she didn't want Raj, how would she face her parents?

Jake wiped his mouth and excused himself. He had to drive to New Jersey to see his mother. They agreed to meet at the Empire State Building later in the day.

Meera walked the few short blocks to Fifth Avenue and looked in the windows of the high-end designer stores. It was too early for the shops to be open, but she enjoyed looking at the beautiful dresses, perfectly lit to showcase their finery. She was never meant to wear any of the dresses here. She was like Eliza Doolittle from *My Fair Lady*. She had watched the movie in the small room at the orphanage and dreamed of what it would feel like to be rescued. Her father had made that happen. Her mother had taken a street urchin and turned her into a princess. Meera had gone from scrapping for a few rupees to buy food to having an unlimited allowance to spend on clothes and accessories. Not once in her life had her father raised an eyebrow at what she charged to the credit card he gave her. She thought about Derek's father forgoing a much-needed CT scan for his son because he couldn't afford it. Did she deserve the life that had been handed to her?

She moved away from the stores, choosing to walk down a side street lined with cafés now filling up with office workers eager to get their morning caffeine.

People often asked if she would track down her biological parents. There was no way to do so, but even if she could trace them, she had no inclination. Her parents had given her everything she could ask for: an education, a home, a life of luxury and fine things. Why would she seek out the people who had willingly given her up? A familiar pain pulsed through her head. Jake had brought up choices; well, her parents had chosen her. And marrying or not marrying Raj was still her choice. Her parents didn't have a gun to her head.

She checked her watch—it was almost time for her appointment. She pulled out her phone to call Lily and check on her and find out why she hadn't made it to the Bull Blazin' Festival. Meera wondered if Lily had heard from Joe. She doubted it. She was pretty sure Lily had been taken advantage of; she only hoped the girl came to her senses and didn't spend the rest of her life waiting for him. Lily didn't answer the phone. Meera sighed and hailed a cab to take her uptown to the Sienna Simone Bridal House on Madison Avenue.

When she got to the door, she called the number she'd been given and was shown in by an assistant who said Sienna was running late. *Great!* The assistant came back a few minutes later, reverently holding a dress. "This dress has created quite a stir in Sienna's fashion house. She's never designed anything like it."

Meera's mother had insisted on working with Sienna because she was hoping the wedding would be featured in one of the prominent English magazines. Meera studied the pale pink dress with delicate, deep maroon embroidery that highlighted volumes of diagonal cut ruffles. A heavily beaded bodice topped it off. The shape was supposed to mimic a traditional Indian *lehngah*. It was a beautiful dress. Meera rubbed her temples.

"This gown will look so good with your skin tone. I bet you can't wait to try it on. Sienna should be here any minute, so why don't you step into this dressing room?"

Meera stared at the dress. She hated it. It was big and bold, flashy and ostentatious; it was not what she wanted, not what she would have chosen. She had been hoping for something simple and elegant. Maybe even a traditional Indian sari, but her mother kept insisting she would love this dress.

Her throat closed. The boutique was getting too hot. Her mouth was completely dry. She needed air and water, and…something else. The overeager assistant was setting up a spacious dressing room, chattering away. Meera gazed at the front door and the world right outside it. There was nothing stopping her; she had choices, she could do what she wanted. She didn't have to wear that gown.

She turned and fled.

JAKE PULLED UP to the house. It was the quintessential, middle-class suburban house, a brick front with a small front yard. He stared at it for a while, trying to understand the life that his mother led in this place. How long had she lived here? It seemed so small compared to the ranch. Was she happy?

The front door opened and his mother stepped out. From afar, she was as he remembered, but as he walked closer, he saw the differences. Her long blond hair was much shorter now, with hints of gray. Her eyes were still blue, but there were pronounced lines around them. She seemed much smaller—shorter than he was—and thinner.

"Jake! I'm so glad you came."

She sounded different. She'd lost her Southern drawl, and her voice was deep and rough, not sweet and high-pitched like he remembered. He stood there awkwardly—how did one greet a mother who'd left a couple of decades ago? Was there a Miss Manners guide to this? She gave him a small smile and held out her hand. It felt fragile in his, and he gave her a limp handshake.

She led him inside to a living room, and he scanned the comfortable space.

He stepped toward the mantelpiece, drawn by the morbid fascination that makes drivers stare at a car crash. He looked at the framed pictures of his mother marrying another man, her and two girls at Disney World, hiking in the Grand Canyon, in front of the Eiffel Tower, on the London Bridge with the iconic Tower Bridge in the background, at the girls' college graduations. An entire lifetime. A whole new family. He picked up the London photo; it shook in his hands. He set it back.

"Those are my stepdaughters," she explained.

"So you raised another man's children but didn't want to see your own?"

Her expression was pleading. "It wasn't like that, Jake. Things were complicated, and I just needed to get away."

"And what did I do to make me unworthy of a second look back?"

She came closer, and he stepped back. "You didn't do anything. I was selfish—I wanted a fresh start, and I thought having you in my life would remind me too much of your father. You look so much like him."

A cold hand squeezed his heart. His father was a good man; he had been a good husband to her.

"Why did you wanna see me now?"

She stilled. "Could we maybe sit down and talk? I made some apple pie. I remember you used to like them a lot."

He shook his head. He didn't want apple pie. He wanted his mother to go back in time and never leave them. "Just tell me why you wanted to see me."

She sighed. "I've been diagnosed with cancer."

Tears stung his eyes, but he blinked them back. She was a stranger, a mere shadow of the woman he remembered. "Is there something you need from me? A kidney? Bone marrow?"

She shook her head. "It's lung cancer—all those years of smoking, I guess. It's still early and I'm getting treatment, but I've been taking stock of my life, and I…" Tears came down her face. "I regret leaving you, Jake, I always have. It was the easy thing to do—like I said, I was selfish. But now, I want to know you. I want to be part of your life. Are you married? Do you have children?"

He shook his head. She was sick. The news should shock him, or at least make him feel sorry for her, but it didn't. He was numb. The woman standing before him was a stranger. She lived an entirely different life, one that didn't include him.

"You think you can just walk back into my life because *you're* finally ready?"

She looked down. "I know I hurt you. I'm so sorry."

"Hurt me? You nearly destroyed me. I've spent my whole life wondering what I did to drive you away."

She closed her eyes, her face strained. "It was just too much for me, Jake—the ranch, your father and his obsession with it. The town hated me, I had no friends and your dad and I never had any privacy with the ranch hands constantly in the house. And then you…you were a sweet boy, but the ups and downs, the sheer energy you required to do basic things… Your dad was so busy with the ranch, he could never help me. I just couldn't handle it all." Tears were still streaming down her face. "I'm not proud of who I was back then. I was young…"

Jake's ears burned. He had suspected it for years. He *was* the reason she'd left. His problems, his deficiencies.

"So I wasn't perfect enough for you."

She moved toward him, her arms reaching out. He stepped back, knocking down a couple of pictures as he swung to avoid her outstretched hand. One of the frames crashed behind him. Neither of them went to pick it up. "That's not it. It wasn't just you, it was the whole life out there in Hell's Bells. Your father never wanted to leave, and I didn't want to stay."

They were the same words that Jolene had once spoken to him. "Well, Mom, I turned out no different than Dad. I have the same life he did, so there's not much you don't know about me. And I love that life—the ranch has given me purpose, a sense of accomplishment. Dad took care of me, and he didn't have trouble dealing with my problems. The townspeople you hate so much? The ranch hands? They all gave me the love you never could." *And that's what I really came here to tell you—that I turned out okay.*

He picked up the fallen picture frame. "This is the family you wanted. Enjoy them." He stormed past her, ignoring her as she called out his name. He went straight to the car and pulled into the nearest gas station. He hit his head on the steering wheel and let out a stream of curses. He'd come here because he wanted his mother to say out loud what he already knew. And yet he didn't feel any better.

He had made the same choices as his father, including the type of woman he'd asked to marry him. He sat up and turned the ignition. He looked at his hands; they weren't shaking anymore.

He was done making the same choices over and over again.

CHAPTER THIRTEEN

"THIS IS UNBELIEVABLE." Jake leaned over the side of the railing and let the breeze cool his skin. He watched the boat slice through the water, its salty smell wafting up. He was looking out at the symbol that defined the United States, the Statue of Liberty. She seemed to rise out of the water ahead of them, her teal form certain and strong. The sun was low on the horizon, and the orange sky made a stunning backdrop to the statue.

"I know, it's quite a sight." Meera stood beside him, her arm linked with his as they looked over the bow of the ferry that would take them to Ellis Island. It was an extraordinary experience, one he had never craved but now inexplicably felt he'd wanted all his life.

What's happening here? He liked spending time with Meera and felt it was important to figure out his feelings for her, but the more he was around her, the more confused he became. Meera hadn't asked about his visit with his mother, and he hadn't mentioned her appointment. He was just as happy as she was to put their issues on hold to enjoy their time together. They'd spent the day wandering the city, taking in Times Square, going to the top of the Empire State Building, eating pizza on the side of the road. The only flaw in the otherwise great afternoon was Meera's insistence on paying for everything. He fought her for the bill every chance he got but stepped back because she seemed adamant and he didn't want to create a scene. *But that stops now. I don't want her thinking I'm some poor rancher who can't afford things.* He had his pride.

He turned to see Meera's ponytail flapping in the breeze. He studied her delicate features: her perfectly straight nose, finely boned cheeks, almond-shaped eyes framed with blankets of dark lashes, her smooth, milk-chocolate skin. And beneath it all, she had a heart of gold and the spirit of a fighter. He thought about his mother, how she couldn't handle the pressures of parenthood and Hell's Bells; about Jolene, who had fled when she didn't get what she wanted. Meera would never do that. She had the strength to face whatever came her way.

He stepped behind her and put his hands on her upper arms. She stiffened, then relaxed against him, and he held on to her as the ferry pulled up to the dock. The Statue of Liberty now looked enormous. He felt like a little kid at a birthday party with the biggest piece of cake. Meera in his arms, the fresh air, a beautiful evening…what more could he ask for?

"Oh, Meera…I just love…" He felt her tense in his arms. What was he doing? "I just love this city." She let out a breath. The boat docked with a clank and workers moored it to the wharf with ropes.

"Me, too, Jake. Me, too."

Her voice was so soft, he almost missed it. He pulled her closer, and she didn't resist.

They disembarked and made their way to the statue. "So why haven't you been here before?" Meera twined her fingers with his as they stood in line to get their tickets. Her touch sent bolts of excitement through him.

He shrugged. "I don't know. After my mom left, Dad and I closed ranks. We stayed close to home—I think we needed the ranch, and each other. And then it just became habit until…"

She clasped his hand tightly, and he squeezed back. It felt good to be so close to her. Somehow, she made him feel as if everything was okay. He hadn't talked about this stuff with anyone…not that all the gossip mongers in town hadn't tried. He'd kept his mouth firmly shut, sent a clear message that Jake Taylor didn't talk about his mother. But he wanted to spill his soul to Meera. It just felt right, as if they were tangled at some deeper level. Sharing himself with her lightened him up, made him feel as though he was letting go of a lifelong burden.

"Until what?" Meera prompted him.

"Till Dad got Alzheimer's. It came on strong, and suddenly, neither of us knew what hit him. One day he was running the ranch, and the next he was driving into town with no pants and talking nonsense." He stared stonily ahead. "I tried to keep him at the ranch as long as I could, but it was just too dangerous with the animals and equipment. Unless I got round-the-clock nursing, I couldn't keep him from wandering off. The doctor recommended putting him in a home."

Meera nodded. "It's a tough disease. You did the right thing."

He looked down, shuffling his feet. "In a way, it's good that my mom left when she did. I don't think she would've taken care of him the way he became, and then I really wouldn't be able to forgive her."

She gazed up at him with big brown eyes.

"You know, the ranch is the only thing that kept me and Dad going. It's our strength, the one place where we've never failed. No matter what's happened, it's been there for us, the only place I've been good enough."

"Good enough for what?" she asked softly.

"Good enough as a man, as a provider. I've always been able to feed myself and take care of a good number of the townsfolk by employing them. That's the mark of a man—someone who can take care of people other than himself. It's how my father raised me, but I wasn't good enough for my mom and I wasn't good enough for Jolene."

Meera gasped. "Jake, you can't think like that. Jolene left because you weren't right for each other. Just because two people want different things out of life doesn't mean you're wrong or in any way inadequate. Better you found out before you were married that she didn't want the same things."

Jake shook his head, a lead weight descending on him. "Nah, Jolene's a smart girl. She has big ambition. Me? I'm content to be a simpleton, live my life the way I've always lived it. That doesn't make me worthy of Jolene or women like her." He stared at Meera, wondering why he was going on the way he was. What did he want her to say?

Meera turned and grabbed his other hand, forcing him to meet her eyes.

"Listen to me. Any woman would be lucky to have you. If this was another world and our circumstances were different, I would consider myself blessed to love you." Her eyes held sincerity and her lips were set in a firm, determined line. It was nice to hear, but they both knew they could never be together because of who he was.

He could never give her the life she wanted. She couldn't see that women like her—smart, accomplished and strong—couldn't be happy with men like him. She was right about one thing, though: it was better he realized that early on, before he lost his heart like his father had.

Meera seemed to have an uncanny ability to read his mind, because she let go of his hand. *Women who wear designer clothes don't go for bargain brands.* He wasn't a doctor like her fiancé; he'd never be able to show her the world. She would never settle for a man like him.

Their turn came up at the ticket counter. Meera reached for her credit card, but he caught her hand and held it. He knew now to be quick on the draw and deftly handed over his own card. He silenced her with a look when she started to protest. He'd had enough. No matter what happened between them, he didn't want her remembering him as some poor redneck.

She exhaled loudly and turned away from him as they walked toward the monument entrance.

"You know, I make money. I don't have your kind of money, but I'm not so poor that I can't take you around the city! Or pay my own way, for that matter."

She whirled on him. "What?"

"I don't like you paying for everything. You

seem to think I'm so poor I can't afford a cup of coffee." There, he'd said it.

Her eyes widened. "That's not why I'm doing it."

He raised an eyebrow.

"I just… I don't want…" She sighed and dropped down onto a bench. He hesitated, then sat down next to her. It would be dusk soon, and the island would close but he didn't care.

"I'm not sure what we're doing, Jake, but I want to keep on doing it, at least while I'm here." She took a deep breath.

"When you pay for things, it makes me feel like you're taking possession of me. It's what my parents do for me, it's what Raj does. Now that I'm away from them, I want to take care of myself. I worked hard and saved up the last few months to pay for this trip. It's not my father's money I'm spending—for the first time in my life, it's my own."

Jake tipped his head. *Well, talk about taking the wind out of my sails.*

She leaned forward and placed her hand on his. "It's important to me. I need to know I can take care of myself, pay my own way. It has nothing to do with you."

"I get that, but why're you payin' for me, too?"

She wrinkled her nose. "I guess I felt guilty making you spend all this money on my trip."

He opened his mouth to protest, and she put a finger on his lips.

"You're right. I'll stop doing it."

He lifted her finger and kissed it.

"You wanna prove to yourself you can make your own way."

She nodded, her eyes shining. "It's the same with you and the ranch, isn't it?"

Jake swallowed to ease the lump in his throat. "My dad didn't think I was ready to take it over—he fought me tooth and nail, even when the Alzheimer's rattled his brain. In lucid moments he'd tell me I shouldn't take it. That I'd run it to the ground." He looked down. "And I'm not so sure he was wrong. I've had a really hard time. I've barely kept it afloat."

He raised his head to see Meera's gaze fixed on him. "And I bet it doesn't help to have a guest setting fire to an entire field."

He smiled. "It's fine. We recovered most of it, and your idea to look at neighboring property saved me from any major losses." She opened her mouth, but he held up his hand. "And before you say anything, yes—I'll let Tom put all replacement supplies on your credit card, unless the insurance covers them."

She rewarded him with a sparking smile and stood up. He followed suit, and they headed off to see the statue. When they were done visiting the monument, they went to the visitor's center to look up records of Jake's great-grandfather coming into America through Ellis Island. "Must be nice to know who your great-grandfather was," Meera said wistfully.

He nodded. "Oh, yes, my dad's quite proud of his heritage and spent a lot of time telling me stories my granddaddy told him about his father coming through here." They waited in line for a computer. He punched in the necessary information and smiled as the screen loaded. "You're not going to believe this."

She bent closer to see the screen. His great-grandfather had arrived on a ship that had come from London, but the vessel's journey had originated in India. His great-grandfather had boarded there.

"He must have been there when the British ruled India." She smiled. "I guess we may not come from such different places, after all." He laughed and printed the information. He grabbed her hand, and they walked back toward the ferry docks.

"Do you believe in signs?" she asked dreamily.

"You mean, do I believe the universe arranges our lives, that things are predestined and no matter what we do, they're meant to happen?"

Meera grabbed his arm. "So I take that as a yes?" Her voice was filled with excitement.

He laughed. "Until today, I would have said no." He waved the printout in his hand. "This may just convince me otherwise. I don't think Dad had a clue that his grandfather spent time in India. We knew he came from Europe, but we were never sure what country." He didn't believe in destiny or karma, and yet… He would never have imagined himself in this place, with a woman like Meera, but it felt so natural, as if it was meant to be.

It was the last ferry for the evening, so there was a long line to board. They stood in companionable silence, holding hands. He felt as if a cosmic force had pushed him and Meera together against all odds, a magnetism that kept them together. There was no other explanation for what was happening between them.

They boarded the ferry and found a quiet spot standing on the aft deck, facing the Statue of Liberty as they pulled away from the dock. It was cooler in New York than it was in Virginia, and a breeze gently washed over the water. He saw goose bumps on Meera's skin and wrapped his arms around her. She relaxed against him.

As they looked at the retreating island, she spoke softly. "What do you suppose they were thinking? All those immigrants who left their homes and livelihoods, came to this strange new place on crowded boats, taking such a risky journey. How did they have the courage?"

Jake gazed up at the clear sky. He had wondered the same thing. "Yeah, 'Give me your tired, your poor, your huddled masses yearning to breathe free'… I guess the promise of a better life was enough motivation."

"Would you have done it? Left your current life in search of a new and better one?"

He took a deep breath. The answer was no. Wasn't it? Jolene had begged, cajoled, threatened… and he hadn't budged.

He felt Meera's slight weight against his chest, and her hair brushed against his chin.

He shrugged. "Depends on what the promise held."

"What if it was to live the life you want, rather than the one you've been told to live?"

She turned to meet his eyes. Instinctively, he bent down and dropped a kiss on her forehead. Her skin felt soft beneath his lips. He heard the sharp intake of her breath. He wanted nothing more than to cup her face and kiss her, let her know just how much he loved her. *Whoa! Who said anything about love? Rein it in.*

He stepped back from her. Her brows furrowed, but he needed to break contact. Being too close to her fried his senses, made him think crazy thoughts.

She held his gaze, then linked her arm with his. *So much for not touching.*

"It's easy to imagine a better life when your current one sucks," he said. "My great-grandfather was probably dealing with oppression or poverty. He probably wanted control over his own life, to make his own his destiny. So he boarded a boat hoping for better. But I have a good life. I have more than a lot of other folks."

Meera nodded. "I feel the same way. When I think of all the kids I grew up with who didn't get adopted, I have no right to complain about anything. Or feel less than grateful for everything I have."

He wanted to reach out and hug the little girl who still saw herself as an undesirable orphan. *When will you realize you don't owe anybody anything?*

She slid her arm away from his, arched her back and set her hands on the railing, raising her face to the wind.

There was a new vibrancy to Meera, an inner brilliance that was shining through.

Was he living the life that he wanted?

"Jake?"

She had asked him a question. What was it again?

"How did it go with your mother?"

He closed his eyes. "It didn't. I should have torn her letter and thrown it away."

She touched his back. "What happened?"

"She made a new life for herself, raised another man's children."

"So why did she want to see you?"

"She has cancer."

Meera put a hand on her chest. "Then you'll see her again." He couldn't tell whether she was asking him or telling him.

He shook his head. "I'm done with her. The townspeople were right. She's always been selfish, and she didn't want me."

Meera stared at him. "You can't be serious. Even if what you're saying is true, she's trying to make amends now. You have to give her a chance."

"No, I don't. She's had years to make amends. It's too late now."

"But she's your mother. How can you cut her out of your life?"

"As easily as she cut me."

"But she's your mother," she said again.

"Look, I wasn't raised to revere my parents. My mother doesn't get my undying devotion just because she gave birth to me—it's not the way I'm wired. Relationships are about give and take."

She looked as though she was about to say

more when her phone rang. She looked at the screen, frowning, and turned as she answered the call. He shouldn't listen, but the look on her face scared him.

"Yes, Mum, I'm in New York. No, I know… I'm so very sorry. I don't know what came over me…"

She sounded like a little girl, apologizing to her mother for breaking a treasured item.

"I understand…I'm sorry. Yes, I know it's not like me, but I…"

She began to tremble, and she wiped her eyes with her free hand. She took several steps away from him, one hand cupped over an ear. Her head was bent, her shoulders drooped. He longed to reach out to her, to let her know that whatever she had done would not be the end of the world.

"No, Mum, I can't come home early, I have patients I'm committed to."

Jake's pulse quickened. *Go home early?*

"I'm sorry. I never meant to put you in this position."

She was rubbing her temples. "I really can't, Mum. I'm not being difficult…my patient… Mum?" She stared at the phone, her face so sad it ripped his heart. She blew out a breath and draped herself over the railing. He put his arms around her.

She pushed him away. "I can't, Jake."

"Is everything okay?"

She shook her head. He stood beside her and let the silence stretch between them. The boat made its way across the Hudson as the sun's last rays disappeared.

"I never tried on my wedding dress. I saw it and hated it and behaved like a spoiled little girl. I didn't think about the fact that my mother pulled a lot of strings to get Sienna to design it… I've embarrassed her. I don't know what got into me today. It was probably all that talk about choices you stuffed into my head."

Despite the pain he felt go through her, Jake felt a flicker of hope in his heart. Was she questioning her plans?

"If you don't like the dress, why do you feel bad about rejecting it?"

She gave an exasperated sigh. "Because it was the wrong thing to do."

"Why's it so wrong, Meera? Why's it so wrong to choose what you want?"

"You don't understand, Jake." She turned away from him.

"I understand more than you see, Meera." He dared not touch her, but he kept his eyes on her, willing her to see what was in his heart. He kept his voice low, his tone even. "Are you questioning whether you should have rejected the dress or whether you should reject your arranged marriage?"

She spun on him. "I'm not like you, Jake. My parents are important to me. I can't slice them out of my life the way you cut your mother off."

His mouth went dry. He should step back, let her go. He didn't need another stubborn woman who didn't see what was right in front of her.

She was chewing her lip. He should let it be, but he couldn't let her off the hook. He held her gaze. "Why would you marry him? You don't love him, Meera. If you did, you'd never respond to me the way you do."

Her eyes blazed.

"You don't understand, Jake. What we have…" She looked away from him, out toward the ocean.

Something burned in his chest.

"What *do* we have, Meera?"

"What we have is a summer flirtation. It's me on holiday."

He put a hand on her shoulder until she met his eyes. "Meera, this right here is not you on holiday. It's you, the real you. The person who's thinking of marrying that fella you don't love is the Meera you pretend to be for your parents."

She shook off his hand.

"You're wrong. The real me, the one you claim to know, is the irresponsible, impulsive Meera I've worked very hard not to be." Tears fell down her cheeks. "This is not real, Jake. I'm not going to throw away everything I've worked for to live on a cattle ranch stuck in a small town."

Jake reeled back as if he'd been slapped.

She's right, of course.

Meera's expression softened. "That was unnecessarily harsh." She moved toward him, holding out her hand in a conciliatory gesture.

He shook his head. "No, you're right. I don't know what I was thinking, giving in to whatever this thing is between us."

It's the dumb rancher in me, going where my heart takes me. He was done falling for women who were destined to leave him.

"We're done, Meera. Let's go back to Hell's Bells."

CHAPTER FOURTEEN

THE DOOR SWUNG open as soon as she pulled into Lily's driveway. Meera took a deep breath. She'd been asleep just two hours when Lily called. After their fight on the ferry, Jake drove them right back to the ranch. Meera started a thousand conversations, and he shut her out every time.

Today was the perfect day to focus on Lily and find out why she hadn't shown up at the festival. The young woman greeted Meera with a wide smile, almost bursting with excitement.

"Oh, Dr. M., about the Bull Blazin'—I came by the ranch yesterday, but…"

"I went to New York." She should have come by to check on Lily before she left. In the excitement following the festival, she had been entirely too focused on Jake.

Lily clasped her hands. "I know I flaked on you, but I had a good reason." Lily was tugging her into the house, bubbling over.

Despite her fatigue, Meera mustered an enthusiastic tone. "Come on, tell me—obviously you have exciting news."

"Joe emailed me." Lily clapped her hands. "I've been dying to tell you!"

Meera smiled. "I'm so glad. What a relief. What did he say? Were you able to talk to him? To tell him about…"

Lily shook her head. "He just said he's been on assignment and didn't have internet access and that he's coming home to see me in a week."

Meera crossed her arms. She didn't want to deflate Lily's happiness, but she also didn't want to see her get hurt.

"Did he say why he was coming back?"

"No, he didn't say much. I wrote back right away and told him he's got to come back now. I told him I was pregnant and that the baby's comin' any day."

"And did he respond?"

She cast her eyes downward. "He probably lost his internet again."

"Let's hope that's what it is." Meera kicked herself for sounding so skeptical. "Did you tell anyone else about the pregnancy?"

Lily nodded. "I went to Norma Jean's first thing on Friday. I was about to leave for the festival when I saw the email on my phone."

"Is it possible Norma Jean told Joe?"

Lily frowned. "That would mean she knew how to get ahold of him, and she said she hadn't talked to him in months—same as me."

Meera wanted to say more, to tell her not to get her hopes up. Then she saw the look in Lily's eyes. The look that mirrored the way Meera felt.

"I know you're thinking that Joe's taken advantage of me, but you don't understand…he loves me. The thing with the license was a mistake."

"Lily, are you sure?"

"I trust him, I believe in our love. He would've written to me if he could have, and if he says he'll be here in a week, he will."

Meera smiled and squeezed Lily's hand.

Lily squeezed back and placed both their hands on her belly. "The baby will wait until his or her father arrives."

Meera nodded, then reached for her purse. She pulled out a little statue. "My father gave this to me. It's the goddess Lakshmi. *Pitaji* says this little woman will bring me luck as long as I keep her close to me." She pressed the finger-sized statue into Lily's hands. "I hope she brings you the luck you and Joe so very much deserve."

Lily wiped tears from her eyes and hugged Meera.

"How did Norma Jean take the news?"

"She was great about it. She even said she'll help me with the baby. I called her after I heard from Joe. She'll wait until he comes before telling her cousin—his mother. She said it wouldn't be right to make an announcement without him. He needs to be the one to tell his folks. It's been a day and then some since I told her, and not a peep." Lily giggled. "Truth be told, I think she's afraid of her cousin and doesn't want to get blamed for introducing me to Joe."

Lily looked down. "She also told me that the girl he was supposed to marry is still waitin' on him. She gave me quite a talking-to about keeping this secret so long, and she's right. It wasn't fair to that girl, us carrying on and him lying to her. Joe should have broken it off the minute he and I fell in love…before we got married."

Meera felt a stab of guilt. She hadn't spoken to Raj in three days. He had called her when she was in New York, and she'd called him back this morning, when she knew he was on evening rounds in London, so she could leave a message.

Lily was saying something, and Meera refocused her attention on the expectant mother. They chatted about baby preparations.

"I would like you to come to the clinic tomorrow during lunch. I want to do another ultrasound, and we can talk about breastfeeding and what to expect after birth."

Lily nodded. "You were right. It feels good now that Norma Jean knows. She said she would drive me to the hospital if need be."

"And you must go as soon as you start feeling

contractions—don't wait for your water to break. The hospital is two hours away. It's a long time to be sitting in the car while you're in labor."

Lily nodded. She leaned conspiratorially toward Meera. "Now, Dr. M., I hear quite the stir about you and the town's number one bachelor."

Meera groaned. When she'd stopped by the diner to eat breakfast, Gloria had scowled and Mrs. Hayes had winked at her. It did seem as though the entire town was buzzing with the news that she and Jake had gone to New York together. Almost everyone stopped by to say hello just so they could pump her for information. "Oh, Dr. M., did you share a room?" and "My, oh, my, Dr. M., must've been hard to keep your hands off that man, especially after the way you two rode that bull…" The entire town was feverish with rumors and innuendo.

"Not you, too, Lily."

Lily grinned at her. "Hey, I won't push ya— it's written all over your face."

"What's written all over my face?"

"That you have it bad."

Meera shook her head. "We're just friends."

"Joe and I were just friends, too." Then she put her hand over her mouth. "That was a terrible thing to say. This is not the same situation at all. At all."

Meera twisted the watch on her wrist, avoiding Lily's gaze.

"For what it's worth, Jolene was a selfish little girl—we went to high school together. She always got what she wanted, never caring who she hurt. She pursued Jake, not the other way around, and then she strung him along for years, never marryin' him and then leaving." She shook her head, gray eyes shining. "Jake's a good man, Dr. M. And you're a good woman. I know you won't leave him like Jolene."

Meera felt as if the wind had been knocked out of her. She was going to leave; Jake knew that. The whole town knew that. How could she stay? Her whole life was in London. She mumbled something about patients to Lily and escaped to her car.

She backed out of Lily's driveway, almost knocking over the mailbox. Her phone rang just as she pulled onto the road. She needed to answer; it was probably Raj. She looked at the door that Lily had just closed and remembered what the younger woman had said about Joe's fiancée. She pulled over and dug out her phone.

She sagged in relief.

"Priya!" It was her favorite cousin. Meera planned to fly down to Florida to see her in a few days. But now Priya told her she wanted to come visit her instead. Her house had been damaged in a storm, and she needed to vacate immediately so it could be repaired. Meera agreed. The cottage had two bedrooms, and she was sure Jake wouldn't mind. Besides, Priya would be a good buffer between them, an excuse to stay away.

Jake! They had gotten home from New York in the wee hours of the morning. He could barely look at her when they parted. They had become so comfortable with each other that the awkwardness was unbearable. He'd shown her a vision of the kind of love that Lily talked about, the kind of love that inspired Shah Jahan to build the Taj Mahal. The kind of love that didn't exist.

Raj's messages were a cold reminder of the real world she lived in. Her parents would never accept a man like Jake. To be with him would be to lose her family, her life, everything she'd worked for in London. Jake's world was a fantasy. *Wasn't it?*

She went back to town and sat on the bench in the town square, content to watch people go about their business.

"Well, hello there, darlin'."

Meera looked up at Mrs. Hayes.

"Mind if I sit down?"

Meera nodded encouragingly, ignoring the painful twisting of her stomach. This had to be about Jake. Mrs. Hayes got right to the point. "I've known Jake his whole life. When Jolene started dating him, I was over the moon. Jake is nothing less than a son to me, but she didn't make him happy." She paused and reached into her purse for a handkerchief. She blew her nose. "I saw Jake's heartbreak coming. Jolene needed him to be a different man—she wanted to travel the world, and he's a homebody."

Meera studied the cloth in Mrs. Hayes's hands. The ranch was more than a home for Jake, she knew that.

"All the townsfolk are gonna tell you two to stop it. There's only one way this is gonna end, and that's in heartbreak. For both of you." She sighed heavily. "And truth be told, that's what I thought, too, but then I remembered my George. I've loved that man my whole life. I'd have followed him to Mars if he asked me."

Meera leaned forward.

"I don't think Jake and Jolene were the real thing. If they were, he'd have given up everything for her, and she'd have done the same. If there's one thing I know, it's that true love comes right up and smacks you in the face. And when it does, you gotta embrace it, 'cause it only comes but once in a lifetime."

Meera's heart slowed so much she was sure it had stopped.

Mrs. Hayes stood up. "I said my piece to Jake

at the festival, and I'm giving you yours now. The rest is up to you."

And with that, she was gone, leaving Meera sitting there staring after her. And more confused than ever.

CHAPTER FIFTEEN

MEERA FROZE. SHE felt him before she heard him.
She was in the kitchen making herself tea. It was
the middle of the day, and she wasn't expecting
anyone. She took a breath to calm the pounding
of her heart. *Time to call a truce—I don't want
things to be awkward when Priya comes.*

She kept her tone light. "I told the town we're
planning on running away to Tahiti."

She turned and saw just the hint of a smile.
She let out a breath. She wanted them to get past
the words said in New York.

"That would explain all the people who've
stopped by the ranch on the flimsiest of excuses.
Mr. Cregg insisted that you ordered a box of Earl
Grey that he had to personally deliver."

"Have you tallied how many are for us getting
together and how many are against?"

"I think it's about three for it and everyone
else against."

"Mrs. Hayes, Lily and who else?"

"Billy John. Boy has a little crush on you."

"That should make him against."

"Yeah, except he's got a wife and two kids, so he wants to live vicariously through me."

Meera smiled and stepped toward him.

"And what about you?"

"What about me?"

"Do you still have a crush on me?"

A shadow crossed his face. He paused, as if contemplating how much to say. "I have more than a little crush on you, Meera, but we both know it's not going anywhere." His voice was hard. He leaned back against the table, seemingly relaxed but obviously alert.

She didn't know what had come over her, but she needed to touch him. She was playing with fire and she knew it, but all of a sudden she hungered for the rush of emotions he brought out in her. She wanted the fantasy. She stepped closer to him. His eyes clouded with confusion. She took another step. He stood straighter. "What if we could run off someplace? Would you?"

His eyes bored into hers.

"Meera, you make me want to do things I've never wanted to do before."

Her body was acting of its own volition. She inched forward until they were so close she could feel his breath. She touched his arm. He stiffened. She moved her fingers down and found his hands. He grabbed hers and held them tightly.

"Meera, what're you doing?"

She leaned forward and rested her forehead on his chest.

"I wish I knew. I wish I knew what I wanted to do. I'm just doing what feels right in the moment."

"Is this a holiday, Meera?"

She heard the bitterness in his voice and pulled back.

"I don't know who Meera is anymore. Every time I turn around, I'm on a new emotional roller coaster. I just need some time to figure out what's in my heart."

Meera closed her eyes as she felt Jake's arms cradle her. Standing in this kitchen, with the bright, warm afternoon sun pouring in, everything seemed just as it should be—her and Jake together, completely natural, as if they'd been doing it forever.

She sighed against him. "If we could, where would we run off to?"

"Anyplace you want." His breath was soft against her ear, teasing her nerves. She wanted to keep her tone light, to keep this flirtation going just a little bit longer.

"Hmm, maybe we should go to Tahiti or Fiji. I've always wanted to go."

He bent down and kissed the top of her head. "You in a bikini with flowers in your hair... I'm getting the tickets."

It was a nice dream. Then she remembered he had responsibilities, too. He couldn't just drop everything.

"Oh, and what would happen to the ranch?" Her voice was more snarky than she intended.

"How about you just burn it down?" He sounded half-serious.

She lifted her head, searching his eyes. *Could it be? Was he thinking about leaving the ranch?*

"I'm only kidding," he said softly. "About burning down the ranch." He cupped her face. "I'm not joking about running away together. Anytime you say the word, I'll take you wherever you want to go."

Her voice was thick. "Jake…"

"I missed you this morning."

She hadn't seen him since returning from New York. She'd gone straight to town, not wanting to stop in the kitchen. "I felt odd this morning, like everything from the festival to the weekend was some dream and I was just waking up. I didn't know how to face you."

He gave her a small smile. "And now?" His voice was shaky, as if he didn't really want to know the answer.

She sighed. "Whenever I'm around you, it just feels right. I forget about my real life."

He tipped her chin so she was looking right at him.

"And what if this was your real life?"

She met his eyes. *What if it were?* She shook her head. "How can it be? This is not my world. What would I do?"

"You'd love me."

She felt light-headed. Her heart screamed, *Yes, yes, sign me up!* Her head resisted. *Be sensible, Meera. What would you do here? Be a rancher? Raise animals so you can kill them?*

As if reading her mind, he said, "You could take over Dr. Harper's practice. He's gonna retire soon."

"And Rose will kill me in my sleep."

He wrapped his arms around her again and pulled her close. "I'll protect you from her."

"And what else, Jake?" She hadn't meant to sound hostile. He wasn't responsible for the promises she was unwilling to break.

He frowned and loosened his arms. "I can't protect you from your inner demons, Meera, but I'll help you face them. If you let me."

She shook her head. She had obligations, not demons, and she didn't have to deal with them; she had to fulfill them.

"It's not that simple, Jake. What would you say if I asked you to come to London with me?"

His face closed. "It's not the same. I'm a rancher—what would I do in your hoity-toity society?"

"It's exactly the same." She hadn't meant to say it that loudly. "You're suggesting I give up my entire life and move here, but you're not willing to do the same for me."

"Ranching isn't a profession for me—it's who I am, Meera. I know that might not be palatable to a vegetarian, but…but…that's the man I am. I'm not asking you to change who you are."

"Yes, you are. By suggesting I live here, you're minimizing the importance of my beliefs. Being a vegetarian is not just about what I eat—it's how I choose to live. I'm a doctor, and I believe in the sanctity of life—all life. I can't just switch these beliefs off and live with you on a ranch where you raise animals just to be killed."

"You're a scientist. Why can't you understand that the animals wouldn't even exist—they'd never be born—if they weren't raised for meat."

She stared at him. How many times could they have this conversation?

"But that's not the only reason why you can't live here with me. How 'bout we talk about your blind obedience to your parents."

She turned around, unable to look at him. *How dare he?*

"I am done talking, Jake. It's clear that you will never understand where I come from. We have different cultural values when it comes to our parents."

She heard him walking away. By the time she turned around, he was on the other side of the room.

"My cousin Priya is coming into town tomorrow to see me. I'd like her to stay with me in the cottage if you would allow it."

He stopped. "Yeah, sure."

Meera looked at the table. She couldn't meet his eyes. "Priya is the daughter of my mother's sister… She…she can't know about… It's just that she wouldn't understand this thing. Not that I'm… It's just we're so…"

"Don't worry, she won't catch on."

She wasn't doing a good job explaining things. She started to try again, but when she looked up, he was gone.

She braced herself against the counter and hung her head over the sink. She didn't realize tears were falling down her cheeks until she tasted the wet salt.

CHAPTER SIXTEEN

"JAKE, WHAT A rustic little ranch you have."

Jake immediately disliked Priya. She said *rustic* in a nasally voice that made it plain she meant *dingy*. She appeared to be in her late twenties, a head taller than Meera, although that might be the high heels she was wearing. She was slim like Meera with the same milk-chocolate skin. He knew he wouldn't get along with Priya. Her complaining had started the moment she stepped out of the car. "It's so hot here!" *The woman is from Florida!* "Why is everything so dusty?" *It's called the outdoors.*

Meera looked at him pleadingly. He took a breath. *It's just the next two days. I can avoid her.*

"Thank you, Priya," he said with exaggerated politeness. "I'm sure Meera will show you around. In the meantime, help yourself to anything you like." He waved toward the fridge and pantry.

Priya scrunched her nose. It was just after lunch, and the smell of hot dogs clung to the air. "I'm sure we'll be eating out."

"Actually, Jake makes a really good grilled cheese." Meera stepped between them. Her eyes met his. He hadn't seen her since yesterday afternoon in the kitchen. Was there a silent apology in her expression? An apology for what? For pushing him away? Or for having to suffer Priya's presence?

He longed to reach out and touch her, to see if what they had was real or a figment of his imagination. As if sensing that, she stepped back.

"Cheese. Ugh! Calories!"

Meera rolled her eyes. "Priya, you're on holiday, let loose a little. We can exercise."

"Exercise? No, dear. First thing, I'm taking you shopping. You seem to have lost all sense of fashion. Where did you get that hideous dress?"

Meera was wearing a beautiful dress with tiny straps and a light, flowery fabric that hugged the right curves and flowed around her when she moved.

"One of my patients made it for me as payment for treating her. It was rather sweet."

Jake smiled. It was Lily. He knew Meera had been treating her because she'd come to Jake to thank him. She had been very anxious when she'd first approached him about the new doctor, but Lily seemed to have found happiness recently. *Must be the Meera effect.*

"What? They don't have money in this town?"

Jake clenched his jaw; Priya was going to grate on his nerves.

"Sometimes, people can offer things more valuable than money, like their time and effort."

Jake suppressed a smile at the irritation in Meera's voice.

Heavy footsteps caught his attention just as Billy John burst through the door. "Jake! Dr. M.! You've got to come right now, something's wrong with Kelly."

Without thinking, Jake grabbed Meera's hand and followed Billy John outside. Kelly was lying on the ground, almost unconscious, a hand on her chest.

"Go get my medical bag." Meera's voice was firm but calm. Jake hesitated for a second, then took off at a run. "Dial 911 and bring the ambulance back here," he heard Meera telling Billy John. His pulse raced as he sprinted to the cottage. They didn't have an ambulance unit in Hell's Bells. It would take the nearest one thirty minutes to get here.

He barged into the cottage and went straight into Meera's bedroom, where he knew she kept the bag. He came back outside seconds later and ran to the field. He saw Priya out of the corner of his eye. *I can't let anything happen to Kelly.*

He raced back to Meera and dropped the medical bag beside her. She opened it and took out her stethoscope. "Take this blood pressure cuff and put it around her arm, like the picture shows." Jake nodded and went to work on Kelly's arm. Meera extracted a bottle of aspirin and took out a pill. She opened Kelly's mouth and put it under her tongue. She took her blood pressure then brought out another bottle and crushed a tablet a little before putting it in Kelly's mouth. Jake read the label and saw that it was nitroglycerin.

"What's wrong with her?" Jake was breathless. *Please let her be okay. Please.*

Meera hesitated.

"Please," he said.

Meera opened her mouth then closed it. "She didn't want to tell you, but she has a medical condition."

He swallowed.

"I can't say more. I think she'll be okay for now."

He wanted to push Meera to tell him everything, but he knew she wouldn't. If Kelly had told her not to tell him, Meera would respect that.

Kelly started moaning after a few minutes. He helped Meera get her into a comfortable sitting position while they waited for the ambulance. Meera fussed about her, checking her heart rate and blood pressure again. Kelly mumbled.

"I'll come with you to the hospital," Meera said reassuringly.

Jake looked at her gratefully. She didn't have to go with Kelly—it was his job to take care of her—but he felt better knowing Meera would be there.

Meera used her hand to wipe the drool spilling from Kelly's mouth. Jake handed her a piece of gauze from the medical bag.

"I'll get you some soap and water."

"It's okay, Jake. Kelly's family."

He closed his eyes, pushing back the tears that threatened to spill out. Kelly was family. *His* family.

The ambulance came and Meera and Jake helped the paramedics load Kelly onto the stretcher. Meera rode in the ambulance so she could keep monitoring her, while Jake followed in his truck. At the hospital, Jake had to settle for pacing in the waiting room. As Kelly's doctor, Meera was allowed to go in with her. She texted him with updates.

Several hours later, Kelly was admitted for overnight observation, and Jake was finally allowed to see her.

His knees buckled at the sight of Kelly lying in the hospital bed, her body limp.

Meera squeezed his arm. "It's okay, she's just sleeping. We gave her morphine, which knocked her out. She's fine—she'll be discharged tomorrow."

Jake sighed in relief. "Thanks, Meera."

He went to Kelly and sat beside her, holding her hand. Several minutes passed before Meera touched his shoulder. "Go home, Jake. Come back tomorrow when she's awake. I'll need to fill out some paperwork, anyway. I'll catch a ride with one of the townspeople. I'll keep an eye on her and call you if anything changes."

"Meera..."

She nodded toward the door. "I'll walk you out."

They found half the town in the waiting room. Each person came and grasped Meera's hand to thank her. Everyone hugged her, too. Jake noted the tears in Meera's eyes, though she kept repeating that she was just doing her job. *What you did for Kelly means more to the people of Hell's Bells than you can know, Meera. It means more to me than I can express in words.*

Jake drove home in a daze, thankful for the empty country roads. When he parked in the carport, he sat still, head on the steering wheel. He eventually turned off the car and staggered into the kitchen.

Priya was sitting at the table. *Priya!* He'd forgotten about her. She was sipping a cup of tea. *Great. This is the last thing I need.*

"How's that woman who collapsed?" she asked politely.

"Kelly's doing okay now, thanks for asking."

Priya nodded. "It's lucky Meera was here. She's an awesome doctor."

Jake nodded woodenly. He busied himself taking food out of the refrigerator. One of the ranch hands had left him a bowl of chili. He began slicing a loaf of bread.

"Raj is a really good doctor, too. Did Meera tell you they're doing research together?"

Jake stopped cutting the bread.

"Yes, it's quite interesting," Priya continued. "During medical school, Meera thought of this compound that could possibly stop plaque from building in arteries. She and Raj started researching it together, and they wrote a paper that won them an award. Now they're doing this laboratory study to develop it into a drug. Raj is going to turn it into something kids can take so they'll never even develop heart disease."

Jake swallowed and went back to cutting bread.

"They're both just so brilliant, you know. I wouldn't be surprised if they won the Nobel Prize one day. What do you think?"

What I think is that Meera's too good for this fella, or anyone, for that matter. Priya was looking at him, waiting for a response.

"I've never met Raj, so I can't comment. Meera can do just about anything she sets her mind to."

"Hmm… I'm surprised Meera didn't tell you about it. The research is her life. You two seem to have gotten so close."

He stiffened at her tone. "Excuse me?"

"I couldn't help noticing that it didn't take you long to find her medical bag. I'd barely run outside and you were already coming out carrying her bag. If it were me, I'd need some time to search the place."

He swallowed.

"She told me where it was," he fibbed.

She narrowed her eyes.

He put the bread in the toaster and the bowl of chili in the microwave.

"You also seemed really comfortable taking her hand when we first heard the news."

Keep your cool, Jake. The least you can do for Meera is be nice to her cousin. "Kelly is like a sister to me, and she needed medical attention. If you were the doctor, I would've taken your hand."

"That's not what it seemed like to me."

Jake remained silent, hoping Priya would tire of his sullen attitude. But Priya wasn't done.

"Well, it doesn't really matter anyway—it's not like she's going to leave a brilliant pediatrician for a redneck."

Jake placed his hands on the kitchen counter and took several breaths. He wouldn't lose his cool, not with this bratty girl, and it wasn't as if he hadn't thought the same thing. It was hard to disagree with what she was saying, even if he didn't like it. "There you are."

Both Jake and Priya turned at the sound of Meera's voice. Jake tried and failed to catch her eye. She was talking to Priya. He hung his head. *Why would she be looking for me?*

When the microwave dinged, he offered them both something to eat.

Priya scrunched her nose. "I'm a vegetarian, like Meera." *Great. Another one.*

Meera sat down wearily. She took off her shoes and tucked one foot underneath her. "Actually, would you mind making me one of those grilled cheese sandwiches, please? I'm famished."

Priya began protesting.

"I'm so sorry, Priya, I have no energy left to go out. I promise I'll make it up to you tomorrow."

Jake pulled out the frying pan, smiling to himself.

"I can make you one, too, Priya." His voice was saccharine.

"No, thank you. I'd rather starve."

"Priya!"

He knew that look on Meera's face. She was mad as hell.

Priya stood up and stalked off.

Meera sighed.

"Give me another minute, I'll have the sandwich ready then you can go after her if you want." Meera smiled at him gratefully, and his heart fired up. "I'll make her one, too."

"Thank you, Jake." She paused as if measuring her words. "I don't know what's gotten into Priya. She's never been this petulant before."

Jake shook his head. "Your favorite cousin, huh?"

"Well, I don't have any brothers or sisters, adopted or biological…that I know of. And Priya and I have always been close. Really, I can't believe she's behaving like this. It's not like her at all."

"Maybe it's not her."

"Excuse me?"

Tread lightly, Jake, this can blow up in your face.

He slid the sandwiches onto a plate and held it out to her. "Maybe it's just that you've changed."

Meera frowned and took the plate from him. "I'm too tired to have this conversation, Jake. Can we call a truce until Kelly's better?"

"Sure. Thank you, Meera, for taking care of Kelly… If you hadn't been here…" His voice cracked.

Meera set the plate down and stood suddenly, throwing her arms around his neck. He bent down and hugged her, feeling the warmth and comfort baked into her touch.

She stepped out of his embrace. "Try not to worry. She'll be okay, I'll make sure of it."

And he believed her.

"PRIYA!" MEERA RAPPED on her bedroom door before walking in. Priya was sprawled on the bed, texting on her phone.

"Why did you bring me here if you were going to be gone the whole day? There's nothing to do here! Even the cell signal goes in and out."

Meera sighed. "First, you asked to come here. And I didn't have any patients scheduled, but Kelly was a medical emergency and the hospital is really far away."

Priya pouted. Meera tried not to bristle. Why hadn't she ever noticed how childish Priya could be?

"How can I make it up to you tomorrow?"

Priya brightened and sat up. "Let's go to Charlotte—I hear there's some great shopping." Retail therapy sounded like a good idea; it always made Meera feel better. And it would give her distance from Bellhaven, or Hell's Bells as she was now beginning to think of it.

"Done. We have to stop by the hospital to check on Kelly, but it's along the way…more or less. I also have to stop by the clinic to make sure

I don't have any patients… I never do," she added quickly in response to Priya's exasperated look.

"Why are you staying here, anyway? I mean, if you don't have patients, why stick around? Why not blow off the medical rotation and go someplace fabulous like New York or LA?"

"I do have a couple of patients here, like the one who made me this dress, and Kelly, who I took care of tonight." Meera took a bite of her sandwich and chewed. "You know, this town hasn't liked me since I got here, but today, they thanked me profusely for taking care of Kelly. The patients in London are always polite, but the way the town was with me tonight…" She couldn't explain it to Priya. It was more than gratitude in people's eyes as they shook her hand and hugged her tight. They'd shown her uncensored emotion unlike anything she'd ever experienced.

"Come on, Meera, don't give me that." She leaned forward and lowered her voice. "It's that totally hot cowboy in the kitchen, isn't it? I saw the way he looked at you when you walked in and how he seems to know his way around this cottage."

"Well, he does own it."

"Uh-huh…you can smoke-screen all you want, but you can't fool me. So spill it!"

Meera sighed. She should have known Priya would see right through her.

"Really, Priya, it's nothing. I won't lie to you, we are attracted to each other, but he knows I'm going back to London to marry Raj and that's the end of that." Meera's face burned. It was a lot more than that, but she wasn't ready to say it out loud. Not yet. And definitely not to Priya.

"Fine, you don't want to tell me…don't." Priya eyed the sandwich, then reluctantly picked it up. She took a tentative bite and then a bigger one. "You know, it may not be a bad idea to sow your wild oats before the wedding. I mean, I love Raj and you two are so, like, made for each other… but… Jake's really hot. Like, really hot! And I don't see any harm in having some fun before you settle down."

"Priya!" Meera threw a pillow at her.

"Oh, come on, Meera, let loose a little. You're always such a rule follower."

Meera shook her head. "And what if he's such a hottie that I fall in love with him?" She took a big bite of her sandwich.

Priya rolled her eyes. "Are you kidding? You and him? What, you'll be the cowboy and the Indian?" She dissolved into giggles. Meera tried to join in, her laugh high-pitched. Her insides churned.

"Meera, guys like Jake have been hitting on

me since high school. They see us as exotic beauties. This is rural America, where everyone is white and grew up eating hamburgers, not vegetable curry. You can't appreciate this coming from cosmopolitan London, but you and I are different, we're a novelty. It's lust—you're like a fine bottle of wine when he's used to the stuff from the box." She studied Meera. "Tell me you haven't fallen for him!"

Meera shook her head vehemently.

Priya sat up straighter. "'Cause, Meera, he raises cattle here, and these rancher types, this is who they *are*. You can't possibly accept—let alone love—someone who kills cows for a living."

Meera stood up and went to adjust the blinds. "Of course not. I've just been teasing with you. There is nothing going on with me and Jake. You're right…he and I are very different." She raised the blinds, then lowered them, adjusting the slats so each one was perfectly straight.

"Then why're you here?"

"What do you mean? I'm doing my rotation."

Priya fixed her with a look. "That's the story you gave your mother. You didn't have to do it right before the wedding. C'mon, Meera, this is me you're talking to."

"I still don't know what you're implying."

"Raj called me. He said you've been distant,

you never call him, you're short with him on the phone. He's worried about you."

Meera's head began to pound. "Did he send you over here to check up on me?"

"I wouldn't say that. My house is under repair, and I couldn't stand the noise so it was a good time to visit. He loves you, Meera. He just wanted to be sure you were okay."

Meera squeezed her hands into fists. *How dare he?* It was true that she'd been avoiding Raj's calls, but sending Priya to check on her was a horrible invasion of her privacy. "And what report will you be giving him, Priya?" Meera asked coldly.

"I won't tell him about the hottie, if that's what you're asking. I believe you. If you'd slept with him, he wouldn't be looking at you like he wants to eat you for dessert."

Meera took a deep breath, trying to contain her outrage. "Priya, I've always thought of you as a sister. You're supposed to be on my side, so when Raj asks you to spy on me, kindly tell him to stuff it. And that's the last I want to hear about Jake. There is nothing going on between us, but we are friends. Your vulgarity cheapens both of us."

She stormed off and slammed the door to her bedroom. She flung herself on the bed, tears streaming down her face.

CHAPTER SEVENTEEN

"THESE SHOES ARE to die for." Priya held up a pair of Via Spigas that were indeed beautiful. Meera started to reach for them but thought better of it. They would just get stuck in the mud. She shook her head at Priya. Once upon a time, shoe shopping was her favorite activity, and a pair of shoes like the ones Priya was holding would have been enough to make her smile for the whole day. Yet today, she felt restless.

"Should we head back? It must be getting late."

Priya glared at her. "Stores won't be closing for another three hours. Tell me you're kidding, please. Especially after you spent all morning seeing patients."

Meera sighed. Three more hours! All she wanted to do was get through the day with Priya without another fight—or worse, an inquisition. Priya had knocked on her door this morning holding a piece of paper that said Sorry. She'd sat down on Meera's bed and apologized sincerely about Raj. By unspoken agreement, she hadn't mentioned Jake all day. They talked about the usual things: Priya's unending string of boy-friends, all of whom were unsuitable husband material; her fledgling interior design business; and her ever-present, domineering mother. Meera let Priya fill the conversation with chatter that normally amused her to no end.

"Hello!"

Meera looked up.

"Huh?"

Priya blew out an exasperated breath. "You've been tuning me out all day."

"I'm sorry, Priya, I'm just worried about Kelly. She got discharged this morning, but I think she's going to need surgery and she doesn't have health insurance."

"Hmm… So back to my original question—what do you do in Hell's Bells when you don't have any patients and you don't have awesome me to keep you company?"

Meera shrugged. "I've been busy the last week and a half. I've been doing physicals on Jake's staff, I've helped him out on the ranch…there was the Bull Blazin' Festival." Meera's cheek's reddened as she thought about the kiss at the festival. She turned to examine a pair of shoes so Priya wouldn't catch her blushing.

"Wait, what did you help him with on the ranch?"

Meera told Priya the whole story about the

fire and ensuing cleanup. When she was done, Priya whistled and sat down on the bench. She motioned to a sales clerk and showed him the shoes she wanted him to bring her.

"No wonder you haven't had time to call Raj. You've been too busy playing little woman on the prairie."

"Priya!"

"It's all right, get it out of your system, be one with the earth and all that. I know you'll never want to live that way."

Meera bristled. "Why do you say that?"

Priya scoffed. "You? Come on! You love designer shoes—which, by the way, you can't wear at that ranch. I ruined my heels yesterday. You're a patron of the arts—you *love* the opera—and you're halfway to being this world-class researcher." She paused as the clerk brought her the Via Spigas. She held out her feet so he could put them on her, rewarding him with a flirtatious smile. Meera watched the salesman literally swoon.

"You're not going to give all that up to be some country bumpkin. You're a princess, and you were meant to live as one."

Meera's mouth went dry. She wanted to get out of the store and get some fresh air. She wasn't a princess. She was a poor orphan who had won the lottery.

Priya stood and walked up and down the store, admiring the shoes in the mirror. She took them off and put on another pair. Meera sighed and wandered to the shelf where a pair of strappy sandals caught her eye. She turned the shoe and looked at the bottom. The price was printed discreetly on a small label. She owned a number of similarly priced shoes. She thought about Kelly, how she hadn't bought health insurance even after finding out she had angina because she couldn't afford it. And Lily…the young woman was nine months pregnant and spent all day on her feet waitressing to make a fraction of what these shoes cost.

"You didn't find anything to try?"

She put the shoe back and shook her head.

Priya held up a pair of sandals. "Check these out, they will go perfectly with your engagement dress. By the way, what're you going to do about your wedding dress?"

The dress! Meera sat down wearily. "Haven't you heard?"

"That you flaked on Sienna Simone? Yes, your mother was massively upset. She called my mother and got her riled up, and then I had to deal with her over a two-hour lunch."

"My mother talked Sienna's assistant into mailing it to England and asked her tailor there to be ready to make adjustments when I come back." Meera's mother still refused to speak to her. All she would do was exchange perfunctory emails and texts with Meera on necessary wedding details. She knew she should feel bad, but she couldn't stop thinking about how wasteful that dress was. It cost more than what Dr. Harper made in several months of treating the people of Hell's Bells. She knew because he'd made her an offer this morning to take over his practice while he cared for his sick wife. For what it cost her mother to have Sienna make that exclusive dress, Dr. Harper treated the entire town of Hell's Bells, including a lot of people who paid him in fresh eggs and meat.

Priya's eyes widened. She dropped the shoe she was holding and grabbed Meera by the shoulders. "Are you crazy? Your wedding is little more than six weeks away. What if it isn't right? The whole point was to have Sienna fit you. Your mother pulled a lot of strings to make that happen."

Meera rubbed her temples. "I know, but there's nothing to be done now."

Priya picked up the shoes she had tried earlier. "I'm paying for these, then we're getting out of here. I think I saw a Carolina Herrera store when we drove in."

They spent the next few hours trying on all kinds of dresses. Their arms were full of bags.

"I'm pretty sure these are all mine," Priya observed. "You haven't bought a single thing."

Meera shrugged. "I really haven't liked anything enough."

"Meera, you need to buy honeymoon clothes, maybe something sexy for your wedding night?" Priya wiggled her eyebrows.

Meera felt nauseous. "I'm not in the mood, Priya."

Priya shook her head disapprovingly. "You shouldn't have taken this trip so close to the wedding."

It was the argument Meera had been having with her mother for the past several months. Mum had wanted her to wait until after the wedding. Meera had argued that she wanted to get the rotation done so she would have her research degree finished. What she hadn't done was acknowledge to herself that a big part of why she wanted to do it before the wedding was to have space from her parents and Raj.

Priya took the bags from Meera's hands and handed her a dress. "Try this on, just for me."

Meera nodded wearily. It was easier to comply than to argue, so she changed into the dress and stepped out to show Priya.

"She'll take it," Priya said to a sales clerk hovering nearby.

Meera shook her head; she had seen the price

tag in the dressing room. It cost more than a CT scan. "No, I won't, but thank you for your help."

Priya let out a cry of frustration. "What's wrong with you? It's beautiful and fits you perfectly."

"It just doesn't feel right, Priya."

"Is it that the dress isn't right, or is it that Raj isn't right anymore?"

Meera rubbed her temples. "You're being difficult, Priya. I don't understand why Raj has anything to do with this. I just don't like the dress."

Priya narrowed her eyes. She started to say something but apparently thought better of it. "Let's just go back to Hell's Bells. You don't seem to be into this today."

They drove in silence back to the ranch.

THE NEXT DAY, Meera took Priya to the airport with a sense of relief. Priya usually came to London a few times a year, and her weeklong trips always seemed too short. This was the first time Priya had shortened her trip and Meera hadn't enjoyed her company.

She gave her cousin a final goodbye hug, and Priya held on to her. "I love you, Meera, and I would never betray you. What I'm about to say is just between us."

She stepped back and fixed Meera with a look. Tears welled in her eyes.

"Even though you don't see it, you've got a crazy thing for Jake. That story you told me about the fire? You wouldn't have gotten down and dirty for someone you didn't care about. You have two weeks left—don't squander them. Go have fun, spend every second with him. Fill your heart with the kind of free love you may never experience again."

Tears spilled onto Meera's cheeks. Priya really was as close to a sister as she'd ever had. She squeezed Meera's shoulders. "But then go home and marry Raj. I know he's not the hero of a romance novel, but he can give you the life you want, the life you've worked so hard for. Jake will never be able to give you anything more than a dirty old ranch."

CHAPTER EIGHTEEN

"You look as bad as I feel."

Jake walked to the kitchen sink and turned on the tap. He washed his hands, then splashed water on his face. He turned the faucet off and stood there, bracing himself against the copper edge. He closed his eyes and hung his head.

Meera got up from the chair. She had been sitting for a better part of an hour drinking tea and waiting for Jake to show up. The sun had set several hours ago, and the kitchen was lit with the soft glow of a single bulb. The other lights in the chandelier were out. She had to talk to Jake, to figure out what this *thing* was between them. Priya's words reverberated in her head. She had a little more than two weeks left. Two weeks to figure out whether she could even consider giving up everything she had ever cared about for what she and Jake had. And if he would meet her halfway.

She went to his side.

"Is everything okay?"

He shook his head.

"Is it Kelly?"

He shook his head again. "Well, partly. She told me about the angina, and that she needs surgery. She's quitting her job here so she can become poor enough to qualify for medical assistance. She's the most experienced person I have, and she's leaving. I don't know how I'm gonna do this without her."

Meera rubbed his arm. "I'm sorry, I'm the one who advised her to quit. I found out about the medical assistance program at the hospital. They said she makes too much money to qualify now, but if she didn't have this job, she would get full health insurance and they would pay her hospital bill. Besides which, she can't be lifting heavy objects anymore. I would have advised her to find another job either way."

"You did the right thing for her, but…" He slammed his hand against the sink. "Aaarrghh!" The cry was primal, and his pain ripped through her. She stood aside to let him vent his anger. He put a fist on the sink and dropped his forehead on it.

She rubbed his back. "Hey, I'm here," she said softly. "Tell me what it is. Maybe we can figure it out together."

He groaned. "I can't seem to make anything right."

He turned toward her, and she let him take her

in his arms. She rested her head on his chest, her arms cuddled underneath his. She could hear the fast beating of his heart, the heave of his chest as he took in a deep breath. She buried her nose in his shirt, inhaling the scent that defined him.

He held her for several minutes. When he spoke, it was so softly that she had to lift her head to hear him.

"I just ran the ranch out of business."

Her eyes widened. "What happened?"

Shadows danced across his face in the soft light. "We have a couple of sick cows we've been treating. I thought I had it under control, but when Kelly and I came back from the hospital, ten more were sick, and they aren't doing well. We're gonna have to put them down. The problem is they were scattered all over, which means more of them will be sick soon."

He dropped his arms, and she moved out of his embrace, staying within touching distance.

"You're afraid you might lose too many animals?"

He nodded. "There's a good chance we're gonna lose a lot. When they're this sick, we have to put them down and we can't sell the meat."

He pinched the bridge of his nose.

"Please tell me, Jake, I want to know."

"The ranch is mortgaged to the max. If we don't have anything to sell in the fall, I won't be able to pay the bank or any of the bills for the rest of the year, and I won't have calves to raise for next year." He closed his eyes, brows furrowed.

Meera twined her hands with his, and he squeezed them. She wished she knew how to make it better.

"Perhaps things look worse than they really are. Have you talked with your accountant?"

"I *am* the accountant, and I know the numbers. The balance sheets are in my head."

"How much do you have in reserves?" He rattled off a number down to the cent. Meera raised an eyebrow.

"I know, I'm dorky like that. I couldn't focus in school long enough, so I got good at just memorizing things."

He bent his head and put his forehead to hers. "I'm gonna lose the ranch, Meera. If I have to sell it, all the hands will lose their jobs. What'll they do? There aren't other jobs in Hell's Bells, and they don't have the skills to do anything else. My dad was right—I couldn't handle it. I shouldn't have tried, and now I've made a real mess of things."

Meera's heart ached for him. She had worked herself to the bone all her life to avoid disappointing her parents. "This is not your fault, Jake, and if you hadn't taken over the ranch, it wouldn't have stood for all these years that your dad's been in the nursing home."

"He would've sold it to someone who could keep it going." He tapped his forehead against hers. "What am I gonna do?"

Meera bit her lip. He sounded weary. The easy answer to both their problems was right in front of her. If he sold the ranch, they would have so many more options. He wouldn't be tied to Hell's Bells, he could come to London with her. *Maybe...*

That wouldn't be fair to him, though. How many times had he told her his life was on the ranch? And she wasn't ready to tell Raj their engagement was off. Not yet.

"Is there anything you can do to raise money? Sell something?"

"I can sell some land, and that's what I'm thinking I'll do for now. But that'll help me get through a year. Maybe even buy some calves. But what if this happens again next year? We need other revenue sources to be sustainable, and I just don't know how to do that."

"Well, I can help you there."

He raised his head in surprise.

"I don't know anything about ranching..."

"That's an understatement."

"But I do know about diversifying revenue and

how to research business practices. I've helped my father set up several new clinics."

"How's that…"

"You can't be the only rancher who's having this problem. So we research what the others are doing about it and figure out how they're making money. The principles of revenue diversification are the same no matter the business."

He studied at her. "And how do we figure all this out?"

She picked up her phone from the table and waved it at him. "You would be amazed at how much information is available on the internet. I can go get my laptop. Do you have one?"

He shook his head. "But I have a computer in the library. We can go in there."

Her eyes were shining.

He smiled. "How do you do it?"

"Do what?"

"Make me feel like I can rule the world?"

She stepped close to him, stood on her tiptoes and placed a light kiss on his cheek, then smiled playfully. "In my eyes, you're the King of America."

He caught her hand just as she started to walk away. His eyes pierced hers. "Meera, is there any scenario where I could make you my Queen?"

His look burned through her. She started to say something, but this wasn't the time to have the conversation she'd planned. They had work to do. She smiled shyly at him, then pulled her hand away. "I'll go get my laptop. Put on a pot of tea."

"YOU COULD HOST cock fights. Apparently, there's big money to be made."

He pretended to choke himself, and she dissolved into giggles.

They had been at it for hours, poring over the ranch's books and reviewing the websites of hundreds of ranches as well as reports from agricultural societies. She should be tired, especially after the emotionally exhausting time with Priya. But she was positively giddy, sitting in the dusty old room with Jake, bantering back and forth. He had an amazing mind; he could recall numbers and facts from websites she could barely remember reading at all.

"Think about it—we'll buy you gold chains to hang around your neck, you can take bets, calculate the odds in your head, put Kelly at the gate to be the bouncer." She started laughing at the image.

"And I'll have Billy John park cars—it'll be valet service. He can wear gold-plated cowboy boots. High-class all the way."

That brought on a new volley of laughter.

"I'll turn the house into a fancy chicken coop,

charge people to board their chicks in the finest surroundings," Jake continued.

"Stop, my insides are hurting."

"I can just see the chickens in here, clucking about, complaining that the ceilings are too low."

She looked up and noticed the white molding inlayed with gold in intricate patterns. Surprised by the elegance, she glanced around the room with fresh eyes, trying to see past the mud-streaked floors, the dusty surfaces and papers piled everywhere. The library was quite beautiful, with a high ceiling and built-in dark wood bookcases along two of the walls.

She stood and pulled the sheet off a large desk. Jake had set up a functional table for his computer. Most of the furniture in the room was covered with sheets. She gasped. The desk was beautiful, a large oak table with finely detailed carvings.

She turned to Jake. "Where did this come from?"

He shrugged. "My grandfather was a senior diplomat. His staff ran the ranch and he turned the house into a retreat for dignitaries. They held grand parties and hosted foreign heads of State here. It was a place where they could make foreign policy away from the prying eyes in Washington."

Meera's eyes widened.

"Are all the rooms here like this?"

He clicked another link on his screen. "I guess."

Meera took his hand and tugged.

"Show me the house."

He raised his eyebrow and stood up reluctantly, stretching as he did. "Okay, you wanna tell me what this is about?"

She shook her head. "I think I have an idea, but show me the house first."

He showed her the living room, which was enormous. It had also been used as a dance hall. Ornate mirrors lined the walls, surrounded by beautiful blue-and-silver wallpaper. He led her upstairs, and she let her hand slide over the dented banister, ignoring the fluttering of her nerves.

He showed her the unused bedrooms first. They were all furnished, mostly with wooden four-poster beds that were covered in sheets. There were seven unused bedrooms and an eighth doorway down the hall.

"Would you like to see my room?"

Her heart was beating so loudly she was sure he could hear it. He took her hand and walked slowly to his door. He stepped aside and let her enter first. It didn't look like any of the other rooms. Floor-to-ceiling windows covered an entire wall, and she noted a door that led onto a balcony. He had a king-size sleigh bed covered with a simple blue-and-white quilt that appeared to be homemade. She touched the fabric.

"My mother used to make quilts. This is one of hers."

Meera raised a brow. *The mother you cut out of your life.* She eyed the quilt. If he didn't care about his mother, why did he keep it on his bed?

There was a dresser and a hook where a bathrobe hung. The wide plank hardwood floors were spotless, as was the rest of the room. The windows shone, and his slippers were tucked neatly in a corner. Nothing was out of place. She looked at him in confusion. "Where did you put the mud and dirt?"

He laughed. "It's a big house—I don't have time to keep it all up. The best I can do is keep my bedroom in order."

She spotted something in the corner and headed over to it. It was an acoustic guitar. "You play?"

He shook his head. "I used to when I was a kid. My momma taught me." She touched the guitar. There was no dust on it.

"I'd love to hear you play sometime."

"I haven't picked it up in decades." He took her hand and tugged on it to take her to the other side of the room.

She noticed a door she had missed before,

which opened into a large bathroom. The wall of windows continued in here, and now she could see the length of the room was the entire front of the house. She took in the large claw-foot tub and brass-framed mirrors over the sink. The bathroom looked as though it had been transplanted from an old Victorian house.

She returned to the bedroom and stepped out onto the balcony. There were a couple of rocking chairs and a small table, and Meera could just barely make out the outline of the trees, rolling fields and her cottage. She'd left the light on in her bedroom, and she could make out the shape of her bed beyond the drapes.

He stepped behind her, and she turned to meet his eyes. "I may have been known to fall asleep in this chair watching the light from your room." His breath was right at her ear, and her nerves came to attention. He ran his hands down her arms, smoothing the goose bumps that prickled her skin.

He buried his face in her hair. She stood absolutely still, afraid to move and ruin the wonderful sensation. He gently turned her so she was facing him. He caressed her cheek with his finger.

"I know I'm gonna sound crazy, Meera, but I can't hide from it anymore. I'm head over heels in love with you."

CHAPTER NINETEEN

Meera's eyes swam with tears, and her heart filled to the brim and spilled over. Jake cupped her face and brushed his thumbs across her cheeks. He bent down and placed a kiss on her lips. It was a tender kiss, full of love and promise.

She opened her eyes and looked up. "I've never felt like this about anyone in my life."

He smiled, leaning his forehead against hers.

"It makes me very afraid."

He nodded. "Scares the heck out of me, too."

"What do you want from me, Jake?"

He lifted her face. "Look at me, Meera." She raised her eyes, warmth spreading in her chest at the intensity in his gaze. "I love you because your heart is filled with the kind of goodness that can redeem a man's worst sins. I love your inner strength, your spunk, your stubbornness, the fact that you're beautiful as all get-out, your red toenails…"

She gave him a small smile. "Sometimes I paint them blue."

"I love you because of…you."

She shifted on her feet. "I'm not sure what I can give you, Jake."

"Meera, I've got nothing to give you. You know the whole truth about my situation. I'm not asking for anything. As corny as it sounds, I just want you to be happy."

Her heart contracted painfully.

"What if my happiness takes me away from you? What if I leave you like your mother and Jolene?"

"Then I'll spend the rest of my life living off this moment. 'Cause in this moment, Meera, you've made me the happiest man alive."

Still cupping her face, he bent down and touched his lips to the corners of her mouth. She felt his love, strong and unconditional, deep in her core. Then he kissed her, sweetly and soundly. She tasted salt from her tears.

He held her for a long time. She waited for him to ask her what she intended to do, but he never did. He just held her, and she enjoyed his warmth, the beating of his heart, the steady rise and fall of his chest.

At some point, he lowered himself onto the rocking chair and pulled her with him. She curled up in his lap. This was what she had craved her whole life, she realized, the comfort of being accepted, of not having promises she needed to fulfill.

"Oh, now, this is heaven," he murmured.

She rested her head on his shoulder. "Mmm..."

"Maybe it's a good thing the cattle got sick. Maybe I should sell the ranch so we can go to Tahiti and just...be."

Meera lifted her head. "I'm not asking for anything, Jake."

"I know, but I want to give you the world."

"Would you be happy doing anything other than ranching?"

She felt him slump. "I don't know how to do anything other than ranching. The hands are my family. I'm responsible for them. I can't just abandon them, no matter how much I'd like to."

"There's nothing else you would consider?" She kept her voice soft and even.

He stiffened. "This is home, Meera. Always has been, always will be."

"And my home is where my parents are."

CHAPTER TWENTY

THE NURSING HOME his father lived in was an hour's drive from Hell's Bells. It was a large house with beautifully landscaped grounds in a suburban community.

"This is rather lovely," Meera observed. "I read that American nursing homes are usually quite shabby."

Jake nodded. "They are. This costs a pretty penny, which is why the ranch is in such dire financial straits. I want the best for my dad if I can't keep him at home."

Meera touched his arm. "My mother says Americans save for their own retirement, while Indian parents consider children their retirement."

"My father's always been there for me, Meera. I'll take care of him as long as he's alive. I just wish I could do better for him."

He caught her staring at him, a bewildered look on her face. "You obviously care about your father, so why is it so easy to cut your mother off?"

This again! How can I make her understand?

"Meera, my father has earned my love and trust by taking care of me all these years. My mother abandoned me."

"So you're saying you owe your dad."

"I'm saying I love him. We've built a relationship over the years."

"Just as I have with my parents. They've taken care of me, given me my life. So just like you're taking care of your father, I need to be there for my parents."

"Providing for your parents, respecting them and taking care of them is very different from giving up your happiness—your entire life—for them."

The thin line of her lips told him he had gone too far.

"Isn't that what you've done by taking over the ranch?"

Luckily, they had arrived at the front desk, and the task of signing in gave him an excuse not to answer.

"He's having a good day," the nurse said as she led them into the common room.

"I'd recognize him anywhere!" Meera exclaimed as they approached his dad.

Jake knew his father looked like an older version of him, with gray hair and the same green eyes. His face broke into a familiar, wide grin.

"Ah, there's m' boy."

Jake bent down to hug him and kissed his cheek. The older man eyed Meera. "Who'd you bring me? That ain't Jolene."

Jake smiled. "It sure isn't, Dad. This is Meera."

"It's a pleasure to meet you, Mr. Taylor."

"Oh, my father was Mr. Taylor. Call me Ted or call me Daddy, baby girl."

Meera smiled. Jake's heart twisted as his father returned Meera's smile with another wide grin. His dad only brought out that big smile when he liked someone. He was the type of man who made snap decisions about someone, and he didn't like very many people. He hated Jolene.

Jake asked his father how he was feeling and went through his mental list of his dad's friends, remembering to ask about the nurse he particularly liked. His father spoke animatedly about recent events at the nursing home.

"Dad, I need to talk to you about something."

His father smiled. "You've got my blessing, boy!"

Jake frowned. "What're you talking about?"

"You're gonna marry this beautiful girl, aren't ya? Well, go on, just be sure to come get me so I can take a picture with that newfangled phone you gave me."

Jake laughed. "That's not what I'm talkin' about, Dad."

"Well, why the heck not! You ain't getting younger, and you ain't gonna find anyone prettier than her." He leaned in and winked. "And I like her accent."

Meera put her hand on her mouth, failing to suppress a giggle. "Very true."

Jake mouthed, "You're not helping."

She stood up, still smiling. "Will you excuse me? I'll get us coffee."

After Meera left, Jake explained what had happened at the ranch. He searched his father's eyes; they were alert today, sharper than they had been in months. He nodded at the right times and asked intelligent questions. Jake felt a sense of relief. It really was a good day when he could talk to his father and pick his brain about what to do. When he finished telling him what happened, he looked down.

"I'm sorry, Dad. You were right about me not being ready to take over the ranch. I shouldn't have insisted on taking the reins when I did, and now I've made a mess of things."

"Look up, boy!"

Jake's head snapped up.

"I'm gonna tell you a story." Jake tried to keep his face neutral. His father was slipping again.

"When you was a little boy, I'd take you with me into town. When the ice cream truck came, that was your treat for hanging 'round all day.

But you always got vanilla—that's what you wanted every time. And one day I said, 'Boy, you gonna get the same thing you always do? You afraid to go with something new?" His father patted his hand. "I was teasing, but you... you marched up to that truck, you read the flavors of the day and you turned around and said you wanted the mint chocolate chip. I said you weren't gonna like it—a boy doesn't go from vanilla to mint chocolate chip. But you was as stubborn as your old man. You insisted I buy it for you, so I did."

Jake vaguely remembered that day. His father smiled widely. "And then you took a bite, and by golly, the look on your face! You hated it."

His father's eyes shimmered, and Jake searched for the glaze but it wasn't there. His dad was still with him. He saw Meera out of the corner of his eye. She kept her distance, but he could tell she was listening.

"So I said, 'I'll eat that. You go on and get your vanilla.' But you just shook your head and kept on eating. And you kept at it till you finished that cone. I thought you was gonna be sick by the time you was done. You is one stubborn boy."

Jake gave him a small smile. "Vanilla's still my favorite flavor."

"Vanilla is what you know." His father leaned in. "You listen and listen good—I didn't want to give you the ranch 'cause I didn't want you saddled with it. It ruined my life, working day in and day out. I lost your momma, and I almost lost you. I didn't want you to have the same sorry life I did on that land. You wanna keep the ranch, you keep it, but if you wanna take your girl and run away, I'll be right there cheerin' you on."

"Dad!"

"Don't you make the same mistakes I did, boy. You live your life the way you want. Don't you keep eating mint chocolate chip just to prove something to this old fart. And whatever you do, if you love that girl, don't you let her go."

Jake swallowed hard.

His father turned and looked out the window. "I shouldn't have let your momma leave. I shoulda sold that ranch a long time ago."

Jake thought about the pictures on his mother's mantel. "I don't think you could have done anything to keep her, Dad. She didn't want us."

"Maybe she'll come back one day. If I keep the ranch, she'll know where to find me."

"Dad?"

Jake waved a hand in front of his father's face, but he didn't blink. He patted his hand, but his father was gone.

Meera set down three steaming cups of coffee. Jake took a sip, burning his tongue. He took another swig. He thought about his mother and how she'd had a different life while his father pined away for her, how Ted Taylor had stubbornly held on to the ranch when what he really wanted was his wife.

They sat in silence drinking coffee.

"Time to go?" Meera asked softly.

He nodded.

"Are you okay?" she said when they reached the car.

Jake nodded. "He told me to sell the ranch and go live my life."

He held the door open for Meera. As usual, she rewarded him with a peck on the cheek before she slid into her seat. He walked over to the driver's side.

He placed his head on the steering wheel, the pounding in his ears drowning out rational thought. "He was having a good day. He meant what he said."

He turned toward her, taking in her big brown eyes. Every time he looked at Meera, he fell in love with her all over again. *Be careful, Jake. Don't push her.* He didn't want to do what every other person in her life had done, make his love conditional.

"What're you thinking?" Her voice was soft.

"What would you do if you couldn't be a doctor?"

She shrugged. "I would work on my research."

"And what if you couldn't be a researcher?"

"I would find something else to do... What's this about, Jake?"

"You have options. If you can't be a doctor, you can be something else. You aren't worried about finding another profession."

"What're you trying to say?"

"I don't have options." He rubbed his neck. He should've told Meera earlier. It hadn't been an issue with Jolene because she already knew. The whole town did. He had never been ashamed of it, but last night with Meera was a new experience. She was enthralled with how good he was with numbers, never once asking him to double-check his math or confirming that the numbers he was giving her were true. She saw him as an intellectual equal. But she needed to know. "I'm dyslexic."

He waited for the sounds of sympathy he was used to hearing from every person he had ever told. Meera just looked at him, encouraging him to say more.

"School was hard for me when I was a boy—it's partly why my mom left. The simplest assignments took me hours, and I got so frustrated that I acted out. I somehow managed to make it to college, and one of my professors figured out I was great with numbers so I went down the accounting path. But I couldn't cut it. I had to drop out."

Meera took his hand in hers. "There are many brilliant people with dyslexia, and these days, there are special educational programs. You *are* good with numbers—I've seen it. You have an amazing mind."

"Yeah, but it only works for so long. I tried getting a job after college... It didn't pan out. The ranch, it's the only thing I've been successful at. It works for me. I can't do a desk job. I need physical labor to give my brain a break, to process things."

"Jake..."

"I'm not being a chauvinistic pig when I say it's not the same whether you move here or I move to London. I don't have the choices you do, Meera."

She dropped her gaze to the dashboard. Minutes passed. When she looked up, her expression was strained. Pain ripped through his body.

He bit his tongue, waiting for the words he knew were coming.

"Jake, you're an amazing man...and the town...it's like nothing I've seen before. This sense of community, of kinship with one's neighbors, I don't know many places on earth where that exists."

"They do have their moments."

"And I love the ranch. It feels like a home. I love your staff—Kelly and Billy John, I get the feeling they would do anything for you." She took her hand back and stared out the window. "For as long as I remember, I've wanted to be a doctor, and I'm invested in my research. But I'm learning that what I love is taking care of people, and I've never had the kind of relationship with my patients in London that I do here. It's making me question what kind of doctor I want to be."

She turned her big brown eyes back to him, and they were full of tears, her face pleading. Jake went cold. "I've been questioning a lot of things lately, but the two things I don't question are my beliefs and the fact that I can't break my parents' hearts. I can't see myself making a living killing cows. I can't get past that, Jake."

"You wouldn't have to be part of the operation."

"How would it work with us on a daily basis? Even if I take over Dr. Harper's practice, you'll sit at the dinner table with a bloody steak on your plate. Am I supposed to sit by eating grilled cheese all my life? And do I watch you raise new calves that will die at your hands? I know you don't understand, but I can't live like that."

Jake shut his mouth. How was he supposed to respond? She was right; he couldn't give her what she wanted.

"And then there's my parents. My father has dreamed of me taking over his medical center in London. It's not blind obedience, Jake—it's love. It's my way of loving them. Just like your way of loving your father is to take care of the ranch—" she nodded toward the nursing home "—and to give him the best."

She twisted her watch around her wrist. "I wish I could wave a magic wand and make myself different…"

"I don't want to change a thing about you, Meera. I love you just as you are. Your beliefs, even the ones I don't understand, make you who you are."

She looked away from him, gazing out the window at something far away. Her voice was so soft, he almost missed what she said. "I'm sorry, Jake. Everything I have is in London. I can't give it all up."

CHAPTER TWENTY-ONE

MEERA STARTED AT the screen. *This could be it! This could be what saves the ranch.* She was sitting in the kitchen with her laptop on the table. Did she *want* to save the ranch? If her idea worked, it would mean a permanent life for Jake in Hell's Bells. But it was clear he would never leave the ranch, anyway. She didn't agree with his claim that he couldn't take up a new profession, but she understood his reluctance. Although she'd been glib about not being a doctor, the truth was she would never do something different. She couldn't imagine giving up her research, which was based in London.

Jake had spent the past week trying everything he could to save the ranch. He'd talked to every bank in the state and had looked for private loans. More cattle were sick and things seemed grim. Jake would have to sell a large portion of land…unless her idea worked. With the crisis consuming him, they hadn't talked any more about her plans, and she was just as happy as he was to ignore it.

"Hi!" Meera looked up to see Jake walk in. She gave him a smile as he went to the sink and poured himself a glass of water. He had been in the field, and Meera savored the smell of Jake and the outdoors.

"You ready to tell me what you've been working on?" He gestured at the laptop.

She nodded excitedly. She had spent the week researching her idea. She hadn't told him about it because she wanted to make sure she had all the pieces lined up, but now that she'd figured out most of it, she couldn't wait to tell him everything.

She patted the seat next to her, and he pulled out the chair and sat down.

"Is it a Hail Mary?"

"What?"

"It's a football long pass, made only when the team's desperate."

"You mean American *foot*ball, the one played with one's hands?"

He smirked. "Yeah, you know, the one where we've lost three games now thanks to you not clearing Derek to play. You're lucky you saved Kelly's life, otherwise the town would never forgive you."

Meera ignored him. She was seeing Derek once a week, way more than necessary, because it was the only way to keep him from playing.

She had been skeptical of Rose's suggestion to keep giving Derek false hope that it would just be a few more days, but even though it didn't make logical sense, the plan was working.

"Yes, it's a Hail Mary, then." She pulled up one of the websites she'd been using for her research. "I've been reading up on dude ranches. It's an interesting concept where you use the ranch for agritourism. I've seen several of these in the Western part of the country, but there aren't very many on the East Coast."

"A dude ranch?"

Meera frowned at the skepticism in his voice. She clicked through various websites to show him what she meant and explained her research. He listened to her without commenting. "You can use this house as a fancy guesthouse, even market it as a historic inn. You already have the cottage—you could live there. It won't take much for you to open this house up as a bed-and-breakfast, sort of like the days when your grandfather used it to entertain dignitaries."

Jake's face was pinched. Meera stomped on her disappointment. He just needed to understand the concept, then he would see what was obvious to her.

"I know this seems overwhelming, but think about it—you already have stables, you can make money boarding horses then charge guests to ride them. You can make a deal with the town restaurant to do dinner for your guests—I'm sure they would welcome the business—and you can organize day trips to other towns as activities. The main attractions here would be visiting a working ranch, horseback riding and staying in a historic house." She stopped to catch her breath.

Why is Jake staring at me so strangely?

"A dude ranch?" His voice had an edge to it. She took a calming breath. Why was he being so obstinate?

"This could be the answer to everything, Jake. You already have most of the infrastructure—you wouldn't need a lot of money to get started." She pulled up a spreadsheet on her computer. "I ran the numbers. It wouldn't cost much to make the improvements needed, and the really good news is that I could probably give you a loan, so you wouldn't need to get one from the bank."

That got his attention. Jake pushed his chair back and stood. "What exactly would this be the answer to? You think this town is fond of welcoming strangers? You think I want a bunch of yuppies traipsing through here? And how would I take care of my staff? They've poured their life into this ranch. You want me to get rid of them…"

"They could work on the dude ranch."

"Doing what? You really see Billy John showing some uppity city folks to their bedrooms or laying out a white tablecloth for breakfast?"

"There would be other work for him to do…"

"And what about the other eleven hands?"

"You might not be able to keep everybody, but let me show you this staffing plan I put together…"

"You put together a staffing plan for my ranch hands without talking to me?"

A fire burned in her stomach. She had devoted every free minute to making a comprehensive plan for him, and he wasn't even giving her the opportunity to explain. Meera stood. "I'm trying to help. If you'd let me get a word in edgewise—'

"I have been listening, Meera. You want me to turn my home into a public spectacle, put most of my hands—who, by the way, will poke their eyes out before they accept a job at a dude ranch—out of work. And to drive the final nail in my coffin, you don't think I can convince a bank to loan me money, so you're gonna give it to me. That sum it up?"

Is that what this is about? Me loaning him money?

"I told you I'm dyslexic, not incompetent. I'll find a way to take care of my ranch and my people."

Meera stepped back. "That's not fair! You know I didn't mean it that way. I was trying to find a solution that would let you keep the ranch and maybe…let us be together."

He clenched his jaw. His eyes held so much anger that she took another step back. *What's going on here?*

"So you're trying to make me into someone more acceptable to you? A businessman? Someone you can take home to your parents? If I'm not a real rancher anymore, you won't be as embarrassed to be with me? You won't have to worry about me ruining your karma?"

Meera slammed her laptop shut. She wasn't going to be his punching bag. She knew he was under a lot of stress, but he had taken everything she'd said the wrong way.

"I don't have to stand here and take this."

"That's right, you don't. You already have plane tickets back to London."

"Is that what this is about?" She stepped closer to him. "Then let's talk about it, Jake, air it out. What do you expect me to do? Call my parents, send them a text saying I'm thinking of calling off the wedding? I'm not going to throw away everything I've worked for my entire life—my research study, my relationship with Raj—for someone I've known for three weeks. Think I can fit all that in a hundred and forty characters and Tweet it to them? I have to go back. I thought you understood that."

He took a deep breath and closed his eyes. When he opened them, he pulled out a chair for her. She glared at him but took a seat. She was angry, but they needed to talk this through. He sat down beside her and took her hand. "Are you canceling the wedding?"

She looked at his hand, feeling the roughness of his skin. "When I came here, my life was cleanly mapped out. I was sure that marrying Raj was the right path for me. Love has always been a logical decision. But now…"

"Now?"

"I don't see how I can ever marry Raj knowing how I feel about you."

He gazed at her with eyes full of hope. She took a shaky breath, stifling the sob that was stuck in her throat. "But that doesn't mean I can drop everything and move here. My research lab is still in London. My father has been dreaming of the day I take over his practice—I can't let him down."

His hand tightened on hers. "Have you ever wondered why they make you feel like you owe them so much? They adopted you, Meera. They didn't buy you."

HE KNEW IT was the wrong thing to say as soon as the words left his mouth.

She was out of the room in a flash. He followed, catching up with her as she reached the front door.

"Meera, I didn't mean to offend you."

She whipped around. Her eyes were hard, her hands on her hips. "Jake, I know there are a lot of things we need to work out, but you need to get it through your head—my parents are a non-negotiable. They mean more to me than anything else in the world, and I will not allow you to drive a wedge between me and them."

She stepped out the front door, then whirled back. "You don't have a right to get upset at me, Jake, not when you're just as unwilling to give up your life as I am."

She ran to the cottage. He thought about running after her, but what would be the point? She was shaking with anger, and talking to her now would just ignite her. Part of him admired her for calling him on his bull. She wasn't wrong; he had no right to be upset at her for leaving. If he really wanted to, he could give up the ranch, go to London and fight for her, make himself a "nonnegotiable" in her life.

He soaked in the vista of his ranch and took a calming breath of fresh air.

He went back to the kitchen. Her laptop beeped, and he opened it up to see that she had an outstanding command so the computer hadn't shut down. His eyes fell on the spreadsheet she had tried to show him earlier. He clicked through the tabs. *She must've spent hours working up all these scenarios.* He knew her heart was in the right place, but she just didn't understand what being a rancher meant to him. It defined him as a man. Looking at her spreadsheets, it was clear she saw the ranch as a business, something that could be neatly planned and put on a clipboard. It was so much more than that.

He closed the document, and her desktop background caught his eye. It was a picture of her with her parents. They were standing on the London Bridge with the Tower Bridge behind them. Meera had one arm around each of her parents, her smile dazzling. He thought about the other picture he had seen with the same background, the one on his mother's mantel…the photo of her with the family she had chosen.

Maybe I'm the one who doesn't get it.

He walked outside and knocked on the cottage door. When she didn't answer, he turned the handle and walked inside. She was sitting on the couch, knees pulled up to her chest, her face buried in her arms. Her sobs seared through him.

"Meera." He dropped to his knees before her. She kept her head buried.

"Meera, I'm so sorry." He reached out to touch her, but she shrugged him off. He sat in front of her, willing her to listen to him. "I didn't have the best parental role models. My mom told me I was too much to handle, and my dad loved me but it was clear he didn't think I could run this ranch. The first woman I loved left me 'cause I couldn't give her the life she wanted. I'm hard-wired to be a cynic—maybe that's why I don't get your relationship with your parents. But that's wrong of me. I don't have a right to judge you."

The sight of her tearstained face sent a knife through his heart. Her expression softened and she loosened her arms.

"I guess I'm a little protective of my parents."

He stood up and sat on the couch beside her. She uncurled and let him put his arm around her.

"How did you open your heart to me?" she asked. "After every person you've loved has betrayed you, how can you find it in you to love me, especially knowing I'll do the same thing?"

He placed his head on her shoulder. "I've been asking myself that same question since I met you. I can't explain it." He took her hand and placed it on his chest. "Feel that pulse that runs between us every time we touch? I've never felt it before. There are times, Meera, when I feel like I can see into your soul."

"And what do you see?" she whispered, her voice cracking.

"I see a girl who just wants to be loved. Without any strings attached."

She dropped her face into her hands. He lifted his head from her shoulder and pulled her closer. He felt her sag against him as she began crying softly.

"Oh, Meera, I didn't mean to upset you." But that only made her sob harder. His stomach twisted painfully. "Meera, please tell me what I've done wrong now."

She shook her head. "No, it's not… Oh, Jake, how is it that you met me all of three weeks ago, and yet you seem to know me better than I know myself?"

He kissed the top of her head.

"What're we going to do, Jake? I don't see a path forward for us."

He lifted her chin and looked into her teary eyes. "For the first time in my life, I have faith. I have faith in you, I have faith in us and, for some inexplicable reason, I have faith in the universe." He smiled wistfully. "You have so much good karma in you, I'm hoping it'll spill over to me."

Her face crumpled. "You have too much faith, Jake."

CHAPTER TWENTY-TWO

EVER SINCE THE incident with Kelly, Meera's appointment calendar was full of patients. She had just finished talking to Marty, who still wanted to know when Derek could play. Meera was tempted to tell him it would be another four weeks, but she bit her tongue and offered to examine him again in a few days. Her father would tell her these "free checkups" were a bad business practice, but she was actually enjoying getting to know Derek and learning about American football. Like Lily, Derek had become a friend. Meera sighed at the thought of Lily; Joe still hadn't returned, but she stubbornly believed he would arrive any day.

Meera made a note to herself to send Mr. Leeland some recipes for meat marinades. She couldn't get him to eat tofu instead of red meat, but he had agreed to try homemade marinades that were lower in salt and sugar than store-bought steak sauce. And he had promised to try a side of grilled vegetables instead of mashed potatoes. Baby steps. Too bad there weren't any baby steps she could take with Jake.

She sat at Dr. Harper's desk and opened the first chart she had to complete. For the past week, he had been taking care of his wife and offered Meera his office so she wouldn't have to endure the cramped closet. Meera felt bad for him; she knew he'd have to find somebody to take over his practice soon. A knot formed in her stomach.

Dr. Harper was offering to sell her his practice for next to nothing. He wanted to make sure there was a doctor in town for the people of Hell's Bells. She hadn't turned him down, but she had suggested he keep looking for another doctor. And she hadn't told Jake about the offer.

Her phone buzzed, and she checked the screen. It was past midnight in London. She'd been playing purposeful phone tag with Raj all week, but she couldn't put him off any longer. She hit the answer button.

"I can't believe I've finally gotten hold of you."

"Good timing. I just finished seeing patients."

"That's what I was counting on."

"It's late there."

"I wanted to talk to you, Meera. You've been avoiding my calls all week."

"I haven't been avoiding your calls," she said defensively, "I've been busy."

"With what?"

"What do you mean?"

"It's a small-town practice. Surely, you can't be busier than I am in London."

She stayed silent. What was she supposed to say?

"Meera, are you okay?" He sounded worried.

"Of course I'm okay. Why wouldn't I be?" She hadn't meant to sound edgy.

"I talked to your mother a few days ago, and she said you ran out on Sienna Simone—something you neglected to tell me the last time we spoke. Priya came back from visiting you and won't talk to me."

Meera blew out a breath. She'd known this was coming. Telling him she was busy was a poor excuse, and he'd seen right through it.

"I've had a lot on my mind."

"Meera, talk to me."

Raj had always been a good friend to her. She'd never made a major decision in her life without talking to her father or to Raj. So how could she keep such a big secret from him?

She sighed. "Raj, I have to tell you something, but I want to do it in person. It's not a conversation we should have over the phone."

She waited. "Raj, are you still there?"

"Meera, you're scaring me."

"I don't mean to, Raj. You are first and foremost my friend, so I don't want to deceive you by pretending everything is all right. But this is a conversation we must have in person, when I get back."

Rose knocked on the door. "I'm sorry to interrupt, but Lily's here and she's in quite a state." By the sympathetic look on her face, Meera was sure Rose had been listening at the door.

"I have to go, Raj."

CHAPTER TWENTY-THREE

"WHAT'S GOING ON?" Meera opened the car door. They had just pulled into Hell's Bells after spending the day driving to Washington, DC, and back. The local bank had put Jake in touch with someone from the Department of Agriculture, and they had gone up together to see if there was any possibility of getting grant money. The meeting was a complete failure, and Jake was even more at a loss for how to keep the ranch going. Not that she was in better shape. It had been three days since her awkward conversation with Raj, and she couldn't shake a funny feeling in her stomach.

She looked around in confusion. The streets were completely blocked. Cars were triple parked on the side of the road and people were walking about purposefully.

She spotted Gloria, teetering on high heels in a short miniskirt and tank top. Meera waved to her. Gloria hesitated, then walked over. She eyed Jake in the truck. "Another trip together? My, my...aren't we getting close."

Meera ignored her. "What's happening?"

Gloria took her eyes off Jake. "You haven't heard? It's only the biggest news of the year. Even bigger than you, Doctor I-don't-have-my-sights-on-Jake…"

Meera took a breath. *No point in correcting her.* "What news?"

Gloria bounced on her feet, obviously torn between punishing Meera by not telling her and bursting to tell someone who hadn't already heard. Jake joined them.

Gloria met him with a stunning smile. Meera blinked against the wattage. "You remember Norma Jean's cousin, Joe?"

"The Army boy?" Jake nodded.

Meera leaned forward.

"Turns out he and Lily ran away when he was in town and got married." She paused for effect, her eyes wide. "And she wasn't eating too many pork rinds at the diner. She's pregnant. Like, really pregnant."

As opposed to slightly pregnant? Meera suppressed the urge to comment. She searched for Lily in the crowd of people milling about the town square. She must have made an announcement to the town.

"And Joe just came back," Gloria continued. "Lily hasn't seen him for the last nine months."

Meera grabbed Gloria's arm. "What did you say? Joe's here? With Lily?"

Gloria narrowed her eyes. "What do you know about this?"

"Just tell me, Gloria!"

Gloria huffed. "Yes, he's back for her, but turns out their wedding wasn't quite legal. The baby is due any minute. So Norma Jean marched over to my uncle Dick, and he opened the clerk's office and issued them a marriage license." She gestured behind her at the activity on the square. "The town's throwing them a wedding. We don't want a baby out of wedlock."

Impulsively, Meera hugged Gloria. "This is such wonderful news. Where's Lily?" Gloria looked in confusion from Meera to Jake, who was grinning from ear to ear.

"She's at her house, getting ready."

Jake took her hand. "Come on, we won't be able to drive."

Sure enough, Jake's truck was now blocked in by a van that had come up behind them.

"Hey! What's going on with you two?" They ignored Gloria as they made their way down the street.

Jake took Meera to the barbershop and poked his head in the door. "Hey, Mr. Alnutt, can I borrow your bike?"

An old gentleman in the middle of giving

someone a haircut glanced up in surprise. "Jake! How are you, boy?"

"Please, we need to go see Lily." He motioned to Meera.

The man nodded and grabbed a set of keys off a hook, then threw them to Jake, who caught them deftly. He pulled Meera around the corner to the back of the barbershop.

Meera caught sight of the motorcycle parked on the side of the road. She shook her head. "No way. I've never ridden one of those."

Jake grinned at her. "It's actually much easier than a mechanical bull. Come on, get on." He handed her one of the helmets that were hanging off the side, then put on his own.

She eyed it warily.

He straddled the seat and kicked the stand. "Come on, you said you've ridden horses. It's just like mounting a horse. I'll hold it steady."

She grinned and swung her leg over the seat. It was a close fit. She wrapped her arms around Jake and leaned into him, feeling the hardness of his chest, the firmness of his back. He turned his head. "Now, why haven't I thought of this before?"

She giggled, a delicious fire spreading through her. He vroomed the motor, turned the bike and revved it onto the street. Meera pressed her face against his back, her legs squeezing the sides tightly. As he turned left out of the alley, she was sure her knee was going to scrape the ground. She clung to Jake with all her might. The sound of the motor reverberated in her head, but somewhere her mind registered a whistle followed by a "hubba hubba."

Jake wove through the parked cars, and Meera laughed with giddy happiness, enjoying the warmth of his body, feeling his chest contract and expand. His breaths were coming as fast as hers.

She felt wild and free, just as she had with the bull ride. It was a heady sensation.

He pulled into Lily's driveway, and Meera noted a number of other cars already parked there. The front door was slightly ajar. Jake held the bike steady while she dismounted. She took off the helmet and shook out her hair. Jake beamed at her.

"That's it, I'm buying us a motorcycle just to see you do that again."

Meera laughed. *Us!* She liked the sound of that.

Jake held out his hand for the helmet and motioned toward the door. She handed it to him and ran the last few steps. She heard voices and raced up the stairs.

Lily squealed as soon as she saw her. She was sitting at her dressing table in a bathrobe with three other women around her. Lily ignored them all as she flung herself at Meera, almost knocking her over.

Meera hugged her back, holding on to her as best she could, considering her baby bump.

"Have you heard?"

Meera nodded excitedly. She was so happy for Lily. Their last conversation had been stressful. Lily had come to the clinic feeling sick, and Meera found that her blood pressure was high. Lily hadn't heard from Joe again, even though the date of his promised return had passed. Meera had encouraged her to accept the fact that he wasn't going to be around. Lily left the office sobbing and hadn't returned Meera's calls. Lily's eyes were shining brightly now; her face positively glowed.

"I want you to be my maid of honor."

Meera's eyes widened in surprise.

"Oh, for heaven's sake, girl!"

Meera looked for the source of the outburst and spotted a woman sitting on the bed, a needle and thread in her hand, bent over a white dress.

"That's Norma Jean," Lily said. "Don't worry 'bout her. So will you, will you please?"

Meera hugged her. "Of course I will. I'm so honored."

One of the other ladies put her hands on Meera's shoulders and pulled her back. "Well, then, we best get you something to wear, too."

"I'm Mrs. Cregg, Mr. Cregg's wife." *That explains everything.*

Meera grinned at Mrs. Cregg. Against all odds, Joe had come back, Lily was getting married and she was the maid of honor!

"Norma Jean's fixin' up a wedding dress for me. Joe's gonna wear his army class A's, and we have to get ready in a couple of hours."

"Why the rush?" Meera asked.

Lily patted her belly. "No one wants to chance this baby being born until Joe and I are all squared away."

Meera wiped tears from her cheeks and Mrs. Cregg put an arm around her. "Now, now, dear." Meera embraced her. She'd known the woman for all of a minute, but she felt her motherly love envelop her.

"How did this happen so fast?"

Lily squealed. "I know, right! He came back last night, and we had a town meeting this morning and they all just put it together."

Meera thought about her own wedding. She and Raj had started talking about getting married almost two years ago. Her mother had begun meticulously planning every detail once Meera committed to an engagement date over a year ago. Invitation cards to the various functions and events, guest lists, seating arrangements, flowers, centerpieces, catering, clothes, jewelry, shoes, bridesmaids dresses. It was endlessly exhausting. And here, a wedding was being planned in hours.

Mrs. Cregg was putting a measuring tape around Meera's waist.

"I'm sure I have something in my closet I could wear."

Norma Jean shook her head. "This is my Lily and Joe's weddin', and I promised her momma I'd take care of her. I ain't letting you wear just any old thing. We'll fix you up with something nice."

Meera laughed and threw her arms up so they could measure the rest of her. She watched Lily try on a veil that yet another woman had shown up with.

"How can I help?" she asked.

"Why don't you go fix up her hair. Us old ladies don't know how you young girls like it these days." Meera laughed and went over to Lily.

"How're you feeling?" she whispered.

"I'm on top of the world," Lily gushed.

"I meant…are you feeling any contractions or pain?"

Lily frowned and placed her hands on her stomach. "Nah, I don't think so. I've just been feeling the baby kicking. He or she must also be really excited."

"That's good." Meera gave her another hug. "I'm so sorry for what I said the last time we spoke. I'm thrilled that Joe came back." Meera felt fresh tears on her cheeks; she was bubbling with joy for Lily.

"It's okay. I know it is hard for you, not loving your fella like I love Joe."

Meera felt a punch to her gut. She meant Raj.

"When you love someone, when you really love someone, Dr. M., you'll know it in here." Lily tapped her heart. "And you'll have faith that it'll all work out."

Jake's words came back to her. "I'm glad you had faith, Lily. It gives me hope to see things work out for you." She smiled, grabbing the curling iron sitting on the dresser. "Now let's get your hair done."

Meera had never done anyone else's hair or makeup, and they giggled together as she tried different styles. The ladies of Hell's Bells kept up a constant chatter.

They spent a couple of hours getting Lily ready. Jake had taken off, presumably to the town square to lend a hand. Meera marveled at the fact that they had sewn a simple white dress for her in no time. It had a tight bodice that billowed out in soft waves to accommodate her belly and didn't have a train.

Meera used the curling iron to frame the bride's face with soft curls. Everyone stepped back and gasped when she put the veil on Lily's head. Lily looked radiant. Norma Jean burst into noisy tears, Mrs. Cregg clutched her chest and Meera beamed.

"All righty now, we need to find something old, something new, something borrowed and something blue." Norma Jean opened her purse and handed Lily a ring. "This was your momma's. She told me to give it to you when you got married." For the millionth time that day, tears flowed down Meera's cheek as she watched Lily hug her aunt. The warmth and love in the room touched her soul.

"What about new and blue?" The room went silent.

Then it hit her. "I have something that's both blue and new. I'll have Jake get it from the ranch."

"And you can borrow this." One of the ladies pulled out a little necklace and put it around Lily's neck.

Meera texted Jake.

"Here you go." Mrs. Cregg handed Meera a dress, and she laughed in surprise. These women were really something; they had sewn her a dress, too. She used Lily's bathroom to change. The dress fit perfectly. It was soft pink, a color she never wore. She studied her reflection in the small mirror. The dress was made of silky cotton, and the fabric slid with her body. It had little spaghetti straps, a tight bodice that fell away at her waist and it ended right above her knee. She twirled around and giggled. She'd never looked better in her life.

She stepped out to show the ladies, who oohed and aahed at her. She used Lily's curling iron to style her own hair. Lily's makeup didn't really work with Meera's complexion, so she washed her face and simply applied a bit of gloss to her lips. She studied her reflection and barely recognized herself. No perfect makeup, no matching jewelry, hair loose and a little wild. It wasn't a Meera she was used to seeing.

As they stepped out of the house, Meera wondered how they would get to town with the streets blocked. The sun was starting to make its way toward the horizon. While the day had been stiflingly hot, it had given way to a pleasant evening with a slight breeze cooling the air.

Jake pulled up in a horse-drawn carriage. He was dressed in a suit topped with a cowboy hat. She laughed as he tipped his hat. "Your carriage awaits, my ladies."

His eyes traveled the length of her body, and her cheeks colored. He gave her a thumbs-up.

Mrs. Cregg leaned over to her. "Pink's his favorite color."

Meera looked at her with wide eyes, and the woman winked.

Jake hopped off to help Lily into the carriage.

It would fit only two people, with Lily already taking up a lot of room.

She turned to Meera. "I want you with me."

Jake held out his hand to help her climb in. As she stepped onto the carriage, he whispered, "You look like my Meera."

Meera sat next to Lily, her heart beating a mile a minute as she watched Jake hop on the small driver's seat and click his tongue to get the horse moving.

As they got into town, there were cheers from people lining the sidewalks. Down the street, Meera could see that the entire town square had been transformed. An archway covered in flowers and lights stood in the center.

"This is unbelievable." Lily looked radiant.

Meera got her first look at Joe as they approached the makeshift altar. He stood in a dark green uniform in the middle of the archway. Joe turned toward them as the sound of clicking hooves was overpowered by people cheering.

Lily blinked back tears. "This town...they take care of their own."

Meera sniffed as she took it all in. This had all come together in a few hours, an act of love from the community. There had been no meticulous planning, no checklists, no prior notification... Everyone had just worked in symphony for one of their own. And as she looked around, she realized she would give up everything she had ever planned in her life to have a celebration like this.

Meera turned to Jake. "Did you bring it?"

Jake nodded and handed her a small box, his eyes sparking mischievously. "Wish you weren't giving this away."

Meera's mouth fell open. "You weren't supposed to look inside."

He shrugged. "It was open when I got it off your dresser."

Meera's face flamed.

She turned her attention to Lily and opened the box. It was a blue-and-white-lace garter. Lily squealed in delight.

"It's brand-new, and I'd like you to have it." Meera surreptitiously slipped it up Lily's leg while pretending to fix her shoe. Priya had bought it for her on their last shopping trip. *Raj loves blue and white—wear it on your wedding day*, she'd said. Meera liked giving it to Lily. Just a few days ago, she was convinced Lily was headed for heartbreak, and here she was living a fantasy.

They were both giggling as Jake helped them out of the carriage.

"You'd better hurry." Norma Jean handed Meera a bunch of roses. Again, Meera was struck by all the details that had somehow come together with impressive coordination. She walked to the archway and turned to watch Lily walk down the "aisle."

A high school band started playing the "Wedding March."

Meera couldn't help grinning like an idiot. She was bubbling inside and wanted to scream from the rooftops. She caught Jake's eye. He was standing in the back, openly staring at her. She turned away, afraid she wouldn't be able to resist the urge to run into his arms.

Joe's eyes were shining and locked on to Lily's as she approached the altar. Lily had been right all along. Against all odds and reason, she believed in her love. *Maybe some things can't be planned. Maybe some things are beyond logic.*

Lily handed Meera her bouquet.

Meera watched as she reached for Joe's hand. The minister nodded to them, and Joe lifted Lily's veil then took both her hands.

"Lily, from the first moment I laid eyes on you, my heart told me you were the woman who was gonna make an honest man out of me."

Meera thought back to her first moment with Jake. She remembered how her breath caught in her throat, how his green eyes sparkled. She glanced back to catch him staring at her.

Her breath stuck in her chest. *Will it be like this every time I look at you?*

"Lily, you make me feel like I've never felt before. My heart hadn't fully loved until I met you."

Meera's fingers curled around the bouquet, a thorn pressing into her finger.

"You've never asked me for anything, but I want to give you the world and I'm so grateful you're giving me a chance to have you, hold you and love you with every breath I take, from now until the Lord takes me away."

Tears rolled down Meera's cheeks. She could feel the raw love in Joe's voice, just like she could hear the silent vows Jake was uttering.

Lily said her vows, and the minister pronounced them husband and wife. Joe kissed his bride, and the couple turned as the townsfolk threw a shower of rice.

The high school band began playing as the entire town cheered and descended on the happy couple.

"You know, everything's already set up here." She trembled as Jake's breath warmed her ear. He had snuck up from behind to put his arms around her.

"I know, I thought about it, too." She closed her eyes and let herself sway with him. It was a tempting idea. She could be Jake's wife, right here and now. He would take her back to the ranch and to his bedroom. She could sleep in his bed tonight. She wouldn't have to dream about it anymore, analyze it to death or make plans that wouldn't work.

"Are you sure you don't want to make this a double weddin'?" She opened her eyes to see Mrs. Hayes staring warmly at them. Meera blushed and stepped out of Jake's arms, suddenly realizing the number of eyes on them.

Mrs. Hayes leaned forward. "Don't even try to give me some hogwash, little girl. I saw that look on your face." Meera covered her face with her hands, unable to look at Mrs. Hayes. She shook her head.

She heard Jake laughing behind her. "Give her time, Mrs. Hayes."

Meera felt herself being hugged and released her face to put her arms around the older woman. "Darlin' girl, welcome to Hell's Bells. You're one of us now."

Meera glowed.

The band struck up a popular country song, and there were hoots as the crowd began to dance. "What else is going on?" Meera asked.

"Well, it's a weddin'!" Jake said. "Mr. Cregg and the rest of us set up a barbecue…and we checked the vent." She laughed. "And I'm not letting you outta my sight for even a moment."

"You promise?"

She stood on her tiptoes and put her arms around his neck. Suddenly, she didn't care who was watching or what they might think. She pulled his head down and kissed him with everything she had.

They danced with the rest of the town, letting the moonlit night charm them into a state of bliss.

After Lily and Joe left, they helped the town clean up. It was late at night by the time everything was done and most people had headed home. Meera and Jake walked hand in hand, enjoying the sudden quiet.

I'll miss this town. Never thought I'd say that, but I'll miss more than just Jake. She knew he knew, but she had to say it out loud. *This is as good a time as any.*

"Jake, I have a plane ticket back to London next week."

CHAPTER TWENTY-FOUR

MEERA PATTED JAKE'S BACK as he coughed. He seemed to be gasping for air.

"I meant just to talk to my parents."

He looked up. "What?"

She smiled reassuringly. "I need to go back and tell my parents, and Raj, in person."

"Tell them what, exactly?" he asked breathlessly.

"To tell them I've fallen madly in love with this redneck cowboy and plan to go back to a town that's inexplicably called Hell's Bells to work as a country doctor whose patients pay her in clothes."

He leaned over and brought his mouth down on hers. She felt his relief and love the moment their lips touched.

When they came up for air, she grinned. "Why is it called Hell's Bells, anyway?"

He laughed. "I'll show you." They began walking and making plans. Meera would go home in a week and talk to her parents. She would come back a few weeks after that, and they would figure out what to do with the ranch and her research in London. Not all decisions had to be made right now. They needed some time to think things through.

She believed they could be together. Surely, there would be a solution that would let them merge their lives? If it could happen for Lily, it could happen for her.

For the first time in her life, Meera felt content. There was an inner peace she'd never felt before. She realized her constant headaches and ever-present anxiety were not hardwired into her.

Jake led her to a bell tower that was easily a hundred feet tall. Meera had driven past it before.

"Back when this town was founded, people believed it was haunted. They installed the bell to warn folks every time there was evil in and about town. Legend has it that every time the bell's rung, something bad happens. That's why we call the town Hell's Bells."

"So no one ever rings it?"

"Oh, teenagers on Halloween will, or the stray tourist. Freaks people out—it's actually fun to watch." His eyes twinkled, and he wiggled his eyebrows.

She shook her head. "Oh, no, I'm not tempting fate."

"Come on, you're a scientist. How can you believe in crazy myths like this?"

"No way. Besides, the rope is too high for me."

"I can fix that."

She yelped as he lifted her.

"Jake, you're such a bad influence on me."

"I try, princess. I try."

She reached as high as she could and grabbed the rope. She tugged and the bell rang out, clanking as the rusted clapper connected with the rim.

"Ok, now let me down!" She giggled.

"Hmm, I don't know, I like holding you hostage like this."

"Meera? Is that you?"

Meera froze. Jake's arms tightened around her hips. *It can't be!* She turned her head as if stuck in a bad slow-motion movie.

"Raj?"

CHAPTER TWENTY-FIVE

HIS FIGURE LOOMED against the moonlight, his head cocked to one side as if he couldn't believe what he was seeing.

Jake's arms loosened around her, and she slid down. As soon as her feet touched the ground, he stepped away from her. Raj approached them, taking in the scene. He was wearing jeans and a polo shirt, and yet he looked way too formal and out of place. She smoothed her dress.

"What the hell is going on here?"

Meera swallowed. Her mouth was completely dry.

"Raj! I was just ringing the bell…the rope was too high for me…and Jake… Oh, meet Jake Taylor."

Raj narrowed his eyes but stuck his hand out. "Raj Sharma." Jake shook it and the men appraised each other. Meera got the distinct impression they were squeezing the life out of each other's hands.

"What're you doing here? How did you even find me?" Meera broke in.

"I helped him." Meera turned to see Gloria standing behind Raj and bit her lip to keep from saying something nasty to her. It wasn't Gloria's fault Raj was here. Meera had brought it on herself.

Raj turned toward her and closed the distance between them. He placed a kiss on her forehead. A chill swept through her body.

"Well, nice to see you, too, Meera. I thought I would surprise you. Perhaps it's not as welcome as I thought it would be?" He glanced meaningfully at Jake and then returned his attention Meera.

Meera suppressed her annoyance. *How could he?* "Raj, you know I'm not good with surprises. Why didn't you ring to say you were coming?" She hugged herself and noticed that Jake had stepped even farther away from her.

"I did ring you. I thought it best to come here and see for myself how you're getting along." He had called her since their last conversation, but she had refused to pick up, texting him to say they'd talk in person. She should have known he would show up.

Meera rubbed her temples. "I was coming home next week, anyway."

He pressed his lips together and held out his hand. "We should go to your hotel room and have this conversation in private." He looked pointedly at Jake.

Meera stared at his outstretched hand. She swallowed again and turned back to Jake. His face was a mask, his arms crossed. He was watching her closely yet seemed a thousand miles away.

She took Raj's hand, and he yanked her toward him. Her legs turned to rubber. She tugged on his arm. "Wait, I left my purse in Jake's truck." Her voice sounded shrill. Raj stopped and spun around.

"It's okay, I'll drop it off at your front door." Jake's voice was completely bland. And yet she could hear a thousand unspoken feelings in those words. His eyes bored into her as he stepped back into the shadows. Her throat closed.

"Meera!" Raj's tone was urgent.

She hadn't heard the thunder over the pounding in her head, and she didn't feel the raindrops until they started coming down hard. She let Raj lead her to his rental car. Rain pelted the windshield, and Raj started the wipers. Her face was wet as she stared into the night.

"What's going on, Meera?" Raj's voice was calm but tense. "Who is he?" She couldn't see him, but she knew Jake was standing in the rain looking at her.

Meera squeezed her eyes shut as pain twisted her insides.

"He's the love of my life, Raj."

She expected him to curse, to get angry at her, to berate her, even. Instead, he calmly turned the ignition and put the car in gear.

"Give me directions to where you're staying."

She laughed mirthlessly. "You can't ignore it, Raj, all roads lead to Jake. I'm staying in a cottage at his ranch."

His knuckles whitened on the steering wheel. He took a purposeful breath. "Meera, I care a great deal about you. I was worried, so I dropped everything back home to fly over here to check on you. I come here to find you in the arms of another man. I know this month was supposed to be a kind of *Rumspringa* for you, but this is a lot to take."

Meera closed her eyes. He was right. She should have told him much sooner, when she first started having feelings for Jake, after that first kiss. Why had she put it off?

"Now you're telling me you're in love with a man you've known for three weeks."

Her stomach flipped. It was exactly the way her parents would see it.

"Whatever you feel, or don't feel for me, we've been friends for a very long time. Can I please ask you to show me just a little respect? I've been traveling for the past twelve hours. I'd like to take a shower and rest before we get into what sounds like a life-altering decision…for both of us."

Meera nodded. It wasn't Raj's fault she had fallen in love with Jake. She tried to put herself in his shoes; he hadn't been expecting to find her the way he had.

When they got to the ranch, she opened the cattle-guard gate. It was raining heavily, and she was drenched by the time she returned to the car. Raj stared stonily ahead, as if in a daze.

She directed Raj to the carport and led him to the cottage.

"So this is his property?"

She nodded. "He lives in the big house we saw on the drive up. This is the guest cottage. You can sleep in here." She opened the door to the spare bedroom.

"I'm going to take a shower. Is there a place to get tea?"

Meera nodded, grateful for an excuse to go see Jake. As soon as she settled Raj with towels, she ran to the main house, rain pelting her the entire way. She sighed in relief when she saw Jake's truck in the carport.

Meera sloshed into the kitchen, and Jake nearly knocked over his chair as he stood to greet her.

She flew into his arms and burst into tears. He held her tightly. She was dripping wet and so was he. It could have been a scene out of *The Notebook*. They held each other desperately.

"I'm so sorry!" She gazed at him pleadingly. "He's tired and wants to rest, so we'll talk tomorrow but I told him I loved you as soon as we got in the car."

Jake kissed her head. "This can't be easy for you."

"I just wish he hadn't come here. I planned to tell my parents first, to make them understand. Raj…" She buried her face in Jake's shirt, needing his strength. Jake held her for some time and she let him.

"I'd better make some tea and head back," she said finally. "I don't want to make things more awkward than they already are."

He nodded and got the teapot out for her. They had bought it together. He helped her find a tray and load it up with the teapot, cups, milk and sugar. She couldn't stop the tears from streaming down her face. At least the thunderstorm had passed; she could no longer hear the incessant pitter-patter. She knew everyone in town would be ecstatic at the end to the summer drought, but for her it felt like the end of something else.

"Meera?"

She turned, and her heart squeezed tightly at the look in Jake's eyes.

"Do what's best for you, okay? I'm not asking for anything."

CHAPTER TWENTY-SIX

"Am I right in assuming that your parents don't know about these…new developments?"

Meera shook her head. She felt like a schoolgirl sitting in the principal's office. They were in the living room drinking tea. Thunder clapped in the distance, threatening more rain. She had dried her hair and changed clothes. Her tea was colder than she liked, but she didn't want to walk back to the kitchen. She was wrung out.

Suddenly remembering that Raj had been traveling a long time, she asked if he wanted dinner. To her relief, he shook his head.

He set his cup down. "Well, I've had quite the day, so I'm going to turn in. We can talk tomorrow morning."

"I would like to personally tell my parents."

He turned from the doorway of his room, his face impassive.

"We'll discuss it tomorrow." He closed the door behind him. Anger boiled inside her. *What right does he have to dictate terms to me?* But the tone in his voice was familiar, and Meera realized that she was the one who had set that dynamic between them.

She thought of how she and Jake fought all the time. She'd initially considered it a sign of their incompatibility. *I'm myself with Jake—I feel comfortable standing up to him.*

She turned off all the lights, then looked out the window at the second-story balcony in the distance. Was it her imagination, or could she see Jake's silhouette?

She slipped under the covers, pulling them around her. She didn't even have the energy to change. She cried herself to sleep.

A LOUD BANGING woke Meera in the middle of the night. She ran to the door—it was Jake. She looked at him in alarm. Raj came out of his room. "What's going on?"

"It's Lily. You left your cell phone in my truck." Jake handed the phone to Meera, and she held it to her ear.

"Dr. M., my water broke. It really hurts, I can't move, I can't even get up to go to the hospital."

"Stay calm, Lily, I'll be right there. Just breathe like I taught you. Is Joe with you?"

Lily confirmed that Joe was there, but she told Meera the contractions were on top of each other, even though her water had just broken moments ago.

"What's going on?" Raj was rubbing his eyes.

"My patient is in labor, and she's had no pre-natal care." Meera grabbed her bag and slipped her feet into a pair of flip-flops.

"Are you going like that?"

Meera looked down. Her dress was rumpled but otherwise intact. Raj appeared perfectly pressed in his pajamas and dressing gown.

"I need to get to my patient."

"I can drive you," Jake said, and she nodded. She didn't care what Raj thought. She had to get to Lily. It was her first baby, and the con-tractions shouldn't be that bad so soon after her water had broken.

Raj put his hand on the door frame. "I'll come. Perhaps I can help."

She hesitated. "Okay, I'll text you the address. You should be able to find it using your GPS."

She walked out. Jake drove fast through the empty town. Meera barely waited for him to stop the car before running through the open front door. Lily was on the couch, writhing in pain. Joe was holding her hand and pressing cold wash-cloths on her forehead. Meera examined her.

"Something's wrong, isn't it? I can feel it."

Meera nodded. "The baby is breech and prob-ably in distress."

She remembered that the paramedics would take thirty minutes just to get to Hell's Bells and the hospital was two hours away. Her heart raced. She tried to move the baby using the techniques she had read about in her medical textbooks. Lily moaned in pain but the baby didn't move. Meera tried to keep calm—she would never forgive herself if something happened to Lily. She should have encouraged her to go to Fort Bragg; they had a hospital on base. This could end very badly.

She heard someone enter the room. "What's happening?" She turned to see Raj and felt an immediate sense of relief. She gave him a recap of the situation, and he examined Lily. "Okay, Meera, I dealt with this on one of my rotations. We can do this together." Raj explained the procedure and began to talk her through it.

"I feel the cord around the neck. I'm slipping it off," Meera told him.

"Good, Meera. I feel the baby moving." Raj had his hand on Lily's abdomen.

Lily was groaning in pain. "Almost there, Lily, just hang in there." Meera saw the head come out and nearly cried. She took out a bulb syringe and suctioned the baby's mouth and nose.

"All right, a couple more pushes and the baby will be out. You can do it!" Raj's voice was strong and reassuring. Lily took a breath and pushed. Meera grabbed the baby as he came out and wrapped him in a towel, suctioning some more. She rubbed the baby, getting him warm. He started to cry.

A collective sigh of relief and excitement went through the room.

"Lily and Joe, meet your new baby boy." Raj showed Joe how to cut the umbilical cord. Tears were falling down Joe's cheeks. Once cut, they wrapped the baby in more clean towels and handed him to Lily, who was also crying.

Raj checked the infant in Lily's arms while Meera took care of Lily.

Lily and Joe took barely any notice of the doctors' work as they studied their newborn baby. The love in the room was palpable.

"You're crying," Raj said softly to Meera as they washed up at the kitchen sink.

She chuckled. "Lily has been a special patient. I thought…I thought I had almost… Thank you for your help. I really don't know what I would have done. I've never delivered a breech birth before."

He nodded and held out his arms. She hugged him.

She looked up to see Jake standing in the doorway. He nodded at her and Raj.

"You guys make a good team."

CHAPTER TWENTY-SEVEN

THE ENTIRE TOWN was buzzing with the news of baby Lucas and the miracle birth performed by their very own Dr. M.

Meera and Raj had gone back to the cottage for a few hours of sleep. The next morning, Raj insisted on coming with her to check on the new mother and baby. Meera checked Lily while Raj checked little Lucas. He was a pediatrician, after all.

"The baby is doing really well, but I would feel more comfortable if you both went to the hospital to get checked out," he told Lily.

She looked at Meera, who agreed. "We can only do so much here. He needs a hearing test and immunizations. And you should see a gynecologist."

Joe promised to take his wife and son to the military hospital that day.

When they were done, Meera thanked Raj. He smiled warmly at her. "Remember that time we did CPR on the guy who had a heart attack at the restaurant?" Meera nodded.

"We can do great things together, honey. We always have."

She gave him a thin smile. She hated when he called her honey, and yet she'd never said anything to him about it.

"Is there a place where we can talk? Not at Jake's ranch."

"Sure." Meera took him to the diner, where they grabbed coffee and pastries. Everyone stopped to hug and thank her. They all shook hands with Raj and politely thanked him, as well.

"Wow, Lily must be a popular girl in town."

Meera shook her head. "She isn't really. The town…it's so hard to explain. They're a family, and they take care of each other. They celebrate and protect one another. Think of it as a big fat Indian family in a small rural town. They gossip, they're really hard on each other, but when it comes down to it, they're there for each other."

He raised his eyebrows.

"Yes, I know, it is pretty extraordinary."

They saw Gloria as they passed the clinic. Gloria waved and came out to greet them. Meera stiffened. She was wearing a tight red dress, and Meera noticed Raj giving her a second look. Had Jake done that, Meera knew she would be green with envy.

Meera braced for Gloria's signature sarcasm.

Instead, Gloria hugged her tightly. "Thank you for saving baby Lucas. I'm really sorry I've been such a...well, you know." She glanced at Raj. "Rose also told me to tell you that she rescheduled your morning patients to this afternoon."

Meera thanked her as they walked away. She was grateful for some time to talk to Raj.

Meera led them to the park. It was the same place where she and Jake had kissed the first time. Meera warmed at the memory. She took a deep breath and looked at the spot where they'd stood. She needed to feel Jake's strength.

"Do you remember the first summer you were home from boarding school?"

Meera nodded. "I was thirteen and desperately wanted to ride horses the way the other girls did, but I hadn't been riding my whole life like they had." She met his eyes. "You spent the entire summer tutoring me." She knew what he was doing, reminding her how close they were.

He nodded. "Your parents bribed me to." Her mouth dropped open in surprise. "I wanted to take you to the formal end-of-summer function my parents throw every year. Your father said you were a special girl and I had to earn the right to be with you."

She blinked back tears. Her father always

treated her as though she was the most precious thing in the world.

Raj clasped her hands. "I've loved you all my life, Meera."

The lump in her throat grew, threatening to choke her. "I've never questioned your love for me, Raj, but we love each other as friends, not as a husband and wife should."

"But that's exactly the basis for a good marriage. We respect each other, we have the same goals in life, we get along. Our love will grow once we're married."

It's a marriage, not a business merger. Jake's words when she had first described her relationship.

"I'm not sure we have the same goals, Raj."

"I know it seems as though we've been on different wavelengths recently, and I admit I've been so caught up in settling in at your father's practice that I haven't paid attention to you..."

"This is not about me feeling like I've been taken for granted."

"Isn't it?"

Meera narrowed her eyes.

"Meera, you are in a completely different world here. I felt the rush last night delivering baby Lucas. It's thrilling to welcome new life—

the adrenaline alone can make you feel things that aren't real…"

She could see where he was going with this, and she wouldn't let him marginalize her love for Jake. "Raj, please don't. My feelings for Jake are not from an adrenaline rush or dopamine release of holiday happiness. I'm very fond of you, we've always gotten along and none of that has changed. This is not about how I feel about you, but what I feel for Jake. He and I have this thing… It's…"

"Exciting, isn't it? Your pulse races, you feel like you can do anything in the world."

Meera glared at him. "It is not just a biochemical reaction, Raj. It's real."

"Okay, then why not come home with me? Wait to make any decisions until you're in your own element. Let me remind you of the wonderful life we planned together. If you're still in love with Jake, we can talk about it as a family, with your parents."

She rubbed her temples. "Raj, I don't want you to hold on to hope. I'm not going to change my mind about Jake."

He smiled indulgently. "I'm not asking you to. All I'm asking is that you come home first. If you still feel the way you do now in London, then you'll know it's real."

Meera closed her eyes. She would never convince him, or her parents, it was real until she could prove that being at home wouldn't change anything. She nodded. "I was planning to come home as scheduled anyway, so I'll do just that."

"Good. I'll stay with you, and we can fly back together."

CHAPTER TWENTY-EIGHT

"DR. M., YOU CAN settle this for us," Billy John said as she walked into the kitchen. She had tiptoed out of the cottage, desperate not to wake Raj. He had been up early the past two mornings, so she'd taken him to the diner for breakfast. Today, she wanted to see Jake. Alone.

"What am I settling?" Meera poured herself a cup of coffee, and Kelly shuffled her chair over to make room for Meera to sit. Meera looked at the smiling faces and realized she missed having breakfast with everyone.

"Who was the last one to get their physical? It's time to clean the house, and we figure it's between Kelly and me." Meera glanced around the table, mentally checking off which hands she'd seen, and in which order. Her eyes landed on Jake. "Actually, it's Jake. He still hasn't gotten his physical." There was a chorus of comments and teasing. Jake held up his hands. "That rule didn't apply to me!"

"Why not? You said everybody had to get one." Jake scowled at Billy John.

"He's right. I remember, we were right here in this room when you said it, Jake."

Jake stood and put his plate in the sink.

"How about I do it after breakfast?" Meera stared at Jake, silently pleading with him to accept so they could talk.

"And after you give him a clean bill of health, he can scrub, scrub, scrub…get to it, Cinderella." There was general merriment as they finished breakfast. Meera laughed with them, grateful for the chance to have a normal morning before she left for London. She went to the car to get her medical bag, relieved she hadn't brought it into the cottage with her last night so she could avoid Raj. When she returned to the kitchen, everyone was filing out and Jake was piling plates into the dishwasher.

"I think they all knew we wanted to be alone. I've never seen them leave the table such a mess."

Meera handed him plates, and he loaded them in. They each grabbed a sponge; she cleaned the table while he scrubbed the counters. When they were done, she had him sit on the table and take off his shirt. She listened to his heart, her own beating wildly at the sight of his naked chest.

"So have you told him to beat it?"

"Yes, I mean…not exactly." She sighed. "Raj is questioning whether my feelings for you are a result of holiday euphoria and has requested that I come back to London with him before I finalize any plans."

Jake's pressed his lips together. "I see. He thinks this is holiday Meera."

"It's not true, Jake. I know how I feel about you, and if I do what he asks, it'll validate my decision for him…and for my parents. Raj and I have been friends for a long time—I'd like to indulge him." She cupped his face and lifted it up. "Think about this from his perspective. We've been friends for almost twenty years, and he's now seeing a new side of me. He needs time to come to terms with this, and I was planning to go to London, anyway."

His back stiffened.

"Please understand."

"And what if he's right?"

Meera stepped back. "He's not."

Jake looked away. "Meera, I meant what I said when I told you I don't want anything from you. If you go back and realize that this—you and me—was a mistake…" His voice thickened. "I just want you to be happy."

Meera put her forehead against his. "I won't change my mind. My heart won't let me."

"What about your father's practice and your research?"

"I haven't figured that part out yet."

"And what about your doomed karma if you live on a cattle ranch?"

She lifted her head. "I don't know, Jake. I don't have the answers. I'm not saying it's going to be easy. We have a lot of things we need to work on together, but first I need to deal with Raj and my parents."

"When do you leave?"

"In three days. Dr. Harper signed off on my medical rotation, so I can leave a little early... and can come back to you sooner so we can figure this out...together."

"Obviously, I'm interrupting."

Meera startled at Raj's voice. She dropped her arms to her side and stepped back from Jake. It looked bad, Jake with this shirt off, sitting on the table, her standing too close, head bent over his.

Remembering the stethoscope around her neck, Meera held it out to Raj. "I was doing a physical."

Raj stayed silent.

Meera went about quietly completing the rest of the checkup, stealing glances at Jake. He refused to meet her eyes, his expression stony. Raj watched awkwardly.

When she was done, Jake's voice stopped her

cold. "Dr. M., thank you for doing the physicals on all my hands. That was the deal we had, and you fulfilled your share of it."

CHAPTER TWENTY-NINE

JAKE TAPPED HIS foot on the floor and took a swig of moonshine.

"It's her party, she'll be here." Jake turned to look at Mrs. Hayes.

"That's not what I'm worried about."

"You're worried she ain't never coming back." He nodded.

"She'll be back."

"I'm not so sure," he muttered. He glanced around at the impressive turnout. Not quite the party they had thrown Lily for her wedding, but it was something. The high school band was playing, all the ranchers brought meat and Mr. Cregg had special ordered tofu dogs for Meera. All for a woman who, just a month ago, had been shunned by the entire town. For the millionth time, he marveled at her. Four weeks ago he hadn't known she existed, and now she permeated his life. *What will I do if she doesn't come back?* Jake thought about his father's words, the regrets he still harbored about not fighting for his momma. Would he go after Meera if she stayed in London? Would he leave the ranch? Was he holding on to it because it was his mint chocolate chip? He shook his head.

What if he was Meera's mint chocolate chip?

The crowd's sudden excitement let him know Meera was here. He stood up straight. She was leaving tomorrow morning, and he was thirsty for a sight of her. And there she was, dressed in a baby-pink T-shirt, jeans and a straw cowboy hat. People surrounded her; everyone wanted to talk to the guest of honor. She locked eyes on him. The crowd thinned, and he saw Raj next to her, his arm linked with hers.

Jake's mouth soured. They looked like a couple. A—*what was the phrase she'd used?*—a well-suited one.

He saw them encounter Gloria. Meera whispered something to her, then slipped her arm away from Raj. He watched Raj's eyes follow Meera as she moved away, but Gloria quickly cornered him.

He set down his cup and strode toward their spot.

"How'd you know I would know?"

She turned and smiled. It was a beautiful smile, but a sad one. "Because you always know what I need."

He wrapped his arms around her, needing to hold her. He bent his head and kissed her lightly on the lips. "*Love* seems like such a small word for what I feel for you, Meera."

She rested her head on his chest. "I know, Jake. I wish I could find a way to free myself from my sense of duty and responsibility and just stay here with you. But I can't."

He nodded. "I'm not asking. I promised you my love wouldn't be conditional, and it isn't. You're not asking me to change who I am, so I'm not gonna ask you to change who you are."

He felt her breaths coming fast and held her tighter. He thought about how she looked when she'd arrived with Raj, as if she'd been doing it all her life. "Do you love him?"

She tipped her head back. "Not the way I love you."

"But you do love him?"

She shifted so she could look him straight in the eye. "We've been best friends for a long time. I can't tell you I feel nothing for him—I wouldn't have agreed to spend my entire life with him if we didn't have something. I know this must be hard for you, but I do care for him. And he cares for me. That's why he wants to make sure that my feelings for you are true. You understand, don't you?"

He understood just fine. He knew she didn't want to hear it, but she had to; he couldn't let her go and get sucked into the vortex of her parents' influence. He wanted her to think for herself, to question their motives before blindly following their expectations.

"Do you have a choice, Meera?"

She untangled herself from him.

"What do you mean by that?"

"Meera, I'll love you no matter what you do, but I need to know you'll do what's right for you and not what works for your parents."

"I've always done what's right for me." Her voice held an edge.

Yeah, right. He thought about Raj's smug expression when he arrived with Meera on his arm, as if he owned her.

"You're not gonna like this, but when it comes to your parents, you seem to suffocate under a sense of debt. All I'm saying is make sure when you get there, you do what *you* want to do. Make sure the choices are yours, and not theirs cloaked in guilt."

She stepped away from him. He went cold.

"Don't you get it, Jake? My parents are a part of me. You say you want me just as I am? Well, my parents are a big part of that. Their values, beliefs, doing what makes them happy…that's the core of my culture. I won't disrespect my parents. You need to trust me to handle this the right way." She wiped her eyes.

"Meera, I'm not asking you to shun your parents, just to be objective. Look at what just happened. Raj guilted you into letting him stay here so we couldn't even spend your last few days together. You don't see how they manipulate you."

"Right, Jake—you'd rather I stop letting them tell me what to do so *you* can tell me what to do."

She turned and walked away.

He rubbed his neck. What was wrong with him? He meant to give Meera a nice send-off, something sweet to remember him by. As usual, he had screwed it up. He watched her retreating figure. He couldn't let her go without a fight.

He walked back to the party and back to the "bar" Mrs. Hayes had set up. She handed him a cup before he even asked.

He strode to the band and asked to borrow a guitar, and all eyes turned to him when he started strumming.

"I haven't heard that boy sing since his momma left."

He closed his eyes and pictured Meera's beautiful smile, heard her intoxicating laugh, felt her sitting beside him on his tractor. The song in his heart poured out. There was pin-drop silence in the room as he sang.

He didn't think about the future, he didn't worry about the sympathetic looks he would get from the town when she left. He wanted her to hear what she meant to him. He wanted her to understand how he felt about her.

When he was done, he opened his eyes and found Meera staring at him, tears streaming down her face. As soon as their eyes connected, she turned and ran, disappearing out of sight.

He went back to Mrs. Hayes, but this time she handed him a cup of water. He felt a tap on his shoulder and turned to see Raj standing there looking...as if he belonged on Meera's arm. *And here's another fight I'm spoiling for.*

"That was a nice song." He might as well have said, *I'm going to crap all over you.*

Raj was shorter than Jake, with the same skin tone as Meera and the same accent. *Well suited, indeed. The King and Queen of England.*

"I just want to let you know that Meera won't be coming back to Bellhaven."

Anger boiled inside Jake, and he clenched his hands into fists. He could wipe the smug right off Raj's face.

"That's for her to decide." He took a step toward the other man.

Raj wasn't done. "I'd like nothing more than for you to punch me right now so I can return the favor, but I care about Meera and for some unfathomable reason, she cares about you."

"Loves me."

"Excuse me?"

"Meera doesn't just care for me—she loves me, and I love her."

Raj's nostrils flared. Jake noted the tightness in the other man's jaw with satisfaction. Jake lifted his cup, daring him to make the first move.

"You've known Meera for four weeks. I've known her for nearly twenty years and loved her just as long. She will come to her senses in London, I'll make sure of it, because I'm not letting her go."

"You don't know the real Meera and never will," Jake muttered. But Raj was long gone, taking Meera with him.

CHAPTER THIRTY

JAKE WAS IN the rocking chair on his balcony. He wasn't sure how long he had been sitting there, but the sun was coming up. For the first time in years, he wasn't in the kitchen making breakfast and barking out orders. His hands knew what he expected; if not, Kelly would whip them into shape. He was giving Kelly light duty, organizing stuff, so she wouldn't have to do any heavy lifting or earn too much to lose her medical assistance. It was freeing to let her handle some of the responsibility that kept him weighed down, and Kelly was good at it.

He watched the light in Meera's bedroom come on and imagined her packing up all the clothes Lily had made her, taking her time in Hell's Bells as a souvenir. Then the light in the room Raj was using came on. Jake wanted to throw up. He knew they'd slept in separate rooms, yet the thought of them sharing the little house... His shotgun was in the closet; he probably had a clear shot at Raj's window.

That was probably how Raj felt about him,

too. He had spent the night oscillating between imagining ways to punch Raj without offending Meera and feeling sorry for the guy. The man had known Meera for two decades. If Jake felt the way he did after just one month, Raj must be in bad shape. And what right did Jake have to steal Meera away from him? Who was he to say she was better off with him? Based on the way the two of them had delivered baby Lucas, it was obvious Raj and Meera were a team. They had history, and that had to count for something. And what did he have? A failing ranch and a broken heart.

He watched them come outside, suitcases in hand. She held the same suitcase she had shown up with a month ago. The one he had carried to the cottage while she struggled to keep up with him in those ridiculous shoes, which she was wearing now, along with a severe dress. His heart ached for the Meera who was already gone.

Jake went to the railing so he could see her more clearly. She looked up and met his gaze. She held up an envelope and slipped back into the cottage. When she came out again, she mouthed, "I love you" and got into her car. She and Raj had separate rentals.

He should have driven her, he should have dropped her at the airport and kissed her with everything he had. Even if she didn't come back, he wanted her to know what she was leaving behind.

He whipped around and tore through his room, taking the stairs two at a time. He burst through the front door and watched the dust as their cars left the driveway.

He grabbed the keys to his truck and slammed the door. He put the key in the engine and turned the ignition. The engine coughed. "Aaarrghh." The truck had been giving him a hard time all week, but it picked this moment to die on him. He tried a few more times, then gave up. It was just as well; perhaps it was one of those signs Meera believed in, a metaphor for what he couldn't offer her.

He walked to the cottage, his bare feet protesting as the gravel cut into his soles. Her scent immediately overwhelmed him. The entire cottage smelled of lavender and vanilla. He saw the envelope sitting on the coffee table along with the keys to the cottage. He picked it up and walked into her room. The bed was neatly made. The closet door was open, and all the clothes Lily had made were hanging tidily, even the pink maid-of-honor dress. He touched the material and pressed his face against it. His throat tightened.

Have you left my Meera behind, or is this a promise you'll be back?

He felt the letter in his hands and tore it open. It was just a few words.

"Have faith that I'll find my way back to you."

He punched the closet door, scraping his knuckles. "Don't lie to me, Meera. I've already lost you."

CHAPTER THIRTY-ONE

MEERA WAS EXHAUSTED. The flight was uneventful, and much to her chagrin, Raj had insisted on upgrading their tickets to first class. She tried to argue that it was an unnecessary luxury but relented when she realized it also meant she wouldn't be sitting next to him. The seats reclined into beds and were in individual "pods" to provide a sense of privacy. Privacy she used well to draft an email to Jake. She told him she missed him and attached all the files she had put together for the dude ranch. Kelly had cornered her at the party last night to tell her that the financial situation was really bad and that if Jake didn't "get his head out of his you-know-what," he would lose everything.

Meera knew what the ranch meant to him. In her email, she laid out a plan where he could keep a good portion of his cattle operation. She should have included it in the first version of her presentation, but at the time, she had rationalized it as a bad business decision.

They landed at London Heathrow. Raj weaved

her through the immigration and customs lines. Although the first-class line was considerably shorter, it was still a slow process. She fidgeted with the handle of her purse and studied the people in line with her. A cowboy hat caught her eye, and her pulse quickened. She averted her gaze; no matter how much she looked, Jake wouldn't magically appear.

Had she let Raj guilt her into letting him stay in Hell's Bells? Maybe she should have sent him back and spent the last few days with Jake, then come home on her own terms.

She had been up half the night trying to figure out what to write in the note she'd left him. In the end, she'd kept it simple, hoping he understood that she left her Hell's Bells clothes in the closet because she planned to return—without the persona of London Meera.

She knew it wouldn't be easy to face her parents, but she needed to be strong, to draw on Jake's strength so she could stand up to them. Surely, they would support her happiness.

They cleared customs and collected their luggage. As they exited the baggage area, Meera searched the crowds for her parents. She couldn't wait to see them; this had been her longest trip away from them. Although time had flown in Hell's Bells, it seemed like a lifetime ago that her father had seen her off in this very terminal.

"There he is."

Meera turned to see Raj pointing to their family chauffeur. Her heart sank. Her father must be busy seeing patients, and her mother was probably at one of her charity events.

As they drove to her house, Meera stared out the window. She loved London, but now it seemed overly crowded, traffic clogged, gray and cold. She missed the scenery along the country roads, the warmth of the air, the brightness of the sun. A light rain began to fall as they pulled into her driveway. Her parents owned a large, modern house right outside the city. Meera was surprised when Raj exited the car and took the umbrella from the chauffeur to hold it out for her. "Don't you want to go back to your place?"

He shook his head. "Your parents are waiting inside. We thought it best to talk first."

"We? Why wasn't I consulted in this *we* discussion?"

"Because you haven't been yourself, Meera, and your parents and I felt it best to talk to you as soon as you got home."

Meera pursed her lips. The new butler, whom she hadn't met, greeted them at the front door and led them to the drawing room. Meera thought about walking through the front door at the ranch every morning, the sounds of everyone talking in the kitchen, the creaks of the wood floor. Her house was blanketed in silence, the lush rugs smoothing the tap of her heels.

Her mother stood when they walked in. "Meera, it's so lovely to see you, dear." She held out her arms, and Meera went to her, eager to feel the warmth of her mother's love. She hugged her tightly, the way the people of Hell's Bells had held her when she left. "Careful, darling, the suit is crepe."

Meera stepped back. "Come here, Meera, my suit's already wrinkled." Meera looked fondly at her father and embraced him. He held her close, and she choked back tears. "It's good to have you home, child."

"Mrs. Cooley made your favorite cookies and Darjeeling tea."

"I'm glad you haven't fired her," Meera quipped, attempting light humor as she sat down. She and her father often placed private bets on how long her mother would tolerate a new servant before letting them go.

Her mother poured tea and added just the right amount of milk and sugar to Meera's drink. She handed the cup and saucer to Meera with a cookie, then served everyone else from a matching teapot. Meera thought about her favorite mug in Jake's kitchen, the one with the chipped rim. She ran her finger over the smooth surface of her mother's fine china.

"So, Meera," her mother said. "Raj called us earlier. He was quite concerned that you've gone off the deep end, as the Americans like to say. What is this I hear about wanting to break off the engagement?"

Meera flashed her eyes at Raj, who stared back blandly. "Mum, that was a private conversation between me and Raj."

Her mother gestured dismissively. "Nonsense. Raj is a part of this family, and your marriage is a family decision. You can't just break it off without talking it over with us. He's already started taking over your father's practice, you're both leasing the laboratory together, his mother and I are chairing several charities together—we're all one big family. Any decision you make affects us all."

Meera swallowed against the lump in her throat. She wanted nothing more than to retreat to her room and spend the next several days in bed. She hadn't slept well since Raj had moved into her little cottage. *Like I have a right to claim that place as my own.*

She looked her mother in the eyes. "Mum, *Pitaji*, I planned to tell you myself…but it appears I wasn't accorded that courtesy…" She glared at Raj.

He shook his head. "All I've told them is that

the engagement may be off—the rest is up to you." *May be? There is no ambiguity about it. It's off!*

"Is there something more?" Her father leaned forward.

Meera's mouth was dry, so she took a sip of her tea. The hot liquid burned her throat. *Might as well get this over with.* "I've fallen in love with someone else."

Silence hung thickly in the air. Her mother took several sips of tea. Her father watched them all carefully.

"And who is this man that you've been taken with?" Her mother's voice was matter-of-fact.

"Jake Taylor. He owns the ranch that I stayed at in Hell's Bells."

"I see, an American. And what kind of rancher is he?"

"One who raises cattle for meat."

Meera glowered at Raj, silently warning him to stay out of it.

Her mother made a strangled sound. "Meera, you can't possibly be serious. You want to cancel your wedding with Raj so you can marry some redneck? Have you also started eating beef?" Her mother's voice dripped with disappointment and disbelief.

Meera felt her heart snap into pieces. This was not how she'd planned the conversation.

"Of course not! I mean, I haven't started eating beef." Meera took a breath. "And he's more than a cattle rancher, he is quite intelligent, he..."

"Really? Did he go to a top medical school to become a doctor? Will he help you complete the research you've been working on for years, help you win a Nobel Prize?"

Meera rubbed her temples.

"Mother, you're talking about a perfect business partner, not about love." She looked to her father to see if he would back her up, but he was staring at the carpet.

"Right you are, Meera. Love is what you enjoy when you're young. It's based on hormones and emotions that fade with time. Marriage is about finding a perfect mate, one who complements you, helps you navigate life, makes sure you achieve your goals. Someone who you can spend the rest of your life with in harmony. A man who will be part of this family. Tell me, do you see this Jake character sitting in this room having tea with us?"

Meera studied her mother's high-end Italian furniture. Cream-colored sofas and chairs. She thought of Jake's cowboy hat and muddy boots. No, she couldn't see him here, but nor could she picture her perfectly coiffed mother in his warm kitchen, with his ranch hands around the table slapping each other on the back. She had an urge to laugh hysterically.

With considerable effort, Meera kept her composure and simply shook her head.

"Well, it's settled then—you're home and back to yourself. Let's put this nonsense aside. Thank goodness for Raj—had it been someone else, he may have taken offense. I hope you'll find some way to thank him."

Her mother stood up, smoothing her immaculate suit. An image of the closet full of clothes she'd left behind flashed through her mind.

"What if I don't fit in here, Mum?"

Her mother's eyes cut to her. "Meera, we didn't pluck you out of that rat hole in India to have you go back to an impoverished life. We raised you, loved you and gave you everything under the sun to make you into the accomplished young lady you are today. This is where we've raised you to belong. Please don't insult our sacrifice by going back to the very life we saved you from." The last words were delivered with ice-cold precision.

A tense silence shrouded the room. Her father cleared his throat and excused himself. Her mother soon followed him. Meera looked at Raj, but he wouldn't meet her eyes.

"This may not have been the best idea," he muttered and left.

Meera stared at her cup of tea, wondering whether Jake was right. Was she repaying a never-ending debt to her parents?

CHAPTER THIRTY-TWO

"YOU'VE MADE EXCELLENT PROGRESS." Meera handed the sheets of data back to her research assistant.

"Well, Dr. Sharma came by once a week to answer my questions. It was very helpful."

Meera gave him a thin smile. She should be thankful to Raj for picking up the slack, but she only felt irritated at him. She was the lead on the project until they got to the pediatric component; he should have called and consulted her. *He did call, several times, and you wouldn't talk to him.* She should have checked in with the lab more frequently while she was in America; instead she'd been distracted by Jake.

She took a good look at the lab. She and Raj had started it together; they had state-of-the-art equipment and three talented assistants. She had received a prestigious award that had enabled her to compete for funding to lease the space. The work she could do here once she got her research degree... She thought about the little town of Hell's Bells. She could never complete her research there. She understood why Jake couldn't give up the ranch, but was it fair to ask her to give up all this? Forget his life in Hell's Bells, he wasn't even willing to stop cattle ranching. Yet he expected her to sacrifice everything she had worked for. She squeezed her eyes shut.

"Dr. Malhotra, are you okay?"

She nodded. "Great work, carry on. I'll be back tomorrow, and we can run those tests we talked about."

She had been in London for a week. Next week was the engagement party, and the wedding festivities would follow soon after. Her mother had planned fourteen days of celebration. She had barely seen Raj since the disastrous conversation over tea, and her mother refused to talk to her unless it related to wedding planning. It was all going so fast. She just needed a moment to think, to come up with a plan.

Jake replied to her lengthy email with one sentence asking her when she was coming back. How was she supposed to respond? She called to check on Lily, who asked her the same question and didn't want to talk about anything else.

Hell's Bells seemed like another life. She texted Gloria and Rose, both of whom were equally single-minded in their responses. Even Dr. Harper's email simply asked whether he should get her name put on the plaque for the front door.

She sighed and stood up. Today was her first day at her father's medical center, and she was expected there soon. It would be good to talk to him alone at the practice. Maybe Raj, too. If she could reason with her father and Raj separately, then she could figure out how to approach her mother. Even if she didn't go back to Hell's Bells, she knew she couldn't marry Raj.

She drove on autopilot, relieved to be back on the right side of the road. She pulled into her reserved parking spot and surveyed the large glass building. It was five stories high and bore a prominent sign that said Malhotra Medical. This was the headquarters that housed the senior doctors. Her father also owned several outlying clinics.

She had time before the first appointment, so she took the elevators to her father's office. Several staff members greeted her with, "Good morning, Dr. Malhotra." She almost corrected them to call her Dr. M.

When she entered, her father looked up and smiled widely. He had a corner office with a spectacular view of the Thames. While in medical school, she would sit in his office for hours, studying in tranquility.

"Welcome, Meera, so glad you made it a bit

early. This is a most exciting day." He put his arm around her. "Come, I have a surprise for you."

"Actually, I need to talk to you."

"That can wait. First I have to show you something."

He led her to the end of the hall, and Meera frowned. It looked different; there were supposed to be examining rooms in this area.

He opened a door that displayed her name. She stepped into a corner office with floor-to-ceiling glass windows that overlooked the river on one side and downtown London on the other. A modern L-shaped desk stood in the center of the spacious room, allowing her a perfect vantage point. She touched the smooth, unmarred surface. She turned to her father.

"I had this office made for you while you were away. I know how much you enjoy the view from mine, so I thought I'd build one for you."

Her heart squeezed painfully. Her father hadn't just handed over his office, he had made a better one just for her. It was the way he'd treated her all his life.

She threw her arms around him, and he held her tightly. "Oh, my child, I'm so happy you're here. I've been looking forward to this moment my entire life."

"*Pitaji*, you didn't have to go through this much trouble for me."

"Yes, I did, Meera. I want you to make your own mark on this practice. Depending on how your research goes, you can make this into a cardiac clinic, a genetics hub…the possibilities are endless. And this—" he gestured expansively "—will be your command center."

Meera struggled to breathe. Her father had spent his entire life building the practice just the way he wanted it, and he was going to turn the keys over to Meera to do with as she pleased.

"And wait, I have something else for you." Meera wiped tears from her cheeks and took the box from her father. She lifted the lid—inside was a flimsy plastic stethoscope. She gasped.

"This is how I knew you were the child for us. When you said it was your favorite toy, I knew in my heart you were meant to be my daughter, and that one day we would be standing here just like this. I've saved it ever since. You are my legacy, Meera."

Fresh tears filled her eyes. Her heart swelled.

"Now, what did you want to talk to me about?"

She gazed down at the stethoscope in her hand, the stethoscope of a little girl who had nothing. She looked out the office window and then back at her father, who beamed with pride.

"It wasn't important. I love this office, and I love you."

CHAPTER THIRTY-THREE

"WHAT DO YOU WANT?" Jake said through gritted teeth. He turned to see Kelly standing with her hands on her hips.

"Don't you get your panties in a bunch—it ain't my fault she left ya. Now pick up your bootstraps and quit making everyone crazy. The hands are working for free, and your bad temper ain't making it easier."

Jake took a deep breath and let it out slowly. Kelly was right. It wasn't hers or anyone else's fault that he hadn't heard from Meera in two weeks. She hadn't answered his email, and her text messages were short and perfunctory.

On top of it all, an invitation to her wedding had arrived today. It was in a fancy envelope with red velvet paper and gold lettering that proudly announced she was marrying Raj in two weeks. *Guess that answers my question!* Although part of him suspected Raj had sent the invitation out of spite.

Old Pete, the town mailman, had seen the invitation and figured out what it was from the envelope, which proudly proclaimed the bride's and groom's names on the return address label. The entire town now knew he'd been left. Again.

He went back to checking cattle, the few he still had, to make sure they were healthy. Working with the animals was one of his favorite chores; he always marveled at how gentle these large creatures could be. A heifer kicked him in the shins, and he cursed loudly. No matter how much he reminded himself that he would miss having the cattle, he was not feeling the love today. He closed the gate and returned to the house with Kelly.

"When are the buyers coming?"

She checked her phone. "They'll be here in a coupla hours." They stepped over the drop cloths that covered the foyer. Several of the townspeople were coming by in the evening to help paint. "The renos are coming along."

Jake nodded. He still couldn't believe the outpouring of support to help him build up the dude ranch. He had assumed the town would turn against him when he decided to make the ranch a tourist attraction, but instead they had offered to help. Apparently, a few temporary tourists didn't bother people as much as "cultureless rich folk" moving into their beloved town. They didn't want to see him lose his property like Mrs.

Hayes had. Plus, Meera had been right: they saw the potential to boost their own businesses.

Kelly surveyed the latest repairs, nodding approvingly. "You know, you're more stubborn than your old man. If you were gonna do all this anyway, why didn't you start when she was here?"

"I didn't want her stayin' or coming back on the promise of something I wasn't sure would work."

Kelly rolled her eyes. "You were testing her."

He rubbed his neck. Was that what he was doing? "I just didn't want her to stay out of obligation. If I'd told her I was gonna put her plan into action, she'd feel like she should be here to help me with it. That pompous fella was right— she needed to go back to London so she could make up her mind on home base. I want her to come back for me, the way I am, not because she thinks she can mold me into something more palatable for her...or her parents."

He turned away from Kelly. He didn't want to talk about Meera, didn't want to think about Meera, didn't want to see her face wherever he went.

After Meera left, he'd started work on the dude ranch. She was right; it was the only solution. She had also been right that keeping the cattle didn't make good financial sense. He had known it all along, but the new spreadsheets she'd sent him had made it even clearer. Why had he been so stubborn about the cattle? Truth be told, he had only turned to cattle ranching when horse training stopped being profitable. A financial decision. Yet that was another fight he'd picked with Meera.

He sighed. "I was testing myself, Kell. I wanna make sure I'm making decisions with a clear head. There's a lot of hands counting on me, and I don't want to do something for my own selfish needs."

"Boy, you're dumber than you look." She walked right up to him. "You want that girl to give up her whole life, and you're willin' to give up nothing? Take it from one stubborn mule to another—love ain't about power, it's about letting go."

She stalked off, shaking her head as she went.

Jake went upstairs and surveyed the work that had been done on the bedrooms. The hands had offered to work overtime for free to get the major renovations done, and the town was chipping in. Mrs. Cregg and Norma Jean were stitching new curtains for the house. Tom had given him a big line of credit so he could buy the necessary tools and materials. He knew he could do this; he had run the numbers, and he would pay them all back.

Kelly had overseen the work on the house

while he took care of the property. He hardly recognized the rooms; the furniture shone with polish, the newly sanded and stained floors gleamed and the linens were spotless.

His own bedroom was untouched. He hadn't decided what to do about it. He walked over to the balcony and sat in the chair, looking out at the cottage. Meera's clothes still hung in the closet, but her scent was gone.

He went back downstairs, walked into the kitchen and stopped.

"Jolene?"

She smiled at him. "Billy John let me in."

"Well, I didn't think I'd ever see you here again."

She was beautiful, her long blond hair falling in layers over her shoulders. Her eyes were lined with blue makeup that made their natural hue even stronger. She looked as if she belonged in his kitchen. Meera would call her an all-American beauty. She sat in the chair that Meera usually used. She was pouring tea from Meera's teapot.

Someone had made coffee, so he got himself a cup and sat down.

"I came to see how you're doing. I'm sorry about Meera."

Good news travel fast.

She studied his face. "You've got it bad, huh?"

He nodded.

"Well, at least you're over me."

He worked his jaw. "She turned out just like you—didn't want to be stuck in Hell's Bells on the ranch. At least you had the decency to tell me face-to-face."

Jolene touched his arm. He remembered how Meera used to do that and pulled away.

"Jake, I didn't leave you because you wanted to live in Hell's Bells. I left because you never wanted to leave."

"What's the difference?"

"The difference is that I want to see the world. I didn't want you to give up the ranch, I just wanted you to step outside of it once in a while—travel, experience new cultures, see what the world has to offer."

She didn't want to be imprisoned here.

His chest tightened. "I didn't *not* want that, it's just we never had the money."

"And you never put in the effort to figure out how to make it happen. Heck, Jake, I didn't think you'd ever give up cattle ranching, but look at you now, turning the place into a dude ranch. That's all I wanted out of you. To be open to possibilities, to make your mark, go beyond what your daddy left you."

The coffee tasted bitter. He suddenly wanted

a cup of tea. "Why were you drinking fertility tea?"

She laughed. "You found that?" She put her teacup down. "I wanted your babies, Jake. I was gonna suggest we get hitched and start a family."

He frowned. "Then why'd you leave?"

"'Cause you were a stubborn something-or-other who didn't want me going to Charlotte to buy a dress. 'Jolene, Mrs. Cregg or Lily can make you a dress.' You wouldn't consider a honeymoon in the Bahamas—'Jolene, we'll stay in the guest cottage, it'll be just like our own private hotel.' I felt like we'd never get off this ranch, and I couldn't breathe." Her voice was filled with a sad longing. "All I ever wanted was for you to love me as much as you loved your cattle."

His gut twisted. Had he really done that?

"I heard you went to New York City with her."

He nodded. "I guess I learned how to get off the ranch."

She shook her head. "You found someone who inspired you to do something more."

He took a big gulp of his coffee, burning his tongue. He focused on the pain in his mouth.

"Someone who also didn't think I was good enough for her to stay."

Jolene put her hand on top of his. "I never thought that, Jake, don't you believe it for one more minute. I've regretted every minute we've been apart. I was impulsive." Her eyes glistened. "Since I left, I've been realizing just how much I miss you. I was crazy to ever let you go, Jake."

His heart pounded. *What was she saying?*

She slid her chair closer until their legs touched. "Jake, I want us to get back together. We've loved each other for so long, we got along so well… I made a mistake. I think we should get married, and this time we won't drag it out. We'll do it the way Lily and Joe did. We can get married tomorrow."

CHAPTER THIRTY-FOUR

"THIS IS A total disaster."

Meera closed her eyes. She was standing in her bedroom, wearing the Sienna Simone wedding dress. Her mother turned her attention to the panicked tailor in front of Meera. No one on Savile Row wanted the wrath of Neela Malhotra.

"You idiot! How could you ruin a Sienna Simone!" He twisted his handkerchief.

"The dress was about a foot longer than she is. I had to take in the bodice to make it flow."

"Well, you have done quite an incompetent job. This dress is not wearable." Neela dismissed the man and turned her fury on Meera. She shrank back.

"This is all your fault. If you hadn't screwed up your appointment with Sienna, we wouldn't be in this situation." She bit her lip and paced the room.

"What if Meera wears the sari you wore at your wedding, Neela aunty?"

Meera looked gratefully at Priya. She had arrived that morning from America. The wedding was two weeks away, and the engagement party was tonight.

"Yes, Mum, it would be so special to wear your sari—you said you've preserved it." Meera began taking off the ruined Sienna Simone as her mother continued to pace.

"No, that wouldn't be suitable."

"But why not?" Priya asked.

Neela did another lap of the room. "No, I don't want her wearing my sari. My poor dead mother would not approve," she said absentmindedly. But there was something in her tone that made Meera's stomach turn. She was about to protest, then thought better of it; she was on thin ice as it was.

"I will just have to go to Southall tomorrow and find her a sari. There won't be a fitting required, and the Indian tailors are much more competent with stitching a blouse."

She glared at Meera. "I hope you're happy. You've ruined the wedding." She shot a glance around the room, and Meera flinched. "And clean up here, it's a pigsty. I don't know what has happened to you since you've returned from America."

She stormed off, and Meera looked miserably at Priya, who put her arm around her. Meera had told her cousin the whole story, including what had happened between her and Jake.

Meera nodded. "She's still mad at me." She stepped out of the Sienna Simone dress and pulled on a dressing gown. "I should go talk to her, try to smooth things over."

"Why don't you give her some time to cool off? You need to get dressed for the engagement party, anyway."

Meera sighed. Priya was right; the party was supposed to start in a couple of hours, and the hairdresser, makeup artist, manicurist and pedicurist would be here soon. She would be wearing a red lace gown by Valentino. She needed to put the dress on before everyone else arrived.

Priya tidied up while Meera stared blankly at her laptop, then went to her own room to get dressed. Jake hadn't written to her. She began a new email to him, but the words seemed hollow and completely wrong. She slammed the screen shut.

She stood and stretched; she was exhausted from the endless ladies' luncheons her mother had insisted on in addition to the work she was doing at her father's practice. She looked around her room. Her mother had designed it, and it had been featured in one of Britain's top home design magazines. It was the best in modern furniture, with sophisticated silver, black and gray accents. She thought back to Jake's room at the ranch, the warm colors, the sense of comfort and home. She needed to talk to him, hear his voice. It would be early in Hell's Bells; he would be doing the morning feed.

She opened her dresser and took out a plain wooden frame with a yellowed picture inside, showing her with her parents the day she was adopted. The peeling walls of the orphanage stood behind them as she held her father's hand, a big smile on her face.

She wiped the tears from her cheeks and gazed around her room again. At least fifty children would have slept in a room this size at the orphanage. Her parents may have brought her back to this house, but her former life was always with her. She never left food on her plate, she enjoyed the feel of fine clothing, she happily wore the sparkly diamonds her parents gave her and she never touched dirty things. It was what she wanted. It was what she'd worked for all her life.

So why did she feel as empty and alone now as she had waking up every day at the orphanage?

She put the picture back in the drawer, burying it under several layers of folded scarves. She needed to put on her dress. Most of the out-of-town guests had arrived and would stay the two weeks until the wedding. There were events each night to keep the six-hundred-person wedding party entertained. Meera shuddered to think what it would mean to send them all home. For the little orphan girl to embarrass the people who had given her everything.

Priya came back. "Meera, you've got to get ready." Meera sat at her dresser, unable to move.

Priya went to her closet to find the dress. "What's this?"

She was holding a package wrapped in brown paper. Meera frowned, then remembered. When she'd driven through Hell's Bells to go to the airport, the townspeople had come out and waved. Meera almost ran Joe over when he stepped in front of her car. He'd handed her the package and said it was a gift from Lily. Preoccupied with thoughts of Jake, Meera tossed the package into her bag and hadn't thought about it since.

She tore the paper and gasped. It was a white wedding dress with a strapless sweetheart neckline and little beads across the bodice that ended in a satin belt. She held up the dress, watching the skirt fall in layers.

She hadn't bought the silky material for Lily. She must have spent a month's salary on the materials.

With Priya's help, she slipped the dress over her head. She studied her reflection. It fit perfectly. Not a stitch out of place. The tight bodice showed off her petite frame and the layers made her look taller than she was. It was exactly what she wanted for her wedding, something simple and elegant.

The hope and love sewn into the dress choked her. She buried her face in her hands and let the tears come. Pain raked through her body.

"Did your patient make it?"

Meera nodded, unable to speak.

"It's actually really nice."

Meera couldn't take it anymore. She slipped out of the dress and handed it to Priya. "Put it away." Priya looked at her quizzically. "Get it away from me. Now!"

Priya folded it and rewrapped it in the brown paper. Meera went to her closet and brought out the engagement dress she was supposed to wear.

She stepped into the dress, and Priya zipped her up. The dress alone could have covered the loans Jake had begged the banks for to save the ranch. He had refused to let her lend him money…not that she had much of her own. Her parents had bought the dress, just like they bought everything else for her.

She sat down gingerly, careful not to snag any of the delicate silk lace.

"Priya, maybe you should just do my hair and makeup. Might be fun to have just us girls get me dressed."

Priya gaped at her, aghast. "Your mother will

have a fit, besides which, I could never make you look as good as the professionals."

Before Meera could argue, the hairdresser and makeup artist arrived with all the other staff that would "process" her until every exposed inch was plucked, teased, polished or painted. The party was starting downstairs; Meera heard tinkling glass and merry laughter. She was supposed to make a grand entrance.

Meera sat all alone while everyone worked around her. She thought of Lily on her wedding day, surrounded by people who loved her, who were there to wish her well and get her spirit ready for the biggest day of her life.

She put a hand on her stomach and took a deep breath.

It was time to call Jake.

CHAPTER THIRTY-FIVE

"SHE RIDES LIKE a beauty. I think she'll do great on the trails."

Jolene dismounted the horse and swung herself onto another one's back. It was late morning but the air had a crispness to it, and the leaves were turning gold. The warm days were slowing, giving way to unseasonably frosty nights.

Things were finally coming together on the dude ranch. The house was almost finished, the stables repaired, the cattle sold for a good price and now that Jolene had helped him find a couple of rescue quarter horses, Jake could offer trail rides until he found horses to board. Jolene was also helping him build a website and had managed to talk a magazine into writing an article about him. She called it free advertising. He even had a booking. At the rates he was charging, if he filled one room each weekend, he'd be profitable within a few months.

He thought about his mother and the new life she had created for herself while his father had been waiting for her. He wasn't going to spend his life like his father had. He saw Jolene galloping in the distance. He might not love anyone like he loved Meera, but obviously love didn't conquer all. Maybe Meera had a point about choosing someone who could be a partner above all else. As Meera had so frequently pointed out to him, she wasn't exactly the type of girl to help him run a ranch.

Jolene approached, slowing the horse to a trot. "This one isn't quite ready, but I'll work with him for a few more days. I think I can train him."

"You sure you have time for that?"

Jolene smiled. "I told you, Jake, I'm moving back to Hell's Bells. I'll be here for you."

He smiled back and took the reins as she dismounted. His phone vibrated in his pocket, and he reached for it. Meera's face flashed on the screen. He closed his eyes and opened them again to make sure he wasn't seeing things. Jolene came around and stared over his shoulder. "Jake, you need to answer it."

He froze. Jolene pressed the answer button and moved his hand to his ear.

"Meera?" Did he sound as desperate as he felt?

"Jake? You sound different."

"That's because you haven't spoken to me in a long time."

"Oh."

He could hear her breathing. He pictured her sitting all alone in her room, rubbing her temples.

"I'm glad you remember my number." He was trying to sound lighthearted, to ease the tension, but it came out as sarcasm.

"You could have called me." Her voice was equally snarky, accusation in her tone. Maybe he had expected too much of her, been too unrelenting in not giving up the ranch, but none of that mattered because she had asked him to have faith that she would be back. And that's exactly what he'd done.

"You're the one who left."

"Jake…"

"When're you coming back?"

Silence greeted him. Heart pounding, he squeezed his eyes shut, trying to get his heart to understand what his brain had already computed.

"*Are* you coming back?" His voice cracked.

"Jake… I…" There were tears in her voice. "Things are just complicated here, I…I…"

"It's okay, princess, I told you I didn't expect anything from you." He hadn't meant to sound so bitter.

"I'm sorry, Jake."

"Goodbye, Meera."

"Jake, wait…"

He stabbed the end button and threw his phone on the ground. It bounced on the gravel path before settling somewhere in the grass.

CHAPTER THIRTY-SIX

MEERA DESCENDED ONE side of the double staircase into the grand foyer. As her hands ran down the smoothly finished banister, she remembered the gritty feel of another handrail, one that was an ocean away. Gazing at the sea of faces smiling, clapping, oohing and aahing at her, she searched for the one face that wasn't in the crowd.

Raj was waiting at the bottom of the stairs, dressed in a traditional Indian *achkan*. He took her hand when she reached the bottom step, and she thought back to the first time Jake had taken her hand, the tingle of excitement that sent shivers up her arm. Raj looked at her fondly. She felt numb.

Neela led the crowd into the ballroom. A traditional Indian music group struck up a popular track. A man began beating a *Dholki* drum, and Raj led Meera to the dance floor.

Meera knew the steps and danced effortlessly with Raj. She thought about the barbecue, the two-step with Jake, the exuberance that had powered her that night. Now, she felt listless, going through the motions in a trancelike state.

She studied Raj's smiling face. He was a good man, a man any girl would be lucky to have. So why couldn't she feel the same excitement with him?

She excused herself from the dance floor and was immediately surrounded by relatives and friends wishing to congratulate her. She put on a smile and said the appropriate words. She knew how to do this, to be on display, to put on a show. She knew her lines.

Raj's voice over the microphone turned everyone's heads. He was singing her a song, a popular *sangeet* commemorating his love for her. She couldn't see Raj; the image of Jake with his guitar filled her vision. She couldn't hear the song Raj was singing; her ears played the words Jake had written for her, the music that had touched her soul. She put a hand to her chest. She couldn't do this.

She bolted onto the patio and sucked in some air. She heard the crowd applauding, and someone called her name, but she ignored it all as she bent over the railing. She needed a minute, just a minute, to clear her head. To clear the image of Jake from her heart. To shake off her memories of Hell's Bells and free up space to make new ones.

She felt a hand on her shoulder. "Meera?"

Raj's face was filled with concern, and she gulped. She could do this. She had practiced all her life. "That was a lovely song, Raj. Thank you."

"Then why do you look like I just took away your most prized possession?" His voice was soft, his tone filled with dread.

She shook her head, the words to deny and soothe at the tip of her tongue. But her vocal cords froze.

Raj took her hand. "Meera, I know you still have feelings for Jake…" *Feelings? Feelings I can control, feelings I can temper. He has possessed my soul.*

"…but these feelings will pass. I know it doesn't feel like it, but they will." *What if I don't want them to pass?*

"Raj, what if Jake is a permanent part of my heart? How could you live with the knowledge that I love another man?"

She searched his eyes for anger, fury, a reaction to the grenade she had thrown in his face.

He stepped back, his lips pinched. "Loved, Meera. You loved him. I've been extraordinarily patient with you, but I do expect you to be over him by the time we get married. I will not tolerate infidelity."

Meera's eyes blazed. "That's not who I am, and you know it. I'm not talking about being unfaithful to you. I'm talking about the fact that he may be a permanent part of my heart. How can you marry me knowing you won't have my heart entirely?"

He took a breath. "Because, Meera, you have all of mine, and I know that I have enough love in me for the both of us." He took her hands. "Meera, you have to see what I see. Close your eyes." She complied. "I see a perfect life together, taking over your father's practice, working side by side in our lab—we could find the key to treating heart disease, we could go global with the medical centers..." Meera opened her eyes.

"We would be the ultimate power couple," she said flatly.

He nodded excitedly.

"And what about having a home? Children?" *What about my fairy tale?*

"Of course, that's part of the package. We've been friends so long, Meera, we know we get along just fine. We'll never be one of those couples that quibbles and fights over little things."

She thought about the ups and downs, highs and lows that Jake brought out just by being in the same room as her. Raj was always a comforting presence, but she didn't want security anymore. She didn't want to operate on autopilot. She wanted to feel alive again, the way she had in Hell's Bells.

"And what if I'm not actually the perfectly pressed Meera you're accustomed to?"

"Meera, it's very understandable to have prewedding jitters. I've known you for almost twenty years, and I know you hate these big showy events. Once all this wedding madness is over, you'll start to feel more like yourself. You just have to get through the next two weeks."

He nodded toward the ballroom full of people. "Look at your mother—she's so happy. She's waited her whole life for this."

Meera followed his gaze. Her mother was resplendent in her own Valentino, a silver gown with a diagonal ruffle that mimicked the lines of a sari. Meera knew her mother had had both their dresses custom designed. The wedding was the event of the decade, and her mother hadn't spared a single expense.

Just like she hadn't spared any expense in sending Meera to the best boarding schools, paying for private tuitions and giving her the resources to make her a world-class researcher. She'd transformed Meera from the poor orphan girl into the belle of the ball.

What right did she have to throw it all away? To squander the chance her parents had given her, an opportunity that so many other little girls in the orphanage never got. Her parents asked for very little in return. What right did she have to destroy their dreams for her own selfish needs?

Raj offered her his arm. "Shall we go back to our party?" With a heavy heart, she followed him inside.

As soon as they were back in the ballroom, Meera's mother called the crowd's attention. She commanded Meera and Raj to the center of the dance floor, where Raj's parents and her father stood. It was time for the official engagement ceremony.

In traditional Indian style, Meera first placed a symbolic ring on Raj's finger. She had never seen the ring before; her mother had picked it out. Raj then produced a gold ring with a very large diamond surrounded by a few other large diamonds. It was big and ostentatious and Meera tried not to wince at how ridiculously showy it would be on her slim fingers. It wasn't what she wanted.

Raj bent his head so he could whisper in her ear. "Honey, I personally chose this ring to show you how grand our life can be." Her breaths were shallow. A little more loudly, he said, "It is believed that the reason this ring goes on the left ring finger is that finger has a vein that goes straight to the heart. Medically, this is not exactly true, but hopefully, with this ring, I'll have a permanent line to your heart." The crowd let out a collective "awwww." Meera felt as if she was going to be sick.

It was all wrong. She couldn't wear this ring for the rest of her life. She tried to take her hand away, but Raj was holding on tight. He was trying to slip it on her finger, but it was getting stuck. He kept twisting and pushing, but the harder he tried, the more the ring caught on her knuckle. He laughed nervously. "I guess it needs a little resizing."

Raj was meticulous with details. He'd had her finger sized for the ring. That it shouldn't fit now was a sign.

She shook her head and snatched her hand back forcefully. "It's no use, Raj. It doesn't fit."

She turned and fled, pushing her way through the crowd. Stunned relatives tried to grab her arm, but she pushed them aside. Her dress caught on someone's watch, and she pulled it roughly, ripping the delicate lace. She heard her mother screaming her name, but she didn't care. The room was too hot, the air too thick. If she stayed, she would die.

She raced upstairs to her room and slammed the door. She tugged on her zipper, trying desperately to reach the back to pull it down all the way. She had to get out of the dress; she needed to breathe.

She pulled viciously and brought the zipper

halfway down, then went out onto the balcony. The cool night air felt good on her heated skin. She needed to think. She looked at her left hand. *The ring didn't fit.*

"Meera!"

The sound of her mother's voice raised the hair on the back of her neck.

"What's gotten into you? How could you be so *laparwah*, create such a scene downstairs and look at you, look at that dress!" Her eyes were filled with fury. "Why are you so intent on making a mess of everything?"

Meera stepped toward her mother, unable to hold back her tears.

"Mum, I can't marry Raj, I just can't. I want to, I know he's a good man and I know I'm disappointing you, but I love Jake. I can't live a lie my whole life—it isn't fair to me and it isn't fair to Raj."

Neela's eyes turned ice-cold. "So what do you propose to do? Give up everything you have—your life, your research, all your nice things—and go live like some poor commoner in America?"

Meera gazed pleadingly at her mother. "I know it sounds impossible, but I'll figure something out…"

"And you're going to break your father's heart by leaving his practice."

"I'll talk to *Pitaji*. I think he'll—"

"Meera, you are nothing but a child from the street."

Meera's heart stopped.

"All along, Prem thought we could educate you and make you our daughter, but how wrong we have been."

Meera opened her mouth to reply, but Neela's face twisted with such intense rage that Meera's legs started to give way and she couldn't speak. "Prem tricked me into adopting you. I didn't know when we married that I was infertile, and the plan was to go to India and get a baby we could pretend was ours. But then he saw you in that orphanage, and he promised me you'd make us proud, that you would be the daughter deserving of our love and sacrifice."

Meera gripped the railing of her balcony.

"Mum, please…"

"No, Meera. If you're so grown-up now that you openly defy your parents, then you're old enough to hear the truth. Prem threatened to divorce me when I first refused to accept you—that's how much he loves you, from the moment he saw you. Why do you think he built up that big practice? It was all for you. And this is how you're going to repay him? You…"

Her mother's mouth was moving but Meera couldn't hear her anymore. Blood pounded in her ears. She placed a hand over her chest. Her legs gave way, and she crumpled to the floor. *Had she died?*

MEERA DIDN'T KNOW how much time had passed. It could have been minutes, or it could have been hours. When her senses finally booted up, Priya was sitting next to her.

"I need a shower." Priya nodded and helped her to the bathroom. She tested the water temperature before letting Meera step in. Meera let the water pummel her face, her eyes stinging against the force of the spray. She wanted to blink but couldn't. She wanted to move but couldn't.

Priya knocked on the shower door.

"Meera, Raj is still outside. You're going to have to come out and talk to him." She motioned to a chair, where she had laid out a change of clothes.

Priya turned off the water and handed Meera a towel. She was so tired, she didn't even have the strength to put on her clothes. Priya slipped a flannel nightgown over her head.

She brushed Meera's wet hair and wrapped it in a towel before leading her into the bedroom.

Raj was sitting on her bed, still dressed in his party clothes. Her balcony door was open, and the guests' laughter floated up to her.

"Are you okay?"

She stared blankly at him. *What exactly does he mean by okay?* Nothing in her life made sense anymore.

He patted the bed next to him, and she sat

down, sinking despite the firm mattress. He took her hand.

"I'm sure your mother didn't mean what she said."

Meera stared into space. "Actually, I think for the first time in her life, she meant every word." Had she said that out loud? Her voice sounded so far away.

Raj patted her hand. "Would you like me to cancel the wedding?"

What a strange question to ask. There's a wedding? Why is there still a wedding? My world has shattered, and there will be a wedding to commemorate it? Dark shadows swam before her eyes.

"What are those shapes?" Her voice was weak.

"Priya, can you get her some paracetamol and my medical bag from the car so I can give her a sedative? I think she needs to rest."

Meera woke up the next morning with a heavy head. Streams of light poured in around the drapes. She looked at the bedside clock. It was well past noon. She rubbed her eyes. *How long have I been asleep?* She never slept in this late. Why was the house so quiet?

Her hair was still wrapped in a towel. She vaguely recalled Priya handing her tablets and water. She remembered Raj tucking her into bed and pulling the covers over her.

She stood carefully and threw open the drapes, wincing at the bright midday sun. She took off the towel and padded into the bathroom. She brushed her teeth and took a shower. She knew she had missed the tour bus that was taking the guests sightseeing. *Why didn't someone come get me?* Then she looked at her finger and remembered.

Meera found her phone on the floor. It had died overnight, but she plugged it in and it came alive. She had five texts from Lily, two from Gloria, one from Rose and three from Billy John, all telling her Jolene was back.

She shook her head, trying to clear the cobwebs. Jake deserved to be happy. Didn't he? She had made her bed, and it was time to sleep in it. She deleted all the messages. There was one from Priya asking her to call when she woke up.

She walked into the closet and flipped through her clothes. What did one wear when one's life was falling apart?

She put on jeans and a T-shirt, clothes she normally reserved for when she was alone in her bedroom. Today she didn't care; she just needed to be comfortable.

Time to face the music.

She made her way downstairs and was pleasantly surprised to find her father alone in the dining room, sitting down to lunch.

"Meera, just the person I was hoping to see. Come sit."

She pulled out a chair next to him. The cook had set the table for twelve people.

He slid a plate toward her and spooned some vegetable curry and rice from his plate onto hers. She shook her head, but he ignored her.

"You need to eat."

She picked up a fork and put some food in her mouth. She couldn't taste it. She swallowed with difficulty and sipped from a glass of water.

"Priya and Raj talked to me last night."

Meera looked up in alarm. *What have they told you?*

"They overheard the fight you had with your mother."

Meera swallowed painfully.

He put his hand on Meera's. "First off, they told everyone at the party last night that you were feeling faint and had to lie down. Your mother smoothed it over with the guests. No harm done."

"You must be so disappointed in me." Her voice was raw.

"Meera, listen to me. You are my daughter, always have been and always will be. I won't justify your mother's behavior. She's always been a selfish woman and there's nothing I can do about it. But you are my daughter. I picked you because—"

"Because you thought I wanted to be a doctor?"

"No, my child. I picked you because I felt a connection to you. The moment I laid eyes on you, I felt this link between us, like maybe you were my daughter from a previous life and I'd been reborn to be your father again. You are my child, end of story."

She sobbed loudly, unable to control her emotions. Her father stood and held her tightly.

"Meera, you need to understand that you will never please your mother. And no matter what you do, you will never disappointment me."

Her heart contracted painfully.

"Even if I go back to America and give up your practice?"

He laughed. "The practice will be yours whether you want it or not. I will run it until I'm old and decrepit, then you can sell it. It's my dream to see you take it over, but it's my sincere wish that you be happy. And wherever happiness is for you, that's where you should go."

"Have you and Mother been happy?"

He raised his eyebrows. "Why do you ask?"

"Because you've always taught me that marriage should be logical, that you should be with someone who supports and complements you."

He shook his head and laughed. "Your mother taught you that." He glanced at his plate and took a few bites of food. "I think you should marry someone you love. I've enjoyed the life I built with your mother, but it's been a lonely one. We've mostly stayed out of each other's way. I can't say I've been unhappy with Neela, but the only true joy in my life has been you."

Meera's heart overflowed with love for her father.

He pushed her plate forward. "Eat—you're going to need some energy today."

She smiled and dug in, savoring the tingle of spices on her tongue. They enjoyed their meal quietly.

When she was done, Meera knew with clarity what she was going to do.

CHAPTER THIRTY-SEVEN

MEERA SLAMMED ON the brakes just past the town square. The road was blocked with orange cones. No sooner had she stopped than half the town descended on her rental car.

She stepped out, frowning.

Gloria reached her first. Meera braced herself, but Gloria hugged her tight. "I knew you'd be back! I just knew it."

She was followed by Rose, Dr. Harper, Mr. and Mrs. Cregg and a dozen others. Meera stood in shock.

"Oh, don't look like that. My cousin Sean works the car rental counter at the airport, so I asked him to let us know when you returned. He called a couple of hours ago."

Meera laughed. "I'm so glad to be back."

Rose smiled kindly at her. "Welcome home."

"Do you know what's been going on here?"

Rose squeezed Meera's arm. "You'd best go to the ranch and talk to Jake yourself, dear. It's not our place to tell you."

Meera bit her lip and nodded, telling herself to expect the worst. She had come back for Jake, but she had also come back for a different life. One where she made her own decisions, one where her patients and neighbors were family. She drove as fast as she dared to the ranch. When she arrived, she noticed the rusted cattle gate with the tricky lock was gone, replaced by a new wrought iron entryway.

She stared at it. There was an old-fashioned bell beside the gate, a small replica of the larger one in town. She hesitated, then rang it.

"Well, aren't you a sight for sore eyes."

Meera let Kelly envelop her in a hug. "Jake's in the old calf barn." *Since when was it old?* Kelly opened the gate, and Meera ran to the barn, this time in flat-heeled sandals.

And there he was. Same white T-shirt. Same dusty jeans and cowboy hat. She wanted to jump into his arms, but she contained herself.

"I don't mean to disturb you, but do you have a room to let?"

He froze, then turned slowly.

Their eyes locked. His green eyes blazed with a mix of sorrow, disbelief and something else.

He shook his head.

"I don't have a room to rent anymore."

Her heart dropped like a lead balloon. He opened the stall door and stepped up to her. He was standing close, too close. She took a deep breath and let his scent wash over her.

He wrapped an arm around her waist and pulled her close. She yelped in surprise.

"I have a room to share, on a permanent basis this time."

She let out her breath and lifted her face so he could kiss her.

She returned the kiss with all she had.

When they finally came up for air, he picked her up and twirled her. She held on to him as tightly as she could. "It's about time you came home."

She smiled at him. "I love you, Jake, more than I could ever imagine."

"Come on, I have something to show you."

"Wait, what about Jolene?"

He frowned. "What about her?"

"The entire town was texting to let me know she moved back in."

"Is that why you came back?"

She shook her head. "I came back despite that."

He laughed. "She's been helping me with some horses for the dude ranch."

"Dude ranch?"

He grinned.

"Why, you…" She punched him playfully.

"I wanted you to come back for me, Meera."

She nodded. "I did come back for you. And for us."

"The hands knew there was nothing between me and Jolene—I half suspect the town did that to get you back here."

She giggled. "I've missed Hell's Bells."

"Where're your bags?"

She shrugged and pointed to her bag. Inside she had the wedding dress Lily had made her. "This is all I need. Everything else is already here."

He took her hand and pulled her toward the cottage. Her nerves tingled; she felt positively giddy. He opened the door, and her heart stopped. The living room was transformed to look as though they were staring at the Taj Mahal. Huge sections of poster print hung on the walls. The furniture was draped in Indian saris.

Tears shimmered in her eyes. "It's the greatest monument to love."

He nodded.

He dropped to his knee, reached into his pocket and pulled out a ring.

"Meera Malhotra, I want us to make a plan tonight, that ten years from now, we'll tell our children exactly how we lived these past weeks without each other and how we vowed never to do it again. Will you marry me?"

She stared at him and then the ring. It was a

simple platinum ring encrusted with small diamonds. It was beautiful.

"How long have you been planning this?"

"I've been putting this room together since the day you left. I had faith, Meera. I had faith in you and faith in us. I knew we'd find a way back to each other eventually."

Her face was wet. She dropped to her knees in front of him.

"Oh, Jake, yes, I will marry you and I will have your children and tell them how treacherous the last few weeks were for me."

He slipped the ring on her finger. It fit perfectly.

He kissed her sweetly, promising with his soul the love of a lifetime.

When they finally broke their embrace, they were both laughing and she linked her hands with his. "I do have some conditions, though."

A shadow crossed his face.

"I mean requests, not conditions. I'll marry you whether you agree or not," she quickly amended.

He relaxed. "Well, you'll be happy to know all the animals on the dude ranch are strictly for entertainment purposes—they aren't being raised to kill."

She squealed and hugged him. "Oh, Jake, you've saved both our karmas."

He rolled his eyes. "I'm not saying I agree with you—it was a business decision. Didn't make sense to keep up all that cattle."

"I'll take it. So just a few other things..." She held up her fingers to tick them off.

"You can of course eat meat, but I ask that we share at least one vegetarian dinner a week."

"I'll do you one better. I won't eat meat when we're together. I'm not giving it up, but I don't need to eat it in front of you."

She smiled.

"Second, I'm not giving up my research, so I'll have to go to London once a month for about a week and Raj is going to continue being my business partner."

Jake frowned. "I'm not sure I like that, especially the bit about Raj."

She started to protest, but he held up his hands in surrender. "I can live with it. In fact, I'll come with you, see the real Queen of England."

"You mean it? You can leave the ranch for that long to come with me every month?"

"I'm making Kelly the ranch manager and giving her a share of the profits so she can buy health insurance and I can get away once in a while. And while we're at it, I want us to see the world, maybe the real Taj Mahal for our honeymoon."

Meera hugged him. "That's a great idea. I love you, Jake."

"Any more conditions? I don't want to wait another day to make you my wife."

She scrunched her nose. "That's just the thing… can we wait until next week to get married?"

He shook his head. "No way. That's not do-able. You know the town's already settin' up the square. They're expecting me to ride into town with you any minute."

She laughed. "I don't doubt it, but my father would like to give me away, and I need some time to get him here."

Jake nodded. "I would like to meet him, ask for your hand in marriage." He paused. "How's Raj?"

She shrugged. "He didn't take it well, but he's my friend and he could tell I was in bad shape. We made a deal that I wouldn't give up on our research together and he would stay behind and cancel the wedding, face our hundreds of guests."

"He took a bullet for you."

She nodded. "He loves me in his own way, but I don't think he's ever had our kind of love. It was hard for him to understand, just like it was hard for me to accept it. But he's a good man and a good friend."

"What changed your mind? That day on the phone, I was sure you were gonna go through with the wedding and I'd be waiting years for you to come to your senses."

She slapped him teasingly on the arm.

"How were you sure I'd *ever* come back?"

He gazed at her warmly. "Because I know you, Meera, and I know what we have. I could feel you in here." He tapped his chest. "I could feel you even thousands of miles away, and I knew that if I felt it, you did, too, and eventually you wouldn't be able to ignore it anymore."

She nodded. "You were right about me not making my own choices. I've been buried under this debt I feel I owe my parents."

"Have you found a way to dig yourself out?"

She sighed. "No, but I've figured out how to peek above the surface and let myself think more clearly about what I want, rather than what I've been told I want."

He pulled her into his arms.

"We can do this together, Meera. We really can."

She felt his chest against her and squeezed him back.

"Come on, let me show you the rest of the cottage. I made us a new kitchen."

"Watch the curling iron—we can't burn down the cottage."

Meera smiled affectionately at Priya and Lily as they fussed about her.

"Now, Meera, I know you're a doctor and everything, but there are a few things I need to tell

you about what to expect on your weddin' night."
Meera smiled at Mrs. Cregg as Priya and Lily
burst into giggles.

"Let her do it, it'll keep you laughing all day,"
Lily whispered in Meera's ear.

Meera nodded seriously at Mrs. Cregg. "That
would be helpful," she said loudly. The ladies
who had come to help get Meera dressed gathered in.

"Well, first, make sure you use the bathroom
before you get started. It can get very..." A knock
on the door interrupted the conversation.

Priya giggled and stood up to answer it. "Wait
until I come back."

Meera heard voices in the hallway and her
pulse sped up. *It can't be!* She walked out of her
room and gasped. Her mother stood there with
her father and Raj in tow. She hadn't spoken to
her mother since the night of the engagement;
she was only expecting *Pitaji* today. She knew
her father had talked to her mother. For once in
his life, he had stood up to her. That's why she
hadn't called Meera every ten seconds or ex-
ploded when the wedding was canceled.

Her mother stood in the tiny living room, holding a neatly folded red-and-white sari. "Meera,
I can't take back the words I said, but I've come
to offer you this—it's my mother's sari, the one

I wore at my wedding. It would mean a lot to me if you would wear it today."

She studied the white gown Meera was already wearing, the one Lily had made her. Lily touched her arm. "Maybe you can wear that to the wedding ceremony and then change into this gown for the dancing?"

Meera took in her mother's outstretched arms and pleading eyes. Her father had joined his hands together in a silent request.

Meera gave her mother a small smile and took the sari. "No matter how you feel about me, you're the only mother I've ever had, and for that, I will love you forever."

Meera's father stepped between them and pulled Meera and Neela into an embrace.

"Okay, enough of this mushiness, we need to get Meera dressed." Priya shooed the men out of the room.

They unwrapped the sari. The blouse that went underneath was too big on Meera. "I can fix that in a jiffy." Mrs. Cregg snatched the blouse from Neela, who stared at her in shock. The older woman was back in five minutes and it fit perfectly.

"You know, I have a Sienna Simone that could use your touch," Neela said laughingly.

Her mother helped Meera wrap the sari, then opened her purse to give her a simple gold necklace, far less ostentatious than the jewelry her mother had planned for Meera to wear at the wedding to Raj. "My parents were not that wealthy, and this is what I wore when I was married. I have been quite happy with my life, and I wish the same for you, Meera."

Meera gave her mother a hug, and this time Neela let Meera hold her tightly.

When she was ready, Neela unwrapped a red *chunni*, which went over Meera's head. Meera studied her reflection. *This is how I pictured myself on my wedding day.*

"Let's go—it's time."

Meera had no idea what to expect; the town had insisted on throwing the wedding. She figured it would be similar to what they had done for Lily. The horse-drawn carriage awaited her, this time driven by Joe. She gave him a grateful smile and asked Priya and Lily to squeeze in with her.

She gasped when she got her first look at the town square. The gazebo had been transformed into a traditional *mandap*. A *pandit* was tending a small fire. Flowers decorated the gazebo, and chairs had been set up for the guests. Meera's eyes filled with tears.

"How...?"

"We know how to use the internet." Lily chuckled. "We figured if you could throw us an

American barbecue, we could throw you an Indian wedding."

She searched for Jake.

"He'll be coming the traditional way," Priya said mysteriously.

Joe helped Meera step down from the carriage. Her parents were waiting for her, and she touched Raj's arm. "Are you okay?" He nodded, standing straight. Meera looked at the gathered townspeople and let the warmth and love envelop her. This was where she belonged.

She caught sight of Jake's father, sitting on a bench. She went to say hello, and he gave her a wide grin.

"There you are, pretty girl. Now come here and sit beside me." Meera smiled and did just that. Ted was definitely having a good day. He pulled out a phone and gave it to Meera. "Now, my girl back at the nursin' home tells me I need to take something called a selfie with this gizmo. You know what she's talking about?"

Meera laughed and showed him how to take a picture with the phone.

The sound of hooves on the pavement caught her attention. She stood up, walked to the edge of the sidewalk and gasped. Jake was riding a horse, dressed in a traditional *achkan* topped with a cowboy hat. She laughed and turned to Raj. "You gave it to him."

Raj nodded. "I didn't need it, and it looks better on him, anyway."

Jake dismounted and approached her. "Do I get to kiss you now?"

Meera's father stepped between them, handing each a rose garland. The two of them had met earlier while she was getting dressed. "Jake, if you accept Meera as your bride, you will place this garland around her head. Meera, you will do the same."

Meera looked up shyly. Jake's green eyes danced with love and amusement. They exchanged garlands.

"*Now* do I get to kiss you?" he whispered as he put the garland around her. She shook her head demurely.

"There is no kissing in Indian ceremonies." Her father's voice was mockingly firm.

"Oh, now, someone sold me a bill of goods."

"As you cowboys like to say, hold your horses, son. After this ceremony, you have an entire lifetime to kiss my daughter."

"And the next life," Meera added.

Everyone laughed. On the way to the *mandap*, Jake stopped and introduced Meera to his mother. Meera glanced at Jake in surprise, and he whispered in her ear, "I thought it was time to give her a second chance. She even made peace with my father."

They stepped onto the *mandap*'s makeshift platform and the ceremony began. Her father took part of the *chunni* that veiled her head and tied it to a piece of pink cloth, which he handed to Jake. "I have now done the *kanyadan*. I've given my daughter to you, Jake—please take care of her."

Jake nodded. "Thank you, sir. I will love and cherish her as long as I live."

The *pandit* asked Jake to hold out a cupped hand, then put Meera's hand into Jake's before dropping scented woodchips into their palms. "We're going to feed the *agni*, the holy fire that symbolizes light, power and knowledge. It acts as a witness to this marriage."

Meera explained the ceremony to Jake as they went. "For the final part, we'll walk seven times around the fire."

When the time came, she stepped in front of him, and they circled the fire.

"With the first round, we will provide for and support each other.

"With the second round, we will develop mental, physical and spiritual strength.

"With the third round, we will share worldly possessions.

"With the fourth round, we will acquire knowledge, happiness and peace.

"With the fifth round, we will raise strong children.

"With the sixth round, we will enjoy our life together.

"With the seventh round, we will always remain friends and cherish each other."

At the end of the ceremony, the townsfolk threw rice and flower petals at them.

"There's really no kissing the bride at the end?"

Meera shook her head.

"Well, time to make new traditions."

He kissed his new wife, promising her the love of a lifetime and the next several lives.

* * * * *

LARGER-PRINT BOOKS!

GET 2 FREE
LARGER-PRINT NOVELS
PLUS 2 FREE
MYSTERY GIFTS

Love Inspired®

Larger-print novels are now available...

YES! Please send me 2 FREE LARGER-PRINT Love Inspired® novels and my 2 FREE mystery gifts (gifts are worth about $10). After receiving them, if I don't wish to receive any more books, I can return the shipping statement marked "cancel." If I don't cancel, I will receive 6 brand-new novels every month and be billed just $5.49 per book in the U.S. or $5.99 per book in Canada. That's a savings of at least 19% off the cover price. It's quite a bargain! Shipping and handling is just 50¢ per book in the U.S. and 75¢ per book in Canada.* I understand that accepting the 2 free books and gifts places me under no obligation to buy anything. I can always return a shipment and cancel at any time. Even if I never buy another book, the two free books and gifts are mine to keep forever.

122/322 IDN GH6D

Name	(PLEASE PRINT)	
Address		Apt. #
City	State/Prov.	Zip/Postal Code

Signature (if under 18, a parent or guardian must sign)

Mail to the **Reader Service**:
IN U.S.A.: P.O. Box 1867, Buffalo, NY 14240-1867
IN CANADA: P.O. Box 609, Fort Erie, Ontario L2A 5X3

**Are you a current subscriber to Love Inspired® books
and want to receive the larger-print edition?
Call 1-800-873-8635 or visit www.ReaderService.com.**

* Terms and prices subject to change without notice. Prices do not include applicable taxes. Sales tax applicable in N.Y. Canadian residents will be charged applicable taxes. Offer not valid in Quebec. This offer is limited to one order per household. Not valid to current subscribers to Love Inspired Larger-Print books. All orders subject to credit approval. Credit or debit balances in a customer's account(s) may be offset by any other outstanding balance owed by or to the customer. Please allow 4 to 6 weeks for delivery. Offer available while quantities last.

Your Privacy—The Reader Service is committed to protecting your privacy. Our Privacy Policy is available online at www.ReaderService.com or upon request from the Reader Service.

We make a portion of our mailing list available to reputable third parties that offer products we believe may interest you. If you prefer that we not exchange your name with third parties, or if you wish to clarify or modify your communication preferences, please visit us at www.ReaderService.com/consumerchoice or write to us at Reader Service Preference Service, P.O. Box 9062, Buffalo, NY 14240-9062. Include your complete name and address.

LILP15

LARGER-PRINT BOOKS!

**GET 2 FREE
LARGER-PRINT NOVELS
PLUS 2 FREE
MYSTERY GIFTS**

Love Inspired®
SUSPENSE
RIVETING INSPIRATIONAL ROMANCE

Larger-print novels are now available...

YES! Please send me **The Montana Mavericks Collection** in Larger Print. This collection begins with 3 FREE books and 2 FREE gifts (gifts valued at approx. $20.00 retail) in the first shipment, along with the other first 4 books from the collection! If I do not cancel, I will receive 8 monthly shipments until I have the entire 51-book Montana Mavericks collection. I will receive 2 or 3 FREE books in each shipment and I will pay just $4.99 US/ $5.89 CDN for each of the other four books in each shipment, plus $2.99 for shipping and handling per shipment.*If I decide to keep the entire collection, I'll have paid for only 32 books, because 19 books are FREE! I understand that accepting the 3 free books and gifts places me under no obligation to buy anything. I can always return a shipment and cancel at any time. My free books and gifts are mine to keep no matter what I decide.

263 HCN 2404   463 HCN 2404

Name	(PLEASE PRINT)	
Address		Apt. #
City	State/Prov.	Zip/Postal Code

Signature (if under 18, a parent or guardian must sign)

Mail to the **Reader Service:**
IN U.S.A.: P.O. Box 1867, Buffalo, NY 14240-1867
IN CANADA: P.O. Box 609, Fort Erie, Ontario L2A 5X3

* Terms and prices subject to change without notice. Prices do not include applicable taxes. Sales tax applicable in N.Y. Canadian residents will be charged applicable taxes. This offer is limited to one order per household. All orders subject to approval. Credit or debit balances in a customer's account(s) may be offset by any other outstanding balance owed by or to the customer. Please allow 4 to 6 weeks for delivery. Offer available while quantities last. Offer not available to Quebec residents.

LARGER-PRINT BOOKS!
GET 2 FREE LARGER-PRINT NOVELS PLUS
2 FREE GIFTS!

HARLEQUIN®

super romance®

More Story...More Romance

READERSERVICE.COM

Manage your account online!
- Review your order history
- Manage your payments
- Update your address

*We've designed the
Reader Service website
just for you.*

Enjoy all the features!
- Discover new series available to you, and read excerpts from any series.
- Respond to mailings and special monthly offers.
- Connect with favorite authors at the blog.
- Browse the Bonus Bucks catalog and online-only exculsives.
- Share your feedback.

Visit us at:
ReaderService.com